First Comes Love

The Kings' Spot

The Oregon Wine Country Romances
Love Comes Once[?]
First Comes Love

DISCARD

The Ages Wine Heirloom Romances
A Taste of Love
A Taste of Sauvignon[?]
A Taste of Merlot
A Touch of Chardonnay

Also by Heather Heyford

The Sweet Spot

The Oregon Wine Country Romances
Kisses Sweeter Than Wine
Intoxicating
The Crush

The Napa Wine Heiresses Romances
A Taste of Sake
A Taste of Sauvignon
A Taste of Merlot
A Taste of Chardonnay

First Comes Love

A Willamette Valley Romance

Heather Heyford

LYRICAL PRESS
Kensington Publishing Corp.
www.kensingtonbooks.com

LYRICAL PRESS BOOKS are published by

Kensington Publishing Corp.
119 West 40th Street
New York, NY 10018

All Kensington titles, imprints, and distributed lines are available at special quantity discounts for bulk purchases for sales promotion, premiums, fund-raising, educational, or institutional use.

Special book excerpts or customized printings can also be created to fit specific needs. For details, write or phone the office of the Kensington Sales Manager: Attn.: Sales Department. Kensington Publishing Corp., 119 West 40th Street, New York, NY 10018. Phone: 1-800-221-2647.

First Printing: June 2018
ISBN-13: 978-1-5161-0257-0
ISBN-10: 1-5161-0257-6

First Electronic Edition: June 2018
eISBN-13: 978-1-5161-0260-0
eISBN-10: 1-5161-0260-6

10 9 8 7 6 5 4 3 2 1

Printed in the United States of America

For Lee, the middle child, who was never far from my mind while I was writing this book.

ACKNOWLEDGMENTS

"Write what you know," goes the old adage. If I stuck to that too literally all I'd ever write about would be sauvignon blanc and kittens.

The fact is that writers don't just write what we know. We write about what perplexes us in order to make sense of the world.

Of course, for answers to questions such as what kind of gun a detective typically carries, the Internet is the place to go. (Answer: 9mm for a semi-automatic pistol or a .38 caliber. Thank you, crimefictionbook.com.)

When you can't find a satisfactory answer online, though, sometimes you have to resort to asking a real human. I always hesitate to bother friends and family with book questions. But when I do, I'm often rewarded with a glimpse into a part of their lives I wouldn't otherwise see. Like the time I texted my sister, who works in law enforcement, asking what she does with her service weapon when she gets home from work, and tacked on to the end of her reply she added that she always takes her shoes off on the porch because she NEVER tracks into her own home what she has walked through in the course of her workday.

Or the thoughtful pauses leading up to answers peppered with legalese like "probable cause" and "reasonable suspicion" from my friend Kathy, a former state trooper. That's not how she talks when we're sipping wine by her pool.

Any errors that slipped through are entirely my own.

Thanks to Lee, Kathy, Art, and everyone else who made it possible for me to write *First Comes Love*. I'm blessed to have you in my life.

was this was the woman ...

Chapter One

A lex Walker stared at the woman fielding re-
porters' questions outside the county courthouse. Along the lower edge of the TV screen
scrolled a continuous line of text: *Breaking news—
Newberry business exec found not guilty of embezzlement.*

Kerry O'Hearn! Alex had known her when she
was a bright young thing at Portland's most presti-
gious law firm. Now, apparently, she was working
her legal charms here, in Newberry.

He squinted hard at the screen. It couldn't be
her. But it was. The dark-framed eyeglasses were
new, but that was definitely Kerry. Even after all
this time, he'd recognize her anywhere.

Just his no-good, miserable, rotten luck.

A commercial came on and he tore his gaze
away from the TV suspended above the bar, just as
a woman slid onto the stool parked at a forty-five-
degree angle from his.

She slipped off her glasses, folded them, and

laid them on the bar. "I'll have the house Riesling," she told Laurel, the bartender, tucking a curtain of golden brown hair behind her ear.

One glimpse at her straight-nosed profile and Alex's blood began raging in his ears, drowning out the buzz of conversation and Taylor Swift's "Begin Again," playing in the background of the tavern.

The woman appeared to have sensed something, too, because she glanced at him from the corner of her eye.

Those navy-blue eyes . . . the resolute line of those lips . . . the ever-present lock of hair running diagonally across her brow . . . confirmation hit him like a jab to the sternum.

He tipped his glass to his lips, his thoughts on fast rewind. The case that had pitted the State of Oregon against Kerry and her crack team of trial lawyers was, to a great extent, to blame for his losing his taste for the fast, furious life of a city cop. He'd hung in a few years longer, his dissatisfaction growing until finally he'd gone on the hunt for a sheltered little town in which to wind up his career. Newberry seemed to fit the bill. But now, it seemed he was right back where he'd started.

Does she *remember* me ?

If she did, she didn't let on.

Then again, he wouldn't want to play poker with her.

Unlike Kerry, whose telegenic face had been plastered all over the Portland news media, Alex's public role in the long-ago trial was that of a bit player. Even though he'd spent countless hours investigating the crime behind the scenes, he'd been on the stand all of an hour and a half. After testifying, he'd slipped back into the courtroom to watch the proceedings every chance he got. But Kerry wouldn't have noticed him sitting there, in the back row. To her, he was just another blue uniform.

Time took its toll. You could go for years feeling invincible, and then one day your barber starts dropping hints that maybe you should go high and tight to give the illusion of more hair, and you take a long, hard look in the mirror and that's when it hits you that you're not the youngest guy on the force anymore. Not by a long shot.

It didn't take a trained observer to see that time had taken its subtle toll on her, too. Her curves had softened a bit and, apparently, his barber wasn't the only one who believed in lopping off length once you hit a certain birthday. Fine lines extended horizontally from the outer corners of her eyes. But the eyes themselves still glittered like cold, hard sapphires.

Kerry was sure they'd never been formally introduced, and yet there was something familiar about the guy sitting kitty-corner from her at the Turning Point Tavern.

Maybe it wasn't who he was so much as what they had in common. Amid the animated small talk punctuated by occasional bursts of laughter, he and Kerry each nursed their drinks, solo. Like her, the man was *in* the crowd, yet not *of* it.

There was a time, back when she was an assistant DA still learning the ropes, that she'd been a card-carrying member of the happy hour tribe. Out every night, getting to know the right people, finding her niche in the big city. Back then, she'd thought she'd said good-bye to her pastoral hometown for good.

An elbow thumped her in the back, sloshing wine over the edge of the glass in her hand.

"Sorry." A young woman in a dress with spaghetti straps—a style that, regrettably, Kerry no longer had the arms for—smiled wryly and raised her glass in apology as best she could. She was hemmed in by an HVAC technician with DAN and HARMON'S ELECTRIC embroidered on his chest and a man who had already loosened his tie and was now undoing his top button.

Relax. Kerry blew out a breath, dabbed her fingers with her bar napkin, and forced her shoulders down. In the twenty years she'd been gone from Newberry, the wine boom had brought an influx of new residents. In addition to the newbies, there were no doubt a couple of old acquaintances in here she didn't recognize due to the passage of time. Still, she felt a kinship with these people that went beyond living in the same town. All of them radiated the same low-grade anxiety that comes from sacrificing forty hours a week, fifty weeks a year to putting a roof over the heads and shoes on the feet of those who depended on them.

"Ready for another?" asked the bartender, bottle poised to pour.

"No, thanks." She put her hand over the top of her glass. "One and done."

She had to pick up the kids at the Community

Center in less than an hour. She pictured Chloé's and Ella's moon faces smiling up at her and was engulfed in a wave of maternal protectiveness, followed instantly by a sinking feeling when she recalled that morning, when Shay, her oldest, had flat-out refused to change out of her too-short skirt.

But the skirt was the least of Kerry's concerns. According to Shay, twelve going on thirteen was way too old to be enrolled in the after-school program. Kerry got it. She did. But she refused to let Shay go home to an empty house by herself. She'd been practicing law too long, seen too much.

As hard as it was being a single, working mom, those kids meant everything to her. In a matter of minutes, little Ella would come barreling into her arms, threatening to topple her off her conservative, two-inch heels, while Chloé, in sixth grade but mature beyond her years, would sling her purple backpack over her shoulder and yak to Kerry all the way out to their 4Runner, as if she had saved up all her thoughts from the whole day and couldn't hold them in another minute. Bless Chloé's heart. Being raised without a father affected every kid differently. Chloé had become glued to Kerry's hip. She couldn't care less if her classmates caught her holding her hand.

As for Shay, Kerry would be lucky if she merited brief eye contact.

"That trial's all anyone's been talking about for weeks," said the bartender.

"I hadn't figured on an embezzlement case being headline news. Back in Portland, it would have been buried beneath a story about the latest protest march or the homeless problem they can never seem to get a grip on."

But she knew the talk around town wasn't 100 percent positive. *Not guilty* wasn't the same thing as *innocent.* Whether the woman had actually diverted company funds into her own account, it had been Kerry's job to defend her, and she had come through with flying colors. Some people had a problem with that.

Maybe that explained the furtive glances of the guy next to her. He had started frowning into his pinot as intently as a wine critic when she caught him looking at her.

And here she'd had the tiniest spark of hope that maybe, just maybe, his interest might be more than idle curiosity over the trial.

Kerry had had her share of admirers in her thirty-eight years, including one who'd actually cared enough to walk down the aisle with her. But parenting three kids by herself while juggling a high-profile caseload had taken its toll. Lately she'd started to feel invisible . . . sexless. It had been a long time since a man had given her a second glance.

Maybe her time was past. She'd had her chances at romance. And she'd blown them.

The man lifted his glass to his lips and she stole a closer look. His uniform consisted of jeans and a gray, V-neck sweater pulled over a red T-shirt. The way his shoulders filled out the fine-gauge wool hinted of regular, serious workouts. No ring. If he'd ever been married, it'd been over long enough for the telltale narrowing at the base of his finger to fill out. Unless he was one of those guys who liked to keep his status on the down low in case something better came along. There were plenty of those around.

No. His eyes were stormy gray and guarded. The inch-long, horizontal scar on the crest of his cheekbone said here was a man who could handle whatever life threw at him. A man who wouldn't be toyed with, who had seen things most people would *never* see, if they were lucky.

And that close-cropped, no-nonsense haircut combined with a utilitarian watch and clean shave couldn't be more straightforward. Whoever he was, he wasn't a player.

He reached into his back pocket in a smooth, controlled movement, revealing the sliver of black leather and gold metal at his hip. Pulling out his phone, he answered it in a deep voice. "Walker."

A cop. *Detective*, Kerry corrected herself. Those gold shields were highly prized. Patrolmen wore blue to make their authority immediately obvious to both criminals and the public they aimed to protect. Detectives delved deeper in their work behind the scenes.

While he propped both elbows on the bar and bit off curt replies at a low volume into his phone, Kerry leaned back slightly, letting her eyes travel from his broad shoulders down to his narrow waist.

There it was, the hard bulge of his service weapon shoved into the small of his back beneath his sweater, only noticeable if you knew where to look.

She should have known. He had cop written all

over him. How had it taken her so long to see it? This case, combined with Shay's issues at her new school, had really done a number on her.

She lifted the edge of her own phone yet again. It would only take five minutes to get to the Community Center. One of the many advantages of small-town living. Back in Portland, there was never a day when there wasn't traffic to contend with.

The detective—Walker—ended his call and slid his phone back into his pocket.

"You didn't grow up in Newberry," she heard herself say.

Oh, Lord. When it came to hanging out in bars, she was woefully out of practice. A few sips of wine and here she was, chatting up a stranger. But cops didn't qualify as strangers, did they? Cops were solid, steady, and true down to the core. Or they were supposed to be.

"Don't tell me you did."

What was that supposed to mean? She should have kept to herself. Too late now. She smiled mildly. "Not far from here. Ribbon Ridge. You probably never heard of it."

"Smallest AVA in the Willamette," he replied without missing a beat.

Kerry cocked a brow. Most people didn't even know what an American Viticultural Area *was.* Even fewer had heard of Ribbon Ridge, precisely because it *was* so small.

"The Willamette, then. Because you don't strike me as a tourist."

He fondled the underside of his balloon-shaped glass as he considered his answer. "Originally? Right over the border in Washington State."

A beer tap near the intersection of Kerry and the cop put Laurel in the perfect position to eavesdrop. As she waited for a pilsner glass to fill, she said to him, "That Friestatt pinot noir you're drinking?" She tipped her head toward Kerry. "That's her family's place."

"That right?" He grunted in reluctant approval, tilting his glass, looking with renewed interest at the transparent, garnet color.

Kerry rolled her eyes and groaned inwardly. Name-dropping wasn't her style.

"The Sweet Spot belongs to my cousin Hank. Well, technically, he's my second cousin. The Friestatts and the O'Hearns are a fertile bunch. You'll find half the valley comes from one side or the other. In some cases, both. That what brought you to the Willamette? The pinot?"

"That," he said, "and the quiet."

Ouch.

Laurel glanced at Kerry's empty drink. "Check, Counselor?"

She nodded once, stood up, and felt beneath the bar for the purse hook.

"Know why a shark won't attack a defense attorney?" the cop asked Laurel, loud enough for Kerry to hear.

Rummaging in her bag for her wallet, Kerry's hand stilled.

"Er . . . why?" Laurel replied, giving Kerry a wary look.

"Professional courtesy."

Laurel laughed in the obligatory way reserved for difficult bar patrons while accepting the bills Kerry held out. "Change?"

"Keep it."

Walk away, Kerry told herself. *Just walk away.* But the litigator in her couldn't resist a parting shot.

"Why does a cop always go by the numbers?" she asked.

The server folded her arms. "Tell me."

"Because he never learned the alphabet."

Chapter Two

Alex had spent all last summer driving around the Willamette Valley's storybook farm towns in search of the ideal spot to relocate.

He wasn't interested in any of the shiny new housing developments sprouting up as a result of the wine boom. Alex was old school, and he didn't care who knew it. He'd take substance over gloss every time.

He'd explored the back roads of McMinnville, Silverton, Troutdale, and Dundee, eating at their restaurants, drinking in their tasting rooms. One Saturday morning on his drive past farm stands selling honey and vegetables on the honor system, he found a seat in the corner of Newberry's Java coffee shop and pretended to read his copy of *Wine Spectator*. But after a half hour he found he was merely flipping the pages. He'd become caught up in watching the stream of young families waiting patiently in line for to-go cups to take to their ball games and the respectful students from the small, liberal arts college . . . listening to the low-key conversations of the workers from the medical center and the Rustical Furniture Company and the weather prognostications of dairy farmers and grape growers.

He became cautiously excited. But Newberry still had to pass the final test. It had to have the ideal watering hole: unpretentious, but with a decent wine list. As far as that requirement went, most of the drinking establishments in the Willamette qualified. But it also had to have a staff that was friendly but not intrusive. And it had to be popular enough so that Alex wouldn't look conspicuous for being the only patron sitting at the bar by himself night after night. He had nothing against company, as long as they kept their distance. You couldn't get rejected if you kept people safely at arm's length.

Then he discovered the Turning Point, and everything clicked.

"Women. Can't live with 'em, can't shoot 'em." A man slid onto the stool recently vacated by Kerry.

Alex looked up at a grizzled face with bloodshot eyes. Just what he needed . . . some old coot about to chew his ear off.

"Kerry O'Hearn always was a piece of work. Smart, sassy, and easy on the eyes."

"You know her?"

"Know her? We went to school together."

How could that be . . . even if this guy were a few classes ahead of her? He had to be fifty if he was a day.

"That right?" It took all kinds. His curiosity got the better of him. Who knew? Maybe he'd learn something.

"She was always quick with a comeback. Hell, I just ran into Danny at the Thrifty Market and her name came up. You know, on account of that trial everybody's been talking about.

"Danny Wilson?" the man clarified at Alex's confused expression. "They were a couple all through junior and senior year. She broke up with him right before she went off to college. Ended up staying in Portland after she graduated and made a name for herself as a big-time lawyer. Wasn't so lucky in the love department, or so I hear tell. But then, that's life. No one has it all. Not even Kerry O'Hearn." He swigged his beer thoughtfully. "Danny said that after all these years, he still dreams about her."

"What's this Danny guy doing now?" Alex harbored a warped hope he was tethered to a demanding wife on a short leash, with a passel of kids and a time-sucking fixer-upper mortgaged to the hilt.

"Danny done pretty good for himself, too. Worked his way up to new head vineyard manager at the Sweet Spot. Kerry's cousin's place. The Friestatts and the O'Hearns run rampant in this valley. Can't move without bumping into one of them."

The guy had neglected the most important part—Danny's relationship status. But Alex had interrogated enough people to know all he had to do was bide his time. The man was a talker.

Of course, a little encouragement never hurt. "Alex Walker," he said, extending his hand.

The man grinned, revealing a missing incisor in

his lower jaw. "Everyone knows you're the new cop in Newberry. Curtis Wallace. I don't come to town much. Prefer to keep to myself. Got a little place on the river south of here. Real private. Don't take much to keep me content."

"Sounds ideal to me. So, what's your beef with women?"

"No beef. Just better off without them. You know how it goes. All rosy when it starts out, but it never ends well."

"I hear you." Alex raised his glass in a toast.

"You, too?"

"Like you said. You don't get through life without a few battle scars."

"Amen to that. But you don't have to lay back down and keep letting yourself get run over, do you?"

"What brings you to town?"

"Monthly supply run. This is my last stop before I head home."

The door opened to the slanting rays of afternoon sunlight and four more chattering patrons. Someone cranked up the music.

"Time for me to head out," Alex said.

"I'm right behind you," said Curtis, guzzling what was left in his glass and digging for his wallet. "I'm too old for any place where you have to yell to have a conversation. Same time next month?"

"We'll see."

Alex paid his tab and drove slowly through peaceful streets, past Craftsman-style bungalows with board siding and distinctive, four-over-one windows and boxy colonials. The green smell of the first lawn mowing of spring lingered in the air.

Once he'd settled on Newberry, the next step was finding a quiet place to rent. It didn't have to be big, but it had to be a house, not an apartment. A single-family house, not some duplex with the potential for screaming kids and barking dogs and all that commotion. Someplace secluded, where he could get away from the crazy, feed the birds, and hunt and peck on his newly acquired laptop for his budding blog on Willamette Valley wines.

His probe unearthed a sixties-era cottage on North Valley Road. Space was at a premium, but all he really needed were two small bedrooms—one for sleeping, the other for his writing desk—and a place to sit outside with a view of the woods.

But in his zeal to find the perfect spot, there was one thing he'd forgotten. He hadn't skimmed down the short list of his enemies to make sure he wouldn't be running into one of them every time he turned a corner.

He kicked himself for his rookie mistake.

Now, every time he was called to testify against an offender, there was a chance he'd have to face Kerry O'Hearn again.

He drove on, past the library to the edge of town where the elementary and middle schools sat adjacent to each other and shared a block-long expanse of athletic fields.

But this evening, the long shadows of the goalposts barely registered. He couldn't get his mind off *her*.

Across the soccer field, he thought he saw something or someone disappear around an outbuilding of the type used to store athletic equipment.

Much as he wanted to get home to his hobbies,

his sense of duty had him detouring. By the time he'd circled the block, whatever he'd thought he'd seen was long gone. His hand reached for his radio to warn patrol to keep an eye out around the school tonight, but then he changed his mind. In this neighborhood? Probably just a couple of kids dragging ass on their way home from soccer practice. No reason to put the fear of God into them by getting them stopped by the cops. They'd be sorry enough for being late for supper when their parents got through with them. At least, they would be if they were his kids.

Kids. Who needed the heartache?

At the next intersection he turned onto the road that wound through farmland and vineyards, eventually leading to his rental.

He had tried time and again over the years to banish Kerry O'Hearn from his memory, but how could he forget her when her perennially serious expression, the way her glossed lips formed around her well-chosen words, the rounded corners of her small, white teeth were still a regular feature of his dreams?

And according to Curtis Wallace, he wasn't the only one.

Alex pulled his county-issued Taurus under the carport, shut off the ignition, and started his day in reverse. Shoes off outside—he never tracked into his home what he'd walked through in the course of doing his job. Then he went in, unloaded and locked up his Glock 22, and took a quick shower.

After he'd changed into clean jeans and a fresh shirt he opened the cupboard and plucked a wineglass from the neat row. When his hand fell on the half-empty bottle sitting on the kitchen counter, he stopped before he poured and held it up by the neck to eye level, to get a better look at its label.

Friestatt Estate. Willamette Valley, Oregon Estate Reserve pinot noir.

So, Kerry O'Hearn was also a Friestatt. Well, whoop de freakin' do. It wasn't enough that she had destroyed the case he and his team had worked so hard to prosecute. Now it seemed she had infiltrated his fledgling wine blog, too.

He'd been struggling for days to find the perfect descriptors for this particular pinot noir, made, ironically, from grapes grown not five miles from his new house. But it was just like the joke she'd told not an hour earlier. Whenever he sat down to write something that wasn't a police report, it was as if he couldn't put together the simplest sentence without it sounding like drivel when he read it back.

He poured an inch of wine into the glass and carried it out back, hoping if he stood still and was patient enough, he might see a robin, or even a rose-colored house finch, another sure harbinger of spring. He stood there for a minute, swirling the liquid in his glass and scanning the trees lining his yard. But apparently, it was still too early in the year for the songbirds to have migrated north.

He shivered in the chilly May evening and went inside and opened the fridge to see what he could throw together to eat. With the best of intentions, he pulled out a wilted head of lettuce and some rubbery carrots from the crisper drawer. Both went straight into the trash.

Then he spread peanut butter on white bread, topped it with sliced dill pickles, a recipe he'd carried over from his childhood. There'd been months when he'd eaten that meal every night, alone in front of the TV, when his mother was out with clients and his dad was at his store. When he was really young, Dad used to take him along with him. But that didn't last.

"Play with me," Alex begged his dad as he followed him back and forth across the showroom.

"Don't you have anything to do?" It was Dad's trademark response.

Alex knew he was a nag. But he was five years old. What was he supposed to do—play a board game with himself? Sit looking at the merchandise catalogs clogging Dad's desk? He wanted to do something important. Whatever his dad was doing, like using a box cutter to slit open the packing tape on big cardboard boxes and pulling out shiny new table lamps and brass drawer pulls, heavy in his palm. Or decipher the mysterious forms on the computer screen.

Dad must have been the last retailer in America to still use handwritten price tags. One Saturday when Alex was in first grade, he'd followed him around the store as usual, watching him hang red sale tags. "Can I help?" he pleaded, mesmerized by the tag dancing from a low-hanging ceiling fan, out of his reach.

"Don't touch that! Get out of here. Go on. Find something to do so you're not in the way."

Alex had wandered back to Dad's desk, where he spotted a neat stack of special sale tickets, white with a red stripe, the size of Dad's cell phone. Next to the pile lay some fat black markers.

Alex looked over at Dad, but he was busy talking to a customer. Alex knew better than to interrupt. He uncapped a marker, smelled its fuzzy tip and wrinkled up his nose. They were learning to write their numbers in school. He got an idea for how he could help Dad.

The sale had brought in more people than usual. Dad didn't notice Alex slinking around the perimeter of the room, replacing the sale tags he could reach with his new ones. Wouldn't Dad be surprised when he saw how good Alex could write his numbers!

"Is this really only eighty dollars?" asked a man examining the tag of a fancy floor lamp with what Alex now knew was a Tiffany-style shade.

"What the—" Dad's head whipped around the showroom. Far from being proud, he was scowling. "Alex!"

Alex stepped out from behind a multitiered display platform. "Here."

"What the hell are you doing?" He turned to the customer. "Heh heh, sorry about that. He thinks he's helping, but all he does is make my job harder."

"The tag says eighty."

Dad's fake smile melted. "Like I said, it's the kid's fault. He took off the real tag and replaced it with one he made." He turned to Alex again, his face mottled purple and white, and growled, "Where'd you put the good tags, the ones you took off?"

Alex froze. He had torn them in half, the way

Dad tore papers in half when he was working at his desk.

"Where'd you put them?"

Alex's heart was about to pound out of his chest. His cheeks burned like fire. Mutely, he pointed to the trash basket.

"Never mind," *said the customer with a wave of his hand as he drifted away.*

"Obviously it's a mistake. It's one twenty," *said Dad, trailing after him.* "Marked down from two thirty-nine."

"I'll think about it."

The customer walked out the door, and so did the other two browsers, but not before giving Dad a scornful, parting look. That left Alex alone to face his punishment.

"Can't you find anything constructive to do?" *Dad repeated in yet another variation of what would become the theme of Alex's life.* "Tell you what. Here's what you're going to do." *In a flash of inspiration, he strode over to the stockroom and held open the door.*

Head bowed, Alex dragged himself into the dim, musty room and watched as Dad wheeled a cobweb-infested desk chair out of a dark corner and spun it around to face him. "You're going to sit in this chair and not touch anything and think about what you did until I say you can get up. Do you understand?"

Slowly, Alex climbed onto the chair and folded his hands between his legs.

"Do you understand?"

Alex nodded, fighting back tears.

"Yes, sir."

"Yessir."

Four hours was a long time for a rambunctious five-year-old boy to sit still. Dad had to know that. In his defense, he must have forgotten about him, because he didn't come back until almost closing time.

Alex couldn't just up and move yet again. Moving was a huge hassle. Besides, he'd signed a six-month lease. Changing jobs again was definitely not an option. What other department was going to hire him when they saw he'd only lasted two months in Newberry?

He would just have to avoid Kerry O'Hearn the best he could. Find a new watering hole. Try doubly hard to wring confessions out of as many of his perps as possible so they didn't have to go to court. And for the ones that lawyered up, hope they didn't hire her to defend them.

He reclined his chair, took a bite out of his sandwich, and started flipping through the channels, trying to look on the bright side.

He had peanut butter, pickles, and pinot. A fresh start. A quiet place of his own within walking distance of world-class vineyards. Using his own two hands, he'd built bird feeders and bluebird houses and installed them out back, and he had a shiny new laptop. He could make this work. What other choice did he have?

And then Kerry's face came onto the screen in the night's top story about her latest legal victory, and he couldn't turn away.

Chapter Three

K erry was fuming as she left the Turning Point. The nerve of that guy! Given the nature of their work, cops and defense attorneys often butted heads. But that didn't mean they couldn't get along. What had she ever done to him?

But a scant five minutes later, when she reached the Community Center, she was forced to put her anger aside. That was one of the beautiful things about kids. They were a reminder of what was really important and what wasn't.

"Shay. Can you maybe give me a hand back here? I'm trying to keep hold of Ella without dropping her backpack and these drawings Mrs. Marshall thrust into my hand as we were walking out the door. Ella, stop pulling."

Shay strode well ahead of her mother and little sisters on legs that seemed to grow longer every day. She whirled around and stood there in the middle of the road in front of the Community

Center, planted her feet, and waited for them to catch up.

At the sight of Shay's furrowed brow, her jaw set in a blend of even greater anger and hurt than usual, a fresh wave of dread washed over Kerry. "Shay? What's wrong?"

"Nothing!"

Kerry tried not to take offense.

"I'm hungry," wailed Ella.

At that, Kerry's stomach rumbled. All she'd had to eat that day was a protein bar on the drive from her office to the courthouse for this morning's nine o'clock proceedings. During any trial, skipping lunch was routine. If it weren't for trying to get some vegetables into her kids at least a few times week, she could go for days at a time grabbing whatever tempting junk was displayed closest to the register at the front of the Thrifty Market.

"Shay got in a fight," said Chloé, shoulders hunched forward with the weight of her own crammed-to-bursting backpack. Chloé was one of those rare kids who adored school. She was also the quintessential middle child who tried never to rock the boat. For that she paid a price. Kerry hated to remember all the times when she'd been in the midst of drama with Ella or Shay, only to spot Chloé standing off to the side, looking down, stubbing her toe on the sidewalk or the linoleum or the grass, depending on where they were and what the latest disaster was they were dealing with.

"You tattletale!" Shay sneered at her sister.

Chloé flinched and Kerry blinked, feeling the sting of Shay's words right along with Chloé. How could middle schoolers be so mean?

Kerry waited for Chloé to catch up, Ella's back-pack sliding down her arm. Boosting it back up over her shoulder, she put her arm around Chloé, who reached up to move Ella's primitive drawings out of her eyes.

"Chloé was only telling me what I should have heard first from you," said Kerry to Shay.

"I'm *huuungry* . . ."

"Hush, Ella," said Kerry. "We're on our way to get you some food. What? Shay, what happened?"

"I said, *nothing*!"

Kerry's voice shifted into ripping-apart-a-prosecution-witness's-testimony gear. "You're the oldest, Shay. Have some consideration. Can't you see how hard it is for me to handle you three after working all day?"

Shay's expression immediately changed to one of remorse. She came back and reached for Ella's hand. "C'mon, Ella."

Now Kerry was the one overcome with misgivings. Shay might be the oldest, but she had taken the brunt of Kerry's poor decision-making when it came to men. She'd never known her birth father. And just when she'd started to trust Dick, the father of Chloé and Ella, Kerry had discovered he was cheating on her and asked him in no uncertain terms to leave. Now Kerry was expecting Shay to act like a grown-up when she was just becoming a teenager.

She touched Shay's shoulder. "I'm sorry. It was wrong of me to yell."

Shay jerked off Kerry's hand even as she spoke tenderly to Ella on their way to the car. No matter how angry she was at the rest of the world, she was never anything but sweet to her baby sister. "We're going to eat, Ella. What do you want? Some French fries, maybe?"

"Fwench fwies!" shouted Ella.

"No fast food tonight," Kerry said firmly. "I know everyone's starving, but we're going to have a good dinner."

Still. If she cooked, it would be at least another hour before the food was ready, and anyplace other than the hot food bar at Thrifty's meant wrestling Ella into a booster seat and trying to keep Shay and Chloé from annoying other diners with their sniping.

"Where are we going?" asked Chloé.

"Ruddock's," Kerry replied, keeping a watchful eye on Shay, strapping Ella into her car seat.

Chloé slid into the back next to Ella while Shay came around to nab her usual, prime spot in the front next to Kerry.

"Ruddock's?" With its stone walls, wood beams, and locally sourced menu, Ruddock's was as nice as any of the places they used to eat in Portland. "They have the best cheeseburgers," Shay said, all traces of snark now gone. "And their apple bread pudding is amazing."

"Pudding!" shouted Ella.

Chloé's head popped up in the rearview mirror. "But what about Hobo?"

Kerry's foot lifted off the gas of its own accord. The puppy they'd gotten a week ago, locked up in the house all day. How could she have forgotten?

"We'll swing by the house and let Hobo out first," she said.

Shay's head fell back against the headrest. "But

we're almost *there*. The farmhouse is fifteen minutes in the other direction. And then we'll have to go back to Ruddock's after we let the dog out. It'll be forty-five minutes by the time we get back and order, and another twenty before we get our food."

Shay was way too smart as far as Kerry was concerned. She turned the car around and headed homeward. "You guys begged me to get a puppy. I told you how much work they are." She'd caved, hoping the distraction of a dog might make their move more palatable. But it was just as she'd feared. She'd ended up taking most of the responsibility for him.

When they were almost home, Kerry said, "Tomorrow's Friday. How about we wait and go out then? I'll ask Grandma to let Hobo out after school." Kerry's parents lived in a newer house on the property, and her brothers and their wives and kids, as well as Jack and Hank Friestatt and their families, also lived close by.

"Or maybe Grandma can babysit Hobo all day, and then we'll go straight to Ruddock's before coming home."

"I knew we weren't going back," whined Shay.

"Hungry!" Ella started to cry.

"Shhh," said Chloé.

"Don't cry, Ellabella," said Kerry, putting the SUV into Park.

From the driveway, they could already hear Hobo barking inside.

"I'll get you some crackers as soon as we get in, Ella. Shay, would you keep an eye on Hobo while he does his business?"

But they were too late. Just over the threshold of the dining room, with its cream-colored walls, its corner cupboards and wainscoting painted smoky green, and the rustic iron chandelier with little checkered shades, Ella toddled into a puddle. She slipped, catching herself with palms planted on the wet floor.

"Oh!" Kerry exclaimed. "Chloé, could you get the paper towels and mop up Hobo's mess while I get Ella cleaned up?"

Dutifully, Chloé slung her book bag onto a chair and made a beeline for the kitchen, while Kerry picked up Ella, slipped off her wet-soled shoes, and tossed them out into the yard to be dealt with later.

After a supper of canned soup and bagged salad, when Chloé was doing her homework and Ella had been tucked in, Kerry went into Shay's room and sat down on her bed and brushed her bangs out of her eyes.

Shay moved her head away.

"You going to tell me what's going on?" Kerry asked softly.

"What do you mean?"

"You know what I mean. The fight."

"It was nothing. Helena Young said I stole her boyfriend. She got some of her minions to come along and cornered me in the gym beside the bleachers when none of the teachers were around."

Kerry frowned. "What do you mean, stole her boyfriend?" *They were only twelve, for Chrissake.*

"Michael Herod. He's been calling me at night, playing me songs over the phone. He sure didn't act like he had a girlfriend." Shay looked down at where she picked at the corner of the page in the book she'd been reading.

It wasn't the first time Shay had had trouble at her new school.

"It all started when I wore that navy mini and my white shirt with the stars on it and the red tie around my waist. Everyone else had on jeans and flannel shirts. I stuck out like a sore thumb. All the boys wanted to walk with me in the hall, and that made all the girls hate me even more. How was I supposed to know? All I was trying to do was look good on my first day at a new school." She dropped her head onto her aqua pillowcase with the little pompoms on it. "I miss Mayree."

Mayree, still Shay's closest friend, though it'd been months since they'd moved away from her.

"I want to move back to Portland." A tear slid down her nose.

Kerry brushed the fine strands of hair away from her daughter's baby-soft cheek. "I'm sorry. That must have been really hard for you." *Terrible*, in fact. But venting her outrage would only ramp up the drama.

"The school year's almost over and they still hate me."

"They don't hate you. They just don't know what to do with you."

Kerry had thought that moving now would give Shay time to blend in before the start of high school. But it was looking more and more like she'd picked the worst possible time for a child to change schools. With all those hormones cranked on like a faucet, adolescent girls didn't even like themselves, much less a stylish new girl from the city plopped down in their midst, attracting the attention of the equally hormonal boys.

"I can't help it that I'm different. That all my clothes are different. These people around here are just hicks."

Kerry smiled. "I guess that makes me a hick, too."

"You're not a hick. You're my mom."

"Hm." Same thing, Kerry thought with a half smile. She rubbed her daughter's back, wishing she could solve Shay's problems the way she used to, with a storybook or an ice cream cone.

"Don't make me go back," she whined.

Kerry's hand stilled in the hollow between Shay's shoulder blades. "You have to go back. Newberry is your school now. This is where we live."

Shay lifted her head, her anger roaring back. "And to top it all off, I'm the oldest one at afterschool care! Do you know how embarrassing that is? How they laugh at me in the hall behind my back, but loud enough for me to hear?"

Chalk up yet another maternal misstep. Kerry had had an inkling that that might be an issue when she'd signed the kids up last fall, but between juggling her caseload, paying the bills on time, and managing some semblance of a normal home life, she'd brushed aside her reservations, hoping against hope it would all magically work out.

She swallowed her guilt, summoning as soothing a voice as she could muster. "You know Helena's just jealous of you, right?"

Shay's head dropped back to her pillow and a tear squeezed out. "Whatever."

"The world was Helena's oyster, and then along comes this pretty, smart new girl and everything changes. She takes away the attention Helena was getting from her friends, the boy she wanted for her boyfriend, whether or not he knew it. She acts tough, but deep down, she's scared. She doesn't know what to make of you. Chances are maybe her parents or her siblings or someone else has bullied her before. That's how we learn, by experience. Helena learned that bullying's an okay way to deal with things. So, when she feels backed into a corner, she lashes out."

"So, what am I supposed to do? I don't try to act better than her. I'm just being myself."

"Here's what we're going to do. I'm going go to your school tomorrow and tell as many adults as possible—"

"Don't do that!" wailed Shay. "If Helena and everybody hears my mom's involved, it'll just make it worse."

"Listen to me. Your guidance counselor, your teachers, and your principal—they all need to know about Helena, and she needs to know that they're on to her and that this behavior has to stop. From then on, she'll know she's being watched. A lot of times, that's all it takes. And here's the hard part: You're going to have to stand up to her, too, and tell her to quit it."

"I can't."

"You can. You have to. If you don't, it could get worse."

Chapter Four

"Walker."

Alex was halfway down the hall to his locker to change into his sweats when behind him, he heard Chief Garrett call his name.

He stopped in his tracks and turned around to see the chief leaning against the wall with his arms folded.

"Nice going today."

"Thanks." It had taken over three hours to talk the guy lying in the bushes alongside a rural road to surrender the rifle he was holding and take him into custody. Alex had spearheaded the team. It was the most action he'd had since switching jobs.

Garrett nodded toward his office. "Got a minute?"

Alex massaged the nape of his neck as he followed behind his boss. After idling by the past five hours reading every dog-eared, germ-infested gossip rag at the Newberry Medical Center cover to cover, waiting for his detainee to be evaluated, he was itching to jump into his athletic shorts and run off the stress of the day. If he were still in Portland, he'd be on his way to his boxing club right now. But Newberry wasn't big enough to warrant its own, dedicated boxing gym. So, instead of venting his pent-up anxiety on a speed bag, he'd been logging about twenty miles a week on the roads.

While Alex squeezed into one of two scuffed, sunshine-yellow plastic seats, Garrett strolled behind his desk and sank into his black vinyl swivel chair. The unlikely decorating scheme wasn't because Garrett enjoyed lording it over his men, but due to simple lack of public funding. Truth was, Garrett was pretty easy to get along with. Didn't micromanage. Let Alex be Alex. But if there'd been any doubt as to who was in charge in this impromptu meeting, the disparity between the chairs made it crystal clear.

Garrett crossed his legs, folded his hands behind his head, and swiveled easily back and forth. "Been two months. How's it going?"

Alex shifted in his seat, but the small chair made it impossible for him to get comfortable.

"Going great."

"Big difference between a major metropolitan agency and a small-town cop shop. Any surprises so far?"

"What with fewer men, I knew there'd be more going it alone with no backup. And I expected having to pinch-hit sometimes, even to the point of answering the phone if I'm the closest one to the desk when it rings. But I got to admit, I might not have made the switch if I'd known I'd be giving up my Dodge Charger for a five-year-old Taurus." He grinned.

"We make do. Like I said when you came on. This is Newberry, not Mayberry, so don't think you can just coast from now till retirement."

Alex shrugged. "Not the first time I've changed my own oil."

"Did I forget to mention in your interview the savings to the department in doing our own vehicle maintenance?" The chief laughed. "But something I did mention . . ."

Here it came. Alex had been waiting for this since his first day of work for the Newberry Special Ops Division.

"The biggest difference between Newberry and Portland is that here, we know most of our citizens by name. We either went to school with them or go to the same church, or our kids go to school with their kids or play on the same baseball team or go to the same ballet school or whatever. To be completely honest, that was a strike against you, coming in. More than one individual strongly suggested I ought to hire a different candidate for that very reason. Have to admit, I gave it some thought. But I saw something in you that the other candidates didn't have."

"You mean, aside from my rugged good looks?" A reference to his bent nose, courtesy of Lucky Joe Johnson in the Annual Boxing Invitational some years back. "My natural charm?"

"If this job were based on either charm or looks, you'd still be driving that Charger. And while I'm being so honest, I'll tell you something else, even though it's far from PC. You were by far the oldest candidate. There was some backroom muttering about that."

Like Alex needed a reminder. He'd only just turned forty, but his lower back was paying for the years he'd spent riding patrol in Portland, before he made detective. And now here he was, stuck in this sad excuse for a chair while his boss took his sweet time coming out with whatever it was he'd dragged him in here to say.

"You're also a little on the surly side."

So that's what this was about. The news anchor Alex had chewed out for being too close to the crime scene today had complained.

Alex felt his self-effacing grin dissolve. "You spend fifteen years working twenty cases at a time with the worst side of humanity for shitty pay and see how sweet-tempered it makes *you.*"

"Heh heh heh. Like I said. Surly."

Alex's patience was wearing thin. "So what'd you call me in here for? You have regrets? You going to fire me? Fire me."

"Fire you? Hell no, I'm not going to fire you. You were right on the money today. I'd hire you all over again for your top-notch training alone. Aside from that, you're confident. You're accountable. And you embrace failure."

"That's what you were looking for? Someone who knows how to fail?"

"Being an outsider, you may not have noticed it yet, but Newberry's growing. It's not the hayseed town it used to be. Wine sales are up forty percent over the past five years. New businesses that support the grape industry are opening, bringing more workers. Tourism's skyrocketing. And I don't have to tell you that when you got more people, you got more people problems. Drugs, crime, and all the rest.

"What works for a small town doesn't necessarily work for a medium-sized burg. And that's where you come in. That heavy caseload you carried all those years? That taught you tenacity. Resilience. You're the kind of experienced officer a growing town like Newberry needs.

"But we can't let go of that personal connection between officers and residents. That's how we obtain and keep respect. To that end, I was talking to my friend Scott Dishman over at the Community Center. Come to find out he's starting up a youth boxing class."

Alex knew he'd eventually have to do something in community relations. He never dreamed it'd have to do with boxing.

"I box. I don't *teach* boxing."

"You volunteered with PAL at Portland State's summer camps for five years."

The Police Athletic League fitness program that kept low-income kids off the streets during the summer and had the side benefit of showing them that cops were human, too, till it closed for lack of funding when the economy tanked. Chief had done his research.

"I'm not certified."

"Don't have to be. Dishman's already got a certified instructor all lined up. We just need you to be more or less a presence. You know. Show up once a week, fill in from time to time when the regular guy can't be there."

"Like I said, I'm not a teacher. I'm a cop. I picked Newberry as my final stop because I was tired of being depersonalized."

Back in the early days of his career, people by and large still had respect for police officers. But by the time he made detective, whenever he lit someone up for running a red light or expired tags, he had learned to brace himself for the inevitable, "Don't you have anything better to do than pull me over?" Those were the *nice* ones.

"Seemed like no matter how hard I beat my head against the wall, I wasn't having any effect. I'm ready to spend the final decade of my career somewhere quiet and low-key. In case you haven't noticed, kids aren't quiet. They're loud. Loud and messy."

"You do know what Community Response Team *means?*"

Alex sighed and folded his arms. "It's a crisis intervention team."

"It's not just that. We have to be genuinely responsive to the community. Interact with them at their level. We go to them before they need us. That way, when the time comes that they're in crisis, they see us as the good guys. Like I said when I took you on, I expect every officer on the CRT to step up to the plate. Like Myers, who does regular safety talks at the schools. Washington, taking her K9 in. Nothing like an animal to connect with kids. Then there's Zangrilli, who organizes the neighborhood watch. I been keeping my eyes peeled for something just for you. Pretty much knew you wouldn't do it yourself, so I did it for you."

"I'd say thanks, but—"

"No thanks needed. I know it might sound corn-ball, but when I started snooping around I got an earful. Your reputation precedes you."

"What exactly did you hear?" Alex asked warily.

"That underneath that aloof exterior, it's all mush."

Alex threw up his hands. "My darkest secret laid bare. How much is it gonna cost me to keep it to yourself?"

"I heard all about the coat drive for homeless kids you started," the chief continued, ignoring Alex's self-effacement. "How you took that boy from the projects under your wing when his dad was murdered, helping him write his college applications . . ."

"Aw, shoot." Alex squirmed. "'T'weren't nothin.'"

". . . the scholarship fund you set up for that brainy girl in the wheelchair whose family didn't have a pot to piss in. By the way. How is it that didn't make it onto your job résumé?"

Alex looked at his watch. "Are we about done here? 'Cause I just remembered, the mayor wants to give me a key to the city."

"Don't get carried away with yourself. Nobody said you were perfect. Despite the snarkasm, you got a lot to offer. You were exactly what I was look-ing for on my team. A straight shooter. A good communicator."

Alex looked around. "You talking to me?"

"Obviously, you're no Shakespeare. Look at it this way. You claim you weren't feeling connected or appreciated. This boxing thing could be just what the doctor ordered." He swiveled around to glance at the big round wall clock. "Well," he sighed, rising from his chair. "It's almost seven. Wife's chorale's putting on a show tonight. Thank God it's finally here. They've been practicing since January. Five months of fending for myself two nights a week is long enough."

"You've missed her," marveled Alex out loud. He'd have thought a man married as long as some-one the chief's age would relish a free pass twice a week.

"You ever been married?"

"Once, a long time ago."

"You might find this hard to believe, but ask anyone. When Louisa's not home, I'm like a lost baby fawn."

Alex regarded Chief Garrett's steely forearms extending from his rolled-up sleeves. Despite the glints of silver in his hair, he was still an impressive male specimen by any standards. He arched a brow.

"Just wait," said the chief. "One day, you'll see what I mean."

Every now and again, another of that rare breed of men who'd found his perfect match hinted at the same. But at Alex's age, it seemed less and less likely that that was what fate had in store for him. A few years after his divorce, loneliness finally forced him to go out again occasionally. But by now, the plaster in the wall he'd built around his heart seemed to have permanently set. He had de-veloped a hard and fast rule—three dates, max, with the same woman.

"This is Louisa's ninth year singing with chorale," said the chief. "You know. 'Orpheus with His Lute'? 'Lift Thine Eyes, Elijah'?" At Alex's blank expres-

sion, he sighed and said, "Maybe you don't.
Chorale music isn't everyone's cup of tea.

"So, barring another crisis like the one we had
today, I can count on you to go over and meet with
Gene Lovatt, the boxing coach, Thursday morning, then?" said the chief, standing and retucking
his shirttail.

Alex stood, grateful to finally stretch his legs.
"Yessir."

Chapter Five

Coach Lovatt was giving Alex the grand tour of the corner of the Community Center set aside for the boxing classes.

"The building is already equipped with free weights and treadmills. I bought an assortment of gloves, some handwraps, jump ropes, a pair of heavy bags, and two speed bags. That's it for now. Most important thing was making sure we're in compliance with state and local regs. That, and liability insurance. And we've already given the school coupons good for a free introductory lesson. They promised to give one to every student."

Alex looked around, hands propped on his hips. "How old does a kid have to be to do this?"

"Holyfield started when he was eight years old and weighed sixty-five pounds."

"You don't think—"

"No. We're not looking for the next Holyfield. I'm not even sure if we'll get into actual sparring.

That's why I didn't invest in headgear. Yet. Would I love to have a ring? You bet. But we don't happen to have an extra five grand lying around. Maybe someday I'll look in to crowd funding. Right now, our goal is to give a foundation in the basics. You know. Conditioning, punching, stance, footwork. In the end, this is just about providing a place where kids can get into shape and feel better about themselves and learn self-confidence."

"Chief said you're a certified trainer?"

Gene nodded. "I've paid my dues. Placed in sanctioned and amateur shows around the state. For me, boxing was an escape from the streets. Now I'm paying it back."

Alex nodded. "I've heard your name somewhere along the way. Didn't know you hailed from around here. So, what's the schedule?"

"Thursdays after school, three thirty till four fifteen."

"I work a ten-hour variable shift, four days a week. There'll be days when I can't show. Plus, any time there's a major incident, there's a good chance I'll get called to the scene."

Gene reached out to shake Alex's hand. "You got a built-in background check, and I'm willing to bet your TB test is up-to-date. I'll take what I can get."

Kerry scheduled an appointment with Shay's guidance counselor during a time when classes were in session. She didn't want kids passing through the halls to see her there and then tease Shay about her mom coming to her rescue.

While she waited in the principal's office, she pulled Ella's stick-family portrait out of her bag and studied it. Ella had drawn Kerry vastly larger than everyone else, a clear sign she saw her as the leader. Then, in descending order of height, came Shay, Chloé, and finally herself. All four were clustered in the center of the paper. At the far edge was a male figure about the size of Shay. That couldn't be anyone else but Ella's father.

Dick had made all sorts of noise when Kerry insisted on separating, but within a year his visits had tapered off to the point where now the girls had stopped asking about him.

And after yet another failed relationship, Kerry had vowed to expend 100 percent of her energy on her girls from now on.

Yet this drawing was a sign Ella hadn't completely forgotten her father.

"Did Shay have any problems with fighting when she lived in Portland?" asked the counselor when they finally sat down together.

"Shay had lots of friends at her old school. That's what makes this so hard. She doesn't know how to deal with it."

"Did Shay in any way use physical force in this confrontation with Helena?"

"Shay? Never. My girls don't fight. I'm a criminal defense attorney. I've seen where physical aggression leads. I'm bringing my children up to settle their differences with words, not their fists.

"Like I told you on the phone, Helena accused Shay of poaching her boyfriend and threatened to punch her. I won't stand for my daughter being victimized."

"Rightly so. If you give me the names of everyone involved, I promise to follow up with her teachers and the administration. And don't worry, they'll never know how I found out. But back to Shay. How are you handling it with her?"

"I told her to stay where there are people at all times and to continue to defend herself verbally."

The guidance counselor picked up a leaflet on the corner of her desk and handed it to Kerry. "I'm not sure what you'll think of this idea, but the Community Center is starting a boxing class."

Kerry took the flyer and skimmed down the page. "Boxing? I just told you, we don't hit in our family. This is the antithesis of what I advised my daughter to do. Not only that, Shay's got a small frame. A great sense of style. And her thing is playing with makeup. I know she's kind of young for that, but she's been really lonely since we moved here, and it's something she can do by herself. My point is, Shay's not exactly what I picture when I think of women boxers."

"I'm not saying it's right for everybody. But if you read further down, it says it's not so much about combat as it is fitness and building self-confidence."

Kerry set the flyer back in the pile. "I don't think so."

"Shay should have already gotten one of these from her teacher. I wonder what she thinks about it."

"She did?"

"You didn't see it in her backpack?"

Kerry shook her head. Between everything else she had to remember to do on a daily basis, going through Shay's backpack had slipped through the cracks.

"Shay's already at the Community Center after school, isn't she? That would eliminate you having to drive her to the class. Why don't you just take this with you and talk to her about it?" the guidance counselor said, handing the flyer back to her with a kind smile.

Kerry bit her lip and sighed. She had to do *something*.

"I'll talk it over with her. But I doubt it's going to work."

"What have we got?" Alex asked Gene on the first day of boxing classes, rubbing his hands together, trying to work up some enthusiasm about his latest obligation.

A couple of nervous-looking kids were hanging in the doorway, stealing curious glances at the bags suspended at varying heights from the ceiling.

Gene read from the forms on his tablet. "Two boys, ten and twelve. And a girl."

"A girl?" Alex hadn't been expecting girls. Though why not, he didn't know. Girls did everything boys did now, didn't they? Still . . . in his dinosaur point of view, there was something about girls and throwing punches that just didn't mix.

"Her guidance counselor suggested it to her mom. She's being pushed around a little at school."

"Good thing I'm not a teacher. If I caught kids bullying, I'd have to use one as a club to beat the other."

Gene coughed and glanced over his shoulder.

"I'm thinking it might be best if you stick to the after-school programs."

The clock on the wall said three thirty. "Time to start," said Alex. "What do you want to do about the girl?"

"I'll be surprised if she even shows. How 'bout I get these two warmed up on the treadmills down the hall? Be back in about five. If the girl shows up, bring her down?"

Left alone, Alex did a slow circuit of the room. If he had to be here, he wished he had more to do than just assist. From other parts of the building he heard kids yelling, the squeal of rubber soles on a gym floor, and the bouncing of basketballs.

He pulled his gloves from his gym bag, Velcroed them on, and started hitting the speed bag, his hands finding a familiar rhythm.

A minute into his warm-up, he saw two figures from the corner of his eye. He stilled the bag between his gloves and turned to greet them, and it was all he could do to hide his shock when he saw Kerry O'Hearn for the second time in as many weeks with her hand resting protectively on the back of a junior version of herself.

The girl Gene claimed was being hassled was Kerry O'Hearn's daughter?

And now, out of every boxing instructor in the Pacific Northwest, it was falling to Alex in his volunteer CRT role, to teach her daughter self-defense? The old adage was true—no good deed goes unpunished.

With his teeth, he ripped back the Velcro on his glove to free his right hand as he walked up to them.

Kerry's eyes met his . . . not from far across the oak-paneled courtroom of Pioneer Courthouse where Alex had watched her forge her reputation as a ruthless litigator, or at an angle in the dimly lit Turning Point saloon. Here, face-to-face in the Community Center, a place built for the very purpose of bringing people together. And her eyes were far from stone cold. In fact, he saw the last thing he'd ever expected to see in them: vulnerability.

Kerry blinked. "Er, hello."

For years, Alex thought there was nothing he wouldn't do to see Kerry O'Hearn squirm. But no matter what their issues, the kid was hardly to blame.

"Aren't you . . . ?"

He looked down at the hand with short, clear-polished nails held out to him in greeting. As well as he felt he knew the counselor, it seemed impossible they had never touched. Now there was no way around it.

"Alex Walker." After all this time, her palm pressed firmly against his felt somehow momentous.

"*Detective* Alex Walker," she said.

"That's right." He dropped her hand and spun on his heel to leave her there to wait for Gene.

"What are you doing"—she looked around—"here?"

Reluctantly, he turned back around. "Community service. New department policy, whether we want to or not." *Just in case he hadn't made enough of an ass of himself at the bar with his stupid lawyer joke.* "If you're looking for the guy in charge, he's down the hall in the room with the treadmills, getting the other kids warmed up. Should be back any minute."

"I'm Kerry O'Hearn," she said with her usual poise. "And this is my daughter, Shay."

He'd momentarily forgotten about the girl. But then, Kerry's personal life had never been of interest to him. His grudge was for professional reasons.

Now he examined her daughter more closely. She had Kerry's facial features in miniature, including those sensitive, intelligent eyes, but she was darker complected, and where Kerry's head was sleek, Shay's was a mass of curls.

Lucky. Envy of Kerry O'Hearn's good fortune stabbed at him, followed immediately by self-loathing for his jealousy.

"Pleased to meet you, Shay."

Her eyes on her feet, Shay accepted his hand in a weak, rubbery grip.

Alex softened. It wasn't the kid's fault she'd been born to a shark without a conscience.

"Always look a person in the eye when you shake hands with him."

The girl blinked and looked up. "Huh?"

He hated that eyes that young could harbor such despair. "Let's try that again. I'm Coach Walker." He extended his hand again. "And you are?"

"Shay," she repeated with an impossible blend of surprise and insolence.

"Better."

"I'm not staying."

"Shay," warned Kerry.

"I'm not staying."

"You got something better to do?" asked Alex.

"Maybe," Shay spat.

"Like what?"

She thought for a second. "Studying."

"Studying what?"

"Pre-algebra."

Alex pulled a face. "You know how much pre-algebra you're going to be using once you're out of school? What do you want to be when you grow up?"

"A cosmetologist," she said, warily, and with a little less attitude.

He frowned. "A cosme—"

"Cosme*tologist*," she repeated with a roll of her eyes at his profound ignorance. "Someone who works at the makeup counter at Sephora, like at the mall at Tigard."

"Oh, *that* kind of cosmetologist. I don't know much about makeup, but something tells me an A in pre-algebra isn't going to help you much."

"Excuse me?" Kerry cocked a brow.

"I've never set foot in a Sephora," he continued, "but their cosmetologists are probably trained to sell that makeup they put on girls like you. Everyone knows selling anything, whether it's cars or insurance or makeup, takes confidence. Get good at selling one-on-one and next thing you know, people are going to want to know how you do it. You're going to be standing in front of groups of people, demonstrating your awesome skills. And you never know where that could lead. *Teaching* cosmetology. Working for a big makeup company. Who knows? You could have your own YouTube channel, showing people how to use makeup."

The spark of hope in Shay's eyes when she looked up at her mother was such a small thing, but it made Alex want to punch the air in euphoria.

"But there's something you need to learn to do that or any one of a million other roads cosmetology might take you down, and that's self-confidence. And I know a surefire way to get that. I can train you to be confident enough to face just about any situation that comes up. Any person, friend . . . or foe."

"Isn't that right, Mom?" Alex asked Kerry without looking at her.

Shay looked at Kerry again for confirmation, but her mother withheld judgment.

"Tell you what," Alex said to Shay. "Give it one session. Forty five—" He glanced at the clock. "Forty minutes. If you don't like it," he shrugged, "don't come back."

"Who's the parent here?" asked Kerry coolly.

His first five minutes as a boxing coach and he'd already blown it. Alex immediately backed away, holding up his hands. "Sorry. I'm new at this."

"What's going on?" asked Gene, walking up behind Alex, trailed by the other students.

Alex and Kerry began talking at the same time.

"Officer Walker has an interesting way of selling your—"

"I was explaining to Shay and her mom that you need to develop self-confidence, that is, unless you want to suck at life—"

Gene silenced Alex with a hand on his shoulder. "You mind showing the boys how to do some stretches, now that they're warmed up?"

"Sure." Alex backtracked to where the boys stood, watching and waiting. "Good to meet you, Shay."

He was certain the next time he turned around, Shay and Kerry would be gone.

"So, you're Shay," said the man in charge.

"Yessir." Shay looked him in the eye as she took his hand.

Kerry took a step toward him. "Look, Mr., um—"

"Gene Lovatt. The kids call me Coach."

"Mr. Lovatt. Coach. I'm not sure this is the right thing for Shay. She—"

"It's fine," said Shay, giving Kerry an exasperated look. "I can talk for myself."

Kerry's mouth dropped open. "But I thought . . ."

"I'll try it one time. Like Coach Walker said. Better than algebra."

"But you don't even—"

"What else did Coach Walker say?" asked Gene.

"He said it could give me self-confidence," Shay mumbled.

"Did he explain exactly what it is you're going to be doing?"

Kerry and Shay shook their heads.

"First off, the most important things about boxing are the key values of respect, camaraderie, and honor. After that, some people think boxing's just punching. But it's actually a full-body conditioning program that will strengthen your core and your cardiovascular system. We'll be doing lots of aerobic and anaerobic conditioning, plyometrics, and agility movements."

"I have a question," Kerry interjected. "What about the fact that she's a girl?"

Shay's jaw dropped and her eyes rolled back in her head. "*Momm*-ah!"

"I know of models and fashion bloggers who box," said Coach. "They put it right up there with ballet and SoulCycle. Are you afraid of her bulking up? Don't worry. Not going to happen.

"In other words," he turned back to Shay and smiled, "boxing'll give you lean, toned arms and legs. And as an added bonus," he paused for effect, "no one will want to mess with you. So. How 'bout it. You in?"

Kerry opened her mouth to answer for her daughter, the way she had all Shay's life, but Coach Lovatt flashed her a veiled warning.

To say Shay wasn't athletic was an understatement. She hated running so much, she'd begged to stay home from school every year on Field Day. She spent most of her free time in front of the mirror, experimenting with the gaudiest colors in Kerry's eye-shadow palettes, the ones that would otherwise have gone unused when all the neutrals were empty.

So why was she now nodding her head in acquiescence?

"Great," said Coach, tossing an arm around Shay's shoulders. "Mom? We'll see you later."

"But I thought I'd . . ." the word *watch* trailed off as Shay was led away by Coach Lovatt without so much as a backward glance.

Shay, who would always be her firstborn. Her precious daughter, whom she never shared with anyone—not even Shay's father, who'd rejected her while she was still in the womb. She wanted to run after her and scoop her up and tell her there was no need to subject herself to this. That her mama would protect her for the rest of her life.

But as much as she wanted to wrap Shay up in a safe cocoon and keep her tucked safely in her bedroom with the aqua bedspread and stuffed animals, the reality was that Kerry couldn't be with her 24-7 for the rest of her life.

She pressed her lips together and furrowed her brow. As hard as it was, maybe it was time for her baby to learn to protect herself.

Chapter Six

A dozen or so officers lounged at rows of tables for the morning briefing. From the Patrol Division were the school resource officer and traffic safety. From the Special Ops Division were detectives assigned to the property crimes and narcotics units.

There was also Alex's unit. Crimes Against Persons was a catchall term that encompassed felonious assaults, abuse, and missing persons, as well as more violent crimes like rape, robbery, and homicide. CAP was also tasked with collecting crime-scene evidence and interviewing suspects, witnesses, and victims to assist in prosecution.

Granger, one of the other five officers in the unit, sat next to Alex, holding his pen between his teeth, frowning down at his tablet.

Tony Zangrilli was relating how around ten thirty on the previous night's patrol he had spotted two kids in the vicinity of the same schools Alex drove past on his way to and from work.

"I gave foot chase, but they were three hundred yards away before I got out of my car. Soon as they saw me, they took off running and fanned out."

Wincing at the bitter taste of the brew from the ancient coffeemaker, Alex set down his cup. "How old did you say you thought they were?"

"The younger one was about eight and the older one, eleven."

"What time's curfew around here?"

"Nine fifteen for kids under fourteen," stated the chief, where he stood at the front of the room.

Zangrilli added, "It's rarely enforced, but it can come in handy when your gut tells you something's off."

Whatever it was that had caught Alex's attention that evening at dusk a couple of weeks back—a fox, a plastic bag blowing in the wind—it hadn't been solid enough to warrant a report.

But after hearing Zangrilli's story, he made a mental note to keep his eyes peeled whenever he was in that area.

Only two nights later, driving past the athletic fields at around eleven fifteen, Alex came upon two thin, shaggy-haired boys walking down the sidewalk.

"This is Walker." Alex's right hand clutched his radio while his left was already on his door handle in readiness to bail. "Signal thirteen. I'm on Northeast Chehalem by the middle school. Going to be two juveniles on foot, one in a white T-shirt, the other in blue."

On seeing headlights coming down the deserted street, the boys turned their heads but didn't startle at the sight of Alex's unremarkable Ford sedan.

Until Alex slid down his window and drove up alongside them. "What are you two doing roaming the street at this hour on a school night?"

They froze in their tracks.

"Don't try to run." In a second, Alex was standing over them, hands on hips.

"What're your names?" he asked in a speaking tone.

"Tyler," said the older of the two.

"Travith," lisped the other boy who, by the green eyes and pointed chins they shared, was obviously his brother.

"Where do you live?"

Reluctantly, Tyler pointed toward multileveled rooftops on a rise, a few blocks away.

"Allen Street?"

He nodded.

The ritziest street in town, where Victorians trimmed in pastel shades sat back in professionally landscaped yards like grand ladies holding court.

"Do your parents know where you are?"

Travis cowered behind his older brother.

"I'm a policeman," said Alex.

The boys' eyes grew wider.

"Where's your uniform?" cracked Tyler, thrusting out his bony chest.

"Not all policemen wear uniforms. See? Here's my badge." The metal glinted in the light of his headlights.

Despite himself, Travis leaned around his brother to ogle it.

Alex clapped a hand on to each of the boys' clavicles and escorted them to the passenger side of his car and told them to slide in to the front seat. They were so small they could both easily fit.

Then he climbed in next to them.

"What's your last name?"

"Pelletier."

"What's your mom going to say when I bring you to the door?"

He peered down into a pair of faces looking mutely up at him. They didn't seem as scared now. More curious about Alex and his dashboard, kitted out with its video screen for running plates and buttons for sirens and lights.

"You ever been in trouble with the police before?" he asked sternly. "Don't lie, because I'm going to check."

They shook their heads while he radioed their names to the dispatcher.

They came back clean—not that Alex was surprised. "I'm going to take you boys home with a warning," he said. "I imagine Mom and Dad will punish you enough for being out at this hour."

As the older of the two solemnly pointed the way to their house, Alex prepared himself for concerned parental anger, profuse apologies, and sworn promises that this would never happen again, to which he would mutter some platitudes, wave, back down the driveway, and forget all about—what were their names, again?

He pulled into the long drive of a house in a leafy enclave that sat back even farther than the others on the block. His headlamps revealed a boxy brick dwelling with darkened windows and a mansard roof that gave the impression that the whole house was frowning.

He rang the bell while the boys stood on either side of him, still seeming more curious than concerned about an imminent scolding.

After thirty seconds, Alex punched the bell again, twice this time for good measure. The sooner he could get this nuisance case off his hands, the sooner he could get home. Maybe he could get some work in on his blog yet tonight.

Still, no one came.

"Newberry Police," he yelled, and pounded on the door hard enough to make the younger boy jump.

Finally, the door slowly opened to a woman with tousled hair who appeared to have fallen asleep in her street clothes, clothes that fit her so perfectly they could have been made expressly for her.

"Lose something?" By this time, Alex was unable to keep the sarcasm out of his voice.

The woman shook back her fashionably cut hair.

"It's hours past curfew. I found these two a block from here wandering around. You want to explain that?"

"They must have slipped out when I wasn't looking."

"These *are* your kids?"

She hesitated, as if undecided. "Yes."

There was something familiar about this woman who had had the good fortune to live in a grand house and have two healthy boys and yet who stood there, silent as a stone. She reminded him of his own mother.

Long ago, Alex had decided that if one of his kids snuck out and was brought home in the middle of the night by a cop, he wouldn't stand there like a bump on a log like this woman was doing. Like his own mother had done when Alex himself had wandered out, seeking nothing more than someone to talk to, to affirm that he was human, that he existed. He'd haul his butt into the house, sit him down, and give him a reaming he wouldn't soon forget. Then again, no kid of his would suffer self-doubt over whether he was worth more than just a pile of professionally wrapped presents at Christmas, picked out by his mother's personal assistant.

Hopefully, these guys didn't have it that bad. Even if they did, emotional neglect was clouded in ambiguity and hard to prove.

He looked them over again. No obvious bruising, no signs of broken bones.

With a hand to their upper backs, he gave them a nudge forward. "Go on inside, boys, and get ready for bed." He'd meant what he'd said to the kids earlier. He really had intended to let this go with just a warning. But he had scant patience for parents like this one.

The woman turned to retreat into the house, thinking she was off the hook, but Alex stuck his foot in the door as he scribbled on his electronic tablet.

"Not so fast. I'm citing you for violation of curfew. Five hundred dollars for each child."

She turned back around, cocking a brow. "Excuse me?" It was the most emotion she'd shown since answering the door. "That's ridiculous."

"Consider yourself lucky. They've been spotted out here before, but this is the first time they've been caught. If it happens again, you'll get slammed with another fine, plus you'll have to go to a three-hour workshop on what happens to kids left alone to walk the streets at night. A third time and you could lose your kids."

Alex printed the citation and ripped it off his device with a flourish. When she simply looked at it, he grabbed her hand dangling limply at her side and stuffed the citation into it.

Then he strode back to his vehicle to the soft click of the ornately carved front door closing behind him, his pulse pounding in his temples.

He fished in his pocket for one of the rolls of TUMS he kept everywhere—his car, his desk drawer, and his nightstand. This was the kind of call that had got him diagnosed with acid reflux in the first place.

Chapter Seven

Shay's attempts to pummel the punching bag into submission would have been funny if they weren't so impassioned. Her cheeks were pink with effort and her brow was furrowed. Unfortunately, the bag was winning. Alex positioned himself across from her and steadied it between his hands while she continued to give it everything she had in her.

"Take it easy, kiddo. I appreciate the effort, but this is only your third class. There's no need to put so much effort into every punch. You don't have sufficient technique yet. That's a good way to tear a muscle or stave your wrist. For now, just concentrate on your form."

He was getting better at this teaching thing. Wasn't sticking his foot in his mouth nearly as much. It helped a lot that the kids never once asked if he didn't have something better to do.

When class was over, Gene let Alex have the last word. He corralled them together and asked them to sit down cross-legged while Gene stood in the background, trying to be unobtrusive.

"Always remember: in boxing, as in life, a good attitude is important. You should be willing to learn, respect others, and try your best. Have fun. Don't be in a hurry. It takes time, but you're learning a skill for life."

When class was dismissed, he helped Shay take off her handwraps.

"You were really giving it to that bag today. Couldn't help but wonder where all that aggression was coming from." He didn't want her to know Gene had been talking about her to him or, worse, that her guidance counselor had been the one to suggest she take up boxing to gain confidence.

Shay didn't respond.

"It's like Coach Lovatt said at the start of the class. What we're mainly concerned with here is conditioning. But if someone is giving you a hard time, it's best to try to talk it out, defuse the situation before it escalates into a physical attack. That's how police officers are trained to deal with bad guys."

He glanced at his watch. He was off for the rest of the day. Spring had arrived, his first spring in the Willamette Valley, and with it the first waves of migrating songbirds returning from where they wintered in the south. The evenings were growing lighter. On nights like tonight, when Alex made it home before sunset, he liked to relax on his back patio with a glass of wine and watch to see which species would finally show up at his feeders.

Before class, he couldn't wait to get home to do just that.

"Where are you headed?" he asked Shay.

"Just back to the cafeteria till it's time for my mom to pick me and my sisters up."

"I'll walk you over."

The cafeteria echoed with the voices of children in groups at the tables, playing card or board games or just goofing off. Shay chose an empty table at a distance and sat down by herself.

Alex's heart tugged. He knew how it felt to be shunned. Small and useless. Being rejected by the people whose validation you craved most made you wonder why you had even been born. Where your place was in the world, if there even was such a thing.

"What did you mean about defusing the situation?" Shay asked.

"That was probably a bad example. Your situation is different from being a police officer. We've got things we can use to protect ourselves from bullies, like handcuffs and—" No need for a young girl like her to know about TASERs and pepper spray. "All you've got is your voice, and the voices of the people who care about you.

"So. The first thing to do when someone is bullying you is to get right in their face and yell, '*Stop it.* I know what you're doing and I'm not going to take it. I'm going to tell everyone, and they're going to be watching you.' "

"That's the same thing my mom said."

"You should listen to her. Your mom's a very smart lady."

"How do you know?"

Alex smiled tightly. "I just know."

"But I'm not like that. Getting in someone's face is really hard."

Alex arched a brow. "It might be hard, but I'm telling you, that's the only way to take back your power."

Shay twisted her mouth and looked at her feet swinging back and forth.

Alex put his hand on her back. "See you at practice next week?"

She nodded.

"Okay. Have a good week." Alex headed back toward the gym as Gene dropped off the rest of the students back at the caf, the designated parental pickup spot.

"Looks like you got a fan," said Gene as they walked back.

"Shay's got a strong mother. But every girl should have a male role model, too, to balance it out."

"Garrett said you were old school. He wasn't kidding."

"Something wrong with believing a kid ought to have both a mother and a father?"

"Nothing. Nothing at all. Just not used to hearing someone admit to such a radical point of view in this day and age."

Chapter Eight

It wasn't until the Friday of Memorial Day weekend that Kerry finally made good on her promise to take the kids to Ruddock's.

"I'll have a burger and fries," Kerry told the server.

"And to drink? We're featuring a newly released pinot this weekend."

"I'll just have water along with the girls," said Kerry. "The little one can share my fries, and would you bring her some fruit, too? Chloé? What do you want?"

Chloé peered up through long lashes at the server. "I want whatever Mommy's having."

"Coach Walker says everyone should eat five fruits and vegetables a day," Shay stated matter-of-factly.

Kerry's relentless drilling into the girls of the need for a balanced diet had always seemed to fall on deaf ears. But since Shay had started boxing lessons, whatever Alex Walker said was gospel.

Chloé frowned at Shay. "Mom said I could get whatever I want and all I want's a hamburger and french fries, so there." She stuck out her tongue.

"Shay?" asked Kerry, ignoring their sniping in the interest of her sanity. "What would you like, honey?" Like she had to ask. Ruddock's juicy cheeseburgers were Shay's favorite, and the main reason Kerry brought them here.

"I'll have a hamburger with just catsup, no bun, a green salad, applesauce, and green beans."

"That's only four vegetables," said Chloé.

"You forgot—catsup is made from tomatoes. Besides, I already had carrot sticks and celery sticks for lunch. That makes seven. So *there*."

The server arched her brows. "I'll be right back with your waters."

"Um, miss?" Kerry called after her. "I'll have a pinot after all."

The weather had been unusually warm that week. Kerry had even let the girls wear shorts to school. Now she slipped out of her suit jacket to her sleeveless red blouse, folded her hands on the table, and smiled at her girls. "It's the Memorial Day weekend. Who's excited about going to the pool tomorrow?"

"I am!" said Chloé.

"I am!" Ella aped her sister, pounding the table with her spoon for emphasis.

Shay's eyes remained downcast.

Kerry put her hand atop Shay's. "The pool's for the whole town of Newberry, honey, not just your school. Maybe you'll meet some new kids this summer."

"Even if I do, I still have to go back to the same school next fall."

"Try to look on the bright side. Meanwhile, I think we should all go to bed early tonight and catch up on our beauty sleep."

"That's not fair," said Chloé. "You said I don't have to go to bed till nine thirty on the weekends."

Kerry waited for Shay to pile on, but she surprised her with, "Coach Walker says everyone needs eight hours of sleep a night."

First the vegetables, now the sleep. "Well. Coach Walker is absolutely right. As soon as we get home—"

"Look!" Shay pointed to the bar area. "There's Coach Walker now! Coach Walker!" She waved wildly.

"Ssshh! Hush, Shay. Don't interrupt his supper."

Too late. He'd seen her and was waving back, revealing a row of straight white teeth.

To Kerry's pleasant surprise, he was an eye-smiler. His eyes crinkled up into slits so you could hardly see them. And his top lip rose a tad higher on one side, balancing out a nose that bent slightly left.

"Look," said Shay, "he's all by himself."

With large hands, Alex crossed his fork and a wicked-looking steak knife on his plate, empty save for a large meat bone. His naked ring finger confirmed what she'd noticed the first night she'd spotted him in the Turning Point.

"Why don't you ask him if he wants to come

over here and eat with us? We can scoot over and make room," said Chloé with an innocence that made Kerry's heart squeeze.

"No, no. Let him enjoy his meal in peace. Besides, I think he's already finished."

"He doesn't look like he's enjoying his meal. He looks lonely and kind of sad," said Chloé.

Kerry watched Alex gaze with empty eyes at the cooks working around the woodstove and the gas ranges behind the bar as he took a sip of red wine.

He *did* look lonely. Or maybe it was just that his everyday frown made him look that way, compared to that 500-watt smile.

Still. The last thing she wanted was to encourage Shay's attachment to yet another cop.

She looked around for the waitress. *Where was that pinot?*

Ah, here she came.

"Now. What were we talking about?" asked Kerry. Better the kids bickering among themselves than begging her to invite Alex Walker over to their table.

But no sooner had they started doing just that than she saw a tall figure approaching from the corner of her eye.

"Thought I'd stop and say hi on my way out."

Shay blushed, suddenly tongue-tied.

Figures, thought Kerry. Shay couldn't wait for him to come over, and now that he had, she'd left Kerry to carry the ball.

"Hello. You remember Chloé and Ella from when I pick up Alex from boxing?"

He nodded. "Girls."

"How was your dinner?"

Alex rubbed his flat stomach. "I eat out most nights. This place has great pork chops."

"Don't you have a wife?"

Leave it to Chloé.

"Do you have a husband?" he shot back. There was that grin again.

Chloé giggled, her teeth clinking against the rim of her water glass. "I'm not old enough to have a husband yet."

"How old are you?"

She wiped her mouth on her sleeve. "Going on eleven. How old are you?"

"I was your age twenty-nine years ago."

Chloé's lips moved as she attempted the math in her head.

"So, that's twenty-nine plus eleven," said Shay, showing off in her role as big sister.

"I know!" Chloé snapped. "Coach Walker is talking to me. Let me figure it out."

The first time Alex had walked into Ruddock's Roadhouse, he was hit with the smoky aroma of grilled meat. He looked around, letting his eyes adjust to the dimness. Its high-top tables constructed of timber, concrete floors, and industrial décor lent it a definite macho feel. And the open kitchen behind the bar provided something more interesting to look at than the usual rows of bottles. Best of all, it seemed an unlikely joint for a girls' night out or supper with young kids.

After a couple of weeks of dining at the copper-top bar populated with other loners like himself, he'd stopped looking over his shoulder and keeping an ear out for Kerry O'Hearn's low-pitched, self-assured voice.

His steak knife froze over his pan-roasted pork chop when he heard not Kerry's but an equally disconcerting voice.

He peered into the dining room.

Shay's tumble of curls was easy to spot. She was sitting with a younger, blond child, a round-faced toddler whose head was barely visible above the table edge, and Kerry.

Alex fisted his knife and fork on the bar and waited for the inevitable irritation to creep up and ruin his mood, like the delayed pain after you stubbed your toe, now that he had to find yet another place to hide out in.

But he was surprised to feel tenderness and goodwill instead.

In the weeks since he'd met Shay, he had gotten to know her not just as a cantankerous pre-teen but as a person. All she wanted was to belong. When it came down to it, that was all anyone wanted. And to his secret delight, Shay had taken a liking to him, too.

He could have simply exited using the door to the bar, but he'd already been spotted. It would've been rude not to stop and say hi.

But he'd paid his respects, and now he was free to go.

"Have a nice evening, ladies," said Alex, turning on his heel.

"Wait!" said Chloé. "You can't leave till I figure out how old you are."

Shay sighed, propped her chin in her hand, and rolled her eyes.

Alex shifted his weight.

Kerry sipped her wine. Finally, she asked, "Would you like to sit down?"

He hesitated. Kerry still didn't remember him. Maybe it was his clothes. Back then, he'd still been wearing the uniform of the Portland PD. Or maybe she was just too caught up in herself to notice anyone else.

"Please, stay a while," begged Chloé.

Though Shay was too bashful to come out and ask, her eyes pleaded.

"For a minute, and then I got to get going."

No sooner had he pulled over a chair, turned it around, and sat down backward in it than Chloé burst out with, "Forty."

"Guess I can go now," he said, rising to a storm of objection from the kids.

Kerry ducked her head, trying to hide her smile.

"If you don't got a wife, then where are you going?" asked the middle one.

"Just because I don't have a wife doesn't mean I don't have a house to go home to."

"Where's your house at?"

"Chloé," said Kerry gently. "Not so many questions."

He had to admit, from what he'd seen, she was a decent mom. Her girls were a handful, but she was committed to raising them right . . . unlike the Pelletier boys' apathetic excuse for a parent.

On the hand dangling her wineglass, he noted her ring-free left hand. A single mom. Why had it not occurred to him before to wonder about her marital status?

Maybe she wasn't as selfish as he'd thought.

"Not far from here."

The server arrived with a round tray and began unloading platters of burgers and fries.

"Just so you know, this is an exception," said Kerry. "Shay told me you've been talking to your boxing students about the importance of good nutrition. We don't eat like this all the time."

He waved a hand. "No judging here. You should've seen the size of the pork chops I just demolished."

"Do you have to work on the weekends?" asked Shay.

"Sometimes. Not this one, unless I get called in for something important." He and Kerry exchanged knowing glances. *Important,* in the context of his work, usually meant something unfit for innocent ears.

"You should come to the pool with us tomorrow," Shay said brightly.

He searched Kerry's face, but her eyes carefully avoided his.

Alex noticed the silky skin on her bare arms and wondered out of the clear blue sky what she looked like in a swimsuit. "I, ah . . ."

"Pleeeze?" asked Chloé.

"Pleeeze?" asked Ella, with no concept of what she was asking for.

"I'm sorry," said Kerry to him.

"Girls. I'm sure Detective—*Coach* Walker—has lots of things he needs to do tomorrow, and so do we."

She was still making him pay for that lawyer joke at the Turning Point. Who could blame her?

But he couldn't bear to shoot Shay down without at least a bit of effort. "The Community Pool?"

Shay's grin lit up her whole face when she nodded enthusiastically.

Talk of the pool had recently come up at work. "That's right next to the empty lot where the parade forms and ends."

"A parade?" shouted the two younger girls. "Let's go. Can we, Mom?"

"It's an antique car parade. Not sure it's something you girls would be interested in."

Kerry's mouth twisted into a smile. "Parade detail, huh?"

He stood up a little straighter. "Don't mind doing my civic duty."

To the girls, he said, "I'm not promising anything. Depending on how my day goes, maybe I'll stop by when the parade's over."

The kids erupted in a chorus of cheers.

"Now I got to get going and let you guys eat."

"Bye! Good-bye!"

He left Ruddock's with a bounce in his step, wondering when he had decided he was definitely going to the pool. It was nothing, really, just a matter of walking an extra fifty yards, saying hi to make the girls happy, and that would be that.

But it was also the first time since he'd hit town that he'd made plans to do something social in his time off and, he had to admit, that was something.

Chapter Nine

Alex approached the Newberry Community Pool, his easy strides belying his anticipation at picking out a slender woman with three cute kids.

A pop song blared from the vicinity of the snack bar, and the shouts and splashes of children echoed from the water. With the sharp smell of chlorine, he recalled his own childhood summers, and his excitement built.

He spotted Kerry first, sitting along the edge of the baby pool with one knee bent, arms locked behind her, hands flat on the pool deck for support.

When he reached the chain-link fence, he folded his arms across the top of it to take full advantage of being able to watch her for a bit, unobserved.

A band of flowered material wrapped around her chest, flattening the two smallish mounds of

her breasts. Strings went up from her cleavage in a
V to tie behind her neck. Instead of matching like
a typical bikini, her swimsuit bottom was turquoise
and cut like a pair of stretchy shorts, highlighting a
narrow waist. She looked like a model in some vintage fashion magazine.

Her head was turned away from him toward the
wobbly blue disc of the baby pool, where a few other
mothers waded, clinging to the hands of their little
ones. Kerry raised a hand to shade her eyes from
the glare of the sun on the water. He followed her
line of vision and saw Ella hinged at the hip, reaching for a bobbing orange toy.

The innocuous splash of another child was
enough to startle Ella and she fell face forward
into the water.

Alex's hands clenched the chain link, instinct
preparing him to hurl himself over it.

But Kerry rose languidly to her feet and was
soon righting the child, smiling reassuringly into
her face.

Ella gasped openmouthed as she tried to catch
her breath. Kerry waited until she had wiped her
eyes, then retrieved the toy that had floated out of
her reach and calmly handed it to her.

Then she rose to her full height and propped
her hands on her hips and watched her daughter
continue to play.

The water sparkled in the sun and shade from
the tree branches overhead, already fully leafed
out.

"Coach Walker!" From out of nowhere, Shay
was running across the grass toward Alex, followed
close behind by Chloé.

"You came! Mom," she shouted over her shoulder, "it's Coach Walker!"

Alex inhaled a breath he hadn't realized he'd been holding and broke out in a grin.

"I almost didn't recognize you in those bug-eyed sunglasses. How come you're wearing a vest?" panted Shay.

"I just came from work."

"How come you don't wear a uniform?" asked Chloé.

"This *is* my uniform," he said, looking down at his jeans and faded blue T-shirt. He turned around so she could read POLICE on the back of his vest.

"Cool," said Chloé.

"Are you going to come in?" asked Shay, squinting up at him in the bright sunshine.

"I don't know." He was just fine here, on the other side of the fence. Going in was a whole different thing.

"How come? Didn't you bring your swimsuit?"

She had unknowingly handed him the perfect excuse. "No," he said apologetically.

Chloé shrugged. "Oh, well. I'm going to go get back in."

He didn't blame Chloé. He hoped he was never too old to forget the magical allure of a newly opened pool, before you started taking it for granted in August.

Yet he held greater sway on Shay than the pool did. She didn't seem to want to leave him yet.

Alex didn't want her to either. He tried to think of something to talk about to prolong their visit. "Coach Lovatt said something about doing a boxing demo here at the pool this summer."

"What do you mean? What's a demo?"

"That's short for a demonstration. Something to show the other kids what we do in class, to drum up interest. Sound like something you'd be interested in?"

"Me?"

"Yes, you. You're progressing really well."

Kids were so refreshingly transparent. Alex could see the pros and cons flicker across Shay's face as they occurred to her.

"But what exactly would I be doing?"

He dug his fingers into the chain link. "Now don't get too excited because it's not a done deal yet, but Coach Lovatt's talking about maybe getting you guys some headgear so we can do a little mitt work."

"You mean, like, instead of just punching the bags, we'd be punching each other?"

Alex nodded. "You'll partner up with someone your size—you'll have to partner with a boy, because there are no other girls—Coach will call a combination, say jab-right cross and jab-jab-cross, and you'll demonstrate what that looks like, using the in and out footwork you've been learning."

Realization washed over Shay. "Me, fighting against a boy, in front of everyone at the whole pool?"

"We'll see. It's still in the planning stages."

Now Kerry was strolling toward them with long, easy strides of her bare legs. She had donned sunglasses and a big floppy hat. This swimming pool–mama Kerry was virtually unrecognizable from the tough-as-nails attorney he had thought of innumerable times over the years. She looked soft and approachable. At her side, Ella toddled as fast as her chubby legs would carry her. Her sunglasses had slipped sideways on her head, their cloth strap hiding her eyes. But that didn't stop her from stooping to examine every dandelion in her path.

At the sight of her, Alex couldn't help but laugh out loud.

"Mom! You're not going to believe this!" said Shay. She related Alex's idea and then ran off toward the pool, yelling, "Chloé! Guess what!"

"I really appreciate everything you're doing for her," said Kerry.

"She's a great kid."

"Moving's been hard on her. She came from a big school, where there was a clique for everyone, to one where, months later, she's still considered the, quote, 'new girl.' "

He huffed a laugh. "Believe me, I get it."

"I'm sure you do, being the new guy yourself," she said, smiling wryly. She took off her glasses and licked her lips.

Alex was glad he didn't have his board shorts on. Its lack of, er, structure always made him feel somehow overexposed.

"So," he asked, watching sweet Ella shred a dandelion to smithereens, "is it just you? Are you all they have?"

A shadow crossed Kerry's face. "I'm perfectly capable of raising my daughters myself, thank you very much." Just as suddenly, the shadow evaporated. "Sorry. When it comes to my kids, I sometimes overreact." She looked down at where she wriggled her bare toes in the grass. "Don't hold it against me for being a little defensive."

A little? thought Alex. *Ya think?*

Maybe it was because it was the first official day of summer, or the barefoot setting, or her girls' innocent infatuation with Alex. Whatever it was, Kerry let down her guard.

"Shay's biological father was a state trooper. I fell in love"—Kerry sighed, standing there on the other side of the fence from Alex—"let's be honest, *lust*—with him during my second year of law school. We met—where else? In a bar . . . the same bar where I found him a few months later when I went looking for him to tell him I was going to have his child."

Chris had taken a swig from his growler and muttered that any girl smart enough to get into the University of Oregon Law School was smart enough to know what to do with an unplanned pregnancy.

True enough, in theory. What Kerry hadn't told him, though, was that she wasn't only one month late. She'd been so wrapped up in her studies and him that her first missed period had come and gone without her noticing. She was already well into her first trimester.

"By the time Shay was born the following August, it had been months since I'd heard from Chris. Except for the times when Shay asks about him, which are getting to be fewer and further apart, it's almost like he never existed. Then, ten years ago, I married a detective and had Chloé and Ella, and for a while, Shay had a stepdad. But within six months of us separating, he admitted he had a new girlfriend and was moving to Boise to live with her. He calls from time to time and makes promises, but he's not very good at follow-through."

Now Shay was paying for yet another of Kerry's mistakes, and so were Chloé and Ella.

At a whoop followed by a splash, they turned to where Shay and Chloé's heads bobbed in the water.

"You've given Shay something positive to focus on. For that, I'm grateful."

But that's where it ended. Kerry was through with cops, even cops as good-looking and generous as Alex Walker.

Chapter Ten

"**D**inner was great, Mom. Thanks for having us."

"When are you going to stop thanking me? This is your home. As I've said I don't know how many times, we're just so very glad you're here. You and your beautiful girls."

"Sorry." Kerry had been thanking her family ever since she'd come back to town. But she was just so grateful to have them and this place as a safety net. Most people weren't so lucky.

Kerry, her father Seamus, brother Ryan, and his wife Indra relaxed around her parents' teak picnic table beneath the shade of a portico around which lavender-colored wisteria bloomed. They were watching the six boisterous cousins chase Hobo, his pink tongue lolling happily out of the side of his mouth, up and down sandstone paving landscaped with low-growing plants and fragrant herbs.

When the farmhouse's steep staircase became too much for her parents' knees, they'd rented it out and put the income toward building this new, light-filled home nearby, complete with a main-floor master suite and all the latest conveniences.

Kerry's brothers were all established in their respective careers. After their father was elected judge, Ryan, the oldest, had taken over his law firm. Marcus and Keith had gone into the family wine business. The Friestatts were one of the earliest landholders to convert from hazelnut orchards to wine grapes, back when most experts still thought Oregon was too cold. And it might have been at one time, pinot noir being a notoriously finicky grape. But climate change had worked in their favor, overheating Northern California and bringing balmier temperatures to the Willamette Valley. Now, three decades later, Marcus was making a name for himself as yet another in a string of wine-makers and Keith was in sales.

All three O'Hearn men had found bright, interesting women and, in O'Hearn tradition, wasted no time starting broods of their own. Ryan had Indra, Marcus had Paige, and Keith was with Sher-ilynn. The staunchly Catholic family of Judge Sea-mus and Rose O'Hearn would be almost freakishly perfect were it not for their only daughter getting pregnant out of wedlock, followed by a short-lived marriage and a divorce.

Kerry and Ryan had always been close, de-spite—or perhaps because of—their eight-year age difference. When she needed an ear, Ryan was the one she called for his wise counsel.

Ryan knew she'd managed to keep it together over the years, despite her ex getting further and further behind on his share of support. Then, one day, she complained without thinking that the rent on her Portland apartment was about to sky-rocket with the renewal of her lease. That was at the same time that Ella had hit the terrible twos and outgrown her crib and would need new bed-room furniture.

Ryan was never cut out to be a defense attorney. He'd won respect doing family law, real estate trans-actions, and dealing with small business issues, mostly relating to the wine industry.

"In a small town, you have to be a generalist," Ryan explained to Kerry.

But it'd been years since Ryan had seen the in-side of a courtroom. Knowing when to challenge evidence and how to negotiate plea bargains were learned skills, skills he didn't possess. So, when Ryan's strongest guy moved on to a bigger playing field at the same time Kerry was having problems, he made her an offer.

Her parents offered up the farmhouse at what-ever rent she could afford. "But you need the rent money for your new mortgage," Kerry argued the day they sat down at her parents' picnic table to talk it out.

"It's not like we're in dire straits," grumbled her father. To his way of thinking, pleading, even with his own daughter, didn't become a man of his gen-eration.

Still, going back to her hometown felt a little like an admission of failure.

"Didn't we offer to help you out after Shay was born, when you were still struggling to get through law school?" asked Mom. "You insisted on doing everything yourself."

"I *am* her mother. It was my responsibility."

"Don't be silly. We love having you and the girls around. Without you, something was missing. Now we have our whole clan back." Mom folded her napkin on the table, resting her case.

With three kids to support and educate, what choice did Kerry have? Kids grew so fast. Before she knew it, Shay would be starting college.

The worst part was, she had no one to blame but herself. Her responsibility to her girls was the bottom line.

In the course of her career, she'd been both an assistant DA and its opposite, a public defender. She had a rare appreciation for both sides. But defense was where the money was, even if she had to cut her hourly fee when she moved to bring it into line with Newberry standards.

"I'm just so glad the lease was up on the farmhouse when it was," said Mom, setting Dad's after-dinner cup of coffee down in front of him.

"While I'm thinking of it," said Dad. "Now that I don't live and die by a calendar anymore and I don't have a picture window that looks out on the meadow every day, remind me to hire someone to mow it when the end of summer comes around."

"That's three months from now. What do I do with it in the meantime?" asked Kerry. It had been ten years since she'd lived on a vineyard, and before that she was just a kid, innocent of how to maintain a large property. She braced herself for yet another in an overwhelming list of tasks.

"That's the beauty of a wildflower meadow. No fertilizing, no watering, and it only needs to be mowed once a year to keep the weeds down."

"So noted."

Kerry's eye traveled over the pleasantly clut-
tered table, including what was left of the banana
bread Mom had baked that morning. She might
have a new house, but Mom was still at it, baking
and cooking and gardening.

At the head of the table, Kerry's dad sat back,
both hands resting on the arms of his white canvas
director's chair. "Alex Walker," he said. "Tell me
about him."

Darn Shay, going on about Alex all through dinner.

Kerry turned her hands palms up. "Shay said all
there is to say. He's her boxing coach."

"By way of forced community service for the
NPD." Dad looked up from under bushy eyebrows.

"He's a cop. Guilty as charged."

"And to think I used to like cops," muttered
Dad under his breath.

Judges spent their careers working closely with
law enforcement. Seamus O'Hearn gave cops the
respect he felt they deserved. Until two of them
had hurt his only daughter.

"Don't tell me you're—"

"*No*, Ryan," Kerry spat to her brother.

"And even if I was seeing him, I'm thirty-eight
years old. I can see whoever I want. I don't need
anyone's permission."

"Don't get your hackles up. I'm just saying. Given
your history, I'd have thought you'd have learned
your lesson."

"I have. Quit jumping to conclusions."

"I'm only looking at the evidence as presented."

"Ding ding ding! Back to your corners, everybody. Let's not ruin a perfectly good dinner," said her mother.

Indra lay her hand on Kerry's forearm. "Guess who was asking about you?" she said, black, doe eyes sparkling. "Danny Wilson."

The only thing surprising about Danny's name coming up was how long it had taken. The O'Hearns had known the Wilsons for generations. Danny was even-tempered, good-looking, and a hard worker. Back when they were teens, he and Kerry looked like a match made in heaven. Everyone had taken for granted they would be together forever.

"Paige said Danny asked how you were doing." Paige worked with Danny at the Sweet Spot.

"Hard to believe Danny never married," sighed Mom. "A nice boy like him. Such a waste."

"That's easy. He never got over Kerry," said Indra with a sideways glance.

Kerry couldn't be mad at her sister-in-law. Indra was just trying to get her parents off her case about Alex Walker. But in doing so, she was putting her thumb on the scales.

"Are you going to the Police Benefit and Fair next weekend?" asked Mom, changing the subject.

Kerry breathed a sigh of relief.

"Yes, she is," Ryan interrupted as he reached for another slice of banana bread, demolishing it in two bites. O'Hearn Associates always sponsored it in exchange for getting their name prominently displayed on all the promotional pieces. "Everyone in the firm needs to make an appearance."

Kerry glared at her brother. "Thank you, Mr. Bossypants." Then she turned to her mother. "Yes, Mom. I was planning on taking the girls."

"This year marks its twenty-fifth anniversary. Your father and I have never missed one, have we, Seamus?"

Behind his beloved, print copy of *The Oregonian*, her father grunted.

"We'll be there around suppertime." Indra winked. "One less meal to cook."

"Come with us," said Mom to Kerry. "I used to bake something for the bake sale every year, but now with all the new health department laws, they can't accept homemade food anymore. Tsk. A shame, if you ask me. Homemade just tastes better than store-bought."

"Sure."

"Good!" She clasped her hands together. "Oh, I'm *so* happy you moved back home."

Kerry smiled. "I am, too." She meant it. Despite the inevitable bickering, it *would* be good for her kids to spend at least some of their formative years around family, even though her brothers and dad would never be a substitute for a real father.

Chapter Eleven

"Thank you for your donation. Would you like some juice?"

If Alex had heard that phrase once today, he'd heard it a hundred times. It came from one of the EMTs at the blood donation booth squeezed next to his in the postage-stamp-sized parking lot of the Newberry Fire Department. The EMT held out a small plastic cup, the donor chugged the juice, tossed the cup into the trash can provided, and then went on his way. Unless he felt faint, in which case he was invited to sit until the feeling passed.

Alex had been flipping burgers and turning hot dogs at the NPD stand since two o'clock that afternoon. Chief Garrett had assigned each available officer on the force a two-hour shift. But when Washington and her K9 got called out to a suspicious traffic stop, Alex volunteered to let Myers go home and pulled a double. Now the suppertime crowd was trickling in.

"Thank you for your donation. Would you like some juice?"

It was a hot day for this early in June, and standing on the macadam over a commercial-sized charcoal grill made it feel even hotter. Alex's NPD T-shirt stuck to his back, and beneath his ball cap his scalp was on fire.

At least there were two people manning the booth at all times, which meant he and Zangrilli could take turns grilling and waiting on customers.

"Switch?" asked Zangrilli, wiping his forehead with his sleeve. "You look about done to a crisp."

"Thanks," said Alex, handing Zangrilli the tongs and stepping up to the window, where a line of a half-dozen people drifted forward. "Next?"

He looked up, straight into the eyes of Kerry O'Hearn.

Kerry seemed as surprised to see Alex as he was to see her. Neither could find the simplest words to say.

"Coach Walker!" shouted Shay. "Look, Grandpa. It's my boxing coach!"

Shay's grandpa had bushy black brows and a tattersall shirt, the kind on the window mannequins at the stodgy men's shop on Main Street. Despite his slight stoop, he towered between the two small girls whose hands he cradled in his. When they recognized Alex, their eyes widened, and smiles blossomed on their faces.

They remember me. Despite the blistering heat, that bolstered his mood.

"Dad. Mom. This is Detective Alex Walker." She turned to the older couple. "My parents, Seamus and Rose."

"Everybody still calls him Judge, even though he's retired," said Shay. By now, she'd all but lost her shyness around him.

Alex slipped off his plastic glove to take Rose's proffered fingertips and shake Seamus's hand, freckled with age.

"How do you like Newberry so far?" asked Rose politely.

"Nice change from where I was."

"Portland, if I heard right," said Seamus.

Alex nodded, wishing he had met the esteemed man on more equal footing instead of looking like a fast-food worker. He recalled Curtis informing him that everybody in town knew who he was. He wondered what else Judge O'Hearn had been told about him.

"Yessir."

"My granddaughter, here, has told me all about her boxing lessons."

"She's a quick study."

Shay peered up at her grandfather. "Coach Walker said I might get to be in a demonstration."

"Is that so?"

"We're working on it," said Alex.

"She's close to her grandpa, aren't you, Shay?" Seamus said, putting a hand on her shoulder. "Tells me everything." His watery blue gaze underscored a distinct message.

Zangrilli brought over their order.

"Well, it was nice seeing you," said Kerry.

Alex held up a hand in farewell and watched the O'Hearns meander off to his left, toward the blood donation booth.

In the brief lull between customers, Alex cracked open another roll of quarters into the cashbox.

There was a break in the live music coming from the makeshift stage.

"Thank you for your donation. Would you like some juice?"

"No, thanks."

Alex's head whipped around in the direction of the blood donation booth. *Nobody* turned down the juice. The juice was a badge of honor. Refusing it was like throwing away a thank-you card without opening it. The juice was part of the whole giving-blood experience.

There he saw an athletically built guy with thick, nut-brown hair, looking fresh and neat in his pressed pants, rolling down his shirtsleeve over the telltale adhesive tape circling his forearm.

"Kerry," Mr. Perfect said, the thick clot of emotion in his throat audible from where Alex stood.

"Danny," Kerry breathed, her voice freighted with history.

The rest of her family had already moved on to one of the silent auction booths. Chloé, on hearing her mother's voice behind her, stopped and pointed backward.

That kid was attached to her mother like glue.

When Rose O'Hearn glimpsed Kerry and Danny talking, she gently urged Chloé onward with a whisper in her ear and a hand on her back.

"Heard you were back in town," said Danny.

"Since last September. Ryan offered me a place at his firm."

"I know. But then, who doesn't? By the way,

props on winning that big embezzlement case. Everybody's still talking about it. I mean, granted, not everyone agrees with the verdict, but . . ." Too late, Danny bit his tongue.

"So," said Kerry. "What's new with you?"

"Nothing. Well, something, come to think of it," he said, jamming his hands into his pockets. "I'm head winemaker over at the Sweet Spot now. Maybe you heard?" His brows met in the middle with so much pride and hope that Alex's heart squeezed for him.

"Oh, sure," she said with forced enthusiasm. "Indra told me."

"Indra. She must've heard it from Paige."

"Paige," she said at the same time, resulting in a little pantomime of shared chuckles, smiles, and nods, in the imitative way of two people who know each other very, very well.

"Well, I should go," said Kerry with a nervous glance toward where her parents examined an auction item. "My family . . ."

"Right. Your girls are getting big."

"Last time I saw you, I don't think I'd even had Ella."

"Between Paige and Marcus and Seamus, I feel like I know all about her."

Seamus? thought Alex. *Apparently, not everyone called Kerry's dad* Judge.

Kerry cocked her head in a question.

"Your dad and I started having breakfast together once a month, after Rotary. He didn't mention it?"

"It hasn't come up."

"Oh. Do you think—can I give you a call some time? We could all go out together—you, me, and the kids—and get something to eat."

Just as Kerry's mouth opened to reply, a couple of teenagers stopped in front Alex's stand, loudly debating burgers versus dogs.

Desperately, Alex tried to read Kerry's lips without being seen but without success.

Then she smiled at Danny and retreated a step.

But before she could escape, Danny took her arm, leaned in, and kissed her on the soft, downy part of her cheek, right in front of her ear, just as she spotted Alex staring daggers at them.

"Bye," she mouthed to Danny with a flutter of her fingers. And then she jogged to catch up with her family while Danny gazed after her with cow eyes before heaving a brooding sigh and heading in the opposite direction, toward Alex's booth.

Unable to make a decision, the rowdy teens took off without ordering anything.

"What can I get you?" Alex's eyes ground into Danny.

"Newberry Police," said Danny, with a nod to the logo on Alex's chest. "Thanks for your service. You guys rock. I'll take one of those dogs and a Coke." He handed Alex a twenty and, when Alex gave him his change, stuffed all of it into the NPD donation jar.

While Danny squirted mustard on his hotdog, the EMT from next door popped his head around the corner.

"How's it going, Officer? Hey, we're coming up a little short of our goal over here. Need every pint we can get. If you got a sec when your shift is up, we'd sure appreciate it."

"No can do."

Danny looked up at Alex in surprise, then walked off, taking a bite out of his dog.

"Just thought I'd ask." The EMT saluted Alex and left.

"I'm not eligible. It hasn't been six weeks yet since my last donation," Alex hollered, looking at Danny's back, hoping he'd heard.

And then, to his immense relief, Cartwright from Traffic Safety and Han from Narcotics appeared. "Great timing," said Alex, ripping off his vinyl gloves and tossing them into the trash on his way out of the booth. "You mind getting them oriented?" he asked Zangrilli. "Something I got to do."

Maybe he could still catch Kerry.

He darted among kids with balloons on strings, thirtysomethings pushing strollers and dogs on leashes, looking for a sleek, golden brown crown of hair in the crowd.

What the hell was he doing? For years, the mere thought of Kerry O'Hearn had sent his blood pressure soaring off the charts. Chalk it up to the jealousy that overcame him, watching Danny boy with her. Apparently, it'd awakened some latent caveman macho gene.

There she was, standing among a cluster of folks listening to the guitarist on the stage.

"Kerry," he panted, embarrassingly out of breath for the short distance he'd run. Or maybe it had nothing to do with running.

She and Chloé looked him up and down. "You look really hot and sweaty," said Chloé.

"Is it any wonder? He's been out here working in the hot sun all day," Kerry said.

"I was just wondering." He suddenly realized he didn't know what he was there to ask her.

"Yes?"

And then the judge and her mother walked up carrying Ella and eating ice cream cones.

"Hello again," said her mother. "Kerry, Ella wanted ice cream. I didn't think you'd mind."

"Why should she mind?" grumbled the judge.

Alex saw his chance slipping away. Then he spotted a wine booth over Kerry's shoulder. "Would you like to go to the wine fest with me next Saturday?"

Genius. What was a wine fest to Kerry? Her family *owned* wineries.

Kerry paused, for once speechless.

Her mother and father stopped licking their cones and waited with bated breath for her response.

Chloé, as always hanging on her mother's every word, squinted up to see what she would say.

Only Ella was indifferent to everything but licking her chocolate cone.

"I have a moratorium on dating," she said regretfully.

"Oh, go ahead," her mother interjected. "Have some fun for a change. I'll watch the girls for a couple of hours."

The judge gazed steadily at his daughter, awaiting her decision.

She sucked in a breath. "Okay."

Alex raised his hand in farewell and began walking backward. "Pick you up at three."

"You don't know where we live," said Chloé.

"Right," he said, holding up a finger. "I'll call you."

Chloé peered up at her mom. "Does he have your phone number?"

"Is she always so logical?" asked Alex.

"'Fraid so."

Chloé cupped her hand around her mouth and yelled Kerry's number to Alex and everyone else within twenty yards.

"Got it," said Alex as he backed smack into a wall. At least, it felt like a wall. He turned and came face-to-face with a Herculean man in a do-rag and a studded, black leather jacket munching pink cotton candy on a stick.

"Oops." Chloé clapped a hand over her mouth, but she couldn't hide the amusement in her eyes.

The patch on the guy's jacket identified him as a member of the most notorious motorcycle gang in the Pacific Northwest. "Careful," he growled.

"Sorry. My bad."

"Mommy, did you see that?" Chloé giggled.

But Alex didn't care. He was too busy mouthing Kerry's number over and over under his breath as he headed toward the parking lot, grinning from ear to ear.

Chapter Twelve

At home in the shower, needles of water stinging his shoulders, Alex envisioned the long, empty evening stretching out ahead of him. That's what he had come to Newberry for, wasn't it? Solitude and stretches of free time in which to write.

Turned out, he had underestimated just how difficult writing an effective blog was. How much self-discipline it took to walk past the TV, past the tempting stack of unread books on the end table, and stop reading about wines and birds on the Internet and start contributing to the body of knowledge.

He wrote until the sun went down, then went to the kitchen for a snack, only to find nothing that interested him. All he had were half-empty jars of condiments and a gallon of milk.

He drove back to town and loaded up his cart with the biggest stockpile of groceries he had bought since he'd moved to Newberry. He got crackers and nuts and chips. Swiss cheese and cheddar cheese and green apples for slicing and good, marinated olives.

It was after ten when he finally headed home, the trunk neatly packed with brown paper bags, when he spotted what looked like a boy standing on the shoulders of another up against a window of the elementary school.

"12-28 Suspicious Persons." Alex whipped the wheel in a hard right, jumped the curb, and raced across the field.

The shock on the boys' faces when they saw the car zooming across the field toward them would have been comical if Alex didn't recognize them. Travis lost his balance and tumbled off Tyler's shoulders to the ground. But in a flash, they were on their feet again and running in opposite directions, in the same strategy that had enabled them to evade Zangrilli.

Alex leaped out, leaving his door hanging open, and tore toward Travis. "Newberry Police. Stop!"

The boy ran straight into a chain-link fence.

"Keep your hands right there where I can see them."

Travis turned around and raised his arm to shield his eyes against the glare of the Taurus's headlights.

Alex turned him around by his arm. "I thought I told you I didn't want to see you out here again this time of night."

Panting for breath, Travis swallowed.

"Don't hurt him."

Next to them, the older boy materialized out of the dark.

His strategy had worked.

"Show me your hands," yelled Alex.

Tyler raised his hands high in the air. "Don't hurt him! It's not his fault. I take the blame."

"What's your fault? What were you up to?" asked Alex as he led him by the arm over to his brother.

"We just wanted something to eat."

"If you're hungry, go home and eat."

Neither boy spoke.

With sudden realization, Alex glanced up at the building. "Does that window go to the cafeteria?"

Tyler sniffed and nodded.

He studied the boys hard. The light from his headlamps carved out the hollows of their cheeks, their clavicles. He turned and started walking them toward his car, one hand on Tyler's shoulder in case he got any ideas about running again.

"When was the last time you ate?"

"At lunch."

"What'd you have?"

"Thum of Thara's thandwich," lisped Travis.

"My friend gave me his chips again," said Tyler.

"What happened to your own lunches?"

But they were back at his car now and his radio was squawking.

"Detective Walker. What's your location?"

"Elementary school. Two juveniles detained for breaking curfew." He didn't mention the attempted break-in.

If he were still in Portland, he would request transport for the boys and then be on his merry way. But here in Newberry, the number of available officers was already strained to the breaking point. Not only that, Alex felt drawn to these two hapless kids.

"Where are we going?" asked Tyler, clutching the seat as the car jolted over the curb onto the road.

"To get you two something to eat."

Alex took his foot off the gas when he realized he didn't know which way to turn. "Where's the nearest McDonald's?"

"McDonald's?" asked Tyler quietly.

Every town had a McDonald's, didn't it? Then again, come to think of it, he couldn't picture one in Newberry.

"Where do you get fast food around here?"

Again, they drew a blank.

"Shoulda figured," muttered Alex. He hopped out, locking the boys in the car. "Be right back. Don't touch anything, you hear?"

Opening his trunk, he called the station, told them he was on his way, and asked for someone from Child Protective Services to meet him there.

Then he rummaged through his grocery bags and carried an assortment of food back to the front seat.

"Let's see here. We got sour cream and chive—"

Travis reached for the bag from Alex's hands and ripped it open, snatching chips out of the air before they hit the car seat and shoving them into his mouth.

"Crackers, Tastykakes—" He handed those to Tyler, who tore into them almost as enthusiastically as his little brother.

"—and," he opened the carton of juice for them, "this. I just cleaned the car, so don't spill it."

Orange juice didn't exactly go great with chocolate, but what the hell. It would take the edge off until CPS could get them a decent meal.

Five minutes later, he accompanied the boys into the station, where Chief Garrett was waiting.

He sat the boys down on a bench and pulled the chief aside.

"These are the kids from Allen Street I picked up a few weeks ago."

Chief gave him a skeptical look. "Curfew violation's hardly breaking news, even in a town like Newberry."

"It's the house that's newsworthy. Last name's Pelletier. What do you know about them?"

From down the hall, Chief studied Travis, swinging his legs, munching chips, and Tyler, swishing orange juice in his mouth. "Mom has a successful computer business. Greg's in banking."

"Not asking what they do. I mean, who are they as people?"

"Go to church. Belong to the country club. Where'd you find the kids tonight?"

"Trying to break into the school cafeteria."

The chief's jaw tensed.

"Mom invoked her Fourth Amendment right to refuse to let me in the house."

A fragile-looking woman with hair the pale straw color of sauvignon blanc breezed into the station. "Hi there." She smiled at the boys. "My name's Ms. Bartoli."

Once Alex and the chief brought her up to speed, she herded the boys into an interrogation room.

Chief Garrett had gone home to his wife. Now that he'd filed his report, Alex was free to go, too. But he decided to wait at his desk to talk to Ms. Bartoli.

Twenty minutes later, he heard the door open and strolled out to the hallway.

"What do you think?"

"I'd say they're definitely underweight. They've got nits. And the older one has a black hole in one of his molars all the way down to the gum. He says it hurts. They claim they've never been to a dentist."

Alex stroked his chin, suppressing his agitation. "What's next?"

"CPS will notify the parents. I'll take them to the hospital to get checked for malnutrition and signs of physical abuse."

"What about the head lice?"

"That doesn't prove anything. Any child can pick up lice at school."

His hands curled into fists. "They're *hungry*, dammit. When kids who come from a house like that, in the most affluent section of town, are hungry, there's something wrong."

"According to them, there's food in the refrigerator, all right. But they're not allowed to touch it. It's Mom's after-workout food, Dad's steak. Nothing for them. They never eat together as a family."

Alex flashed back to a time when he, too, experienced hunger. He'd pulled on the cereal cupboard with all his strength, but the padlock his mom had put on it wouldn't budge.

His face grew warm. "Then how——?"

"Don't worry. I'll get them a decent meal on the way."

"Then what?"

Ms. Bartoli raised a brow. "Intact, two-parent home? Pillars of the community with spotless records?"

"This is the third time they've been found out on the streets at night," spat Alex, his frustration creeping into his voice. "They were breaking into the goddamn school cafeteria because they needed food. If that's not neglect——"

"We'll do the best we can," she said, calmly slipping into her jacket.

Alex stood steaming at the glass door of the NPD and watched the boys walk out of the station to Ms. Bartoli's minivan. Over the course of his career, he'd seen more despicable acts of violence than he could count. Shootings . . . knifings . . . beatings. When it was grown-ups waging war against each other, he could deal. But when defenseless kids got the shaft, that got his blood boiling.

He took a deep breath. Whatever happened next, it was out of his hands. He had done his job. He didn't have to worry about Tyler and Travis anymore. There was a system in place for kids like them. He was free now, free to go back to his place and enjoy a decent dinner. Anything he wanted, plus a nightcap.

Thing was, his appetite had vanished.

Chapter Thirteen

"What do you think?" Alex asked.

Kerry took another sip of her wine. "It's good."

"Good? That's it? That's all you have to say?"

She and Alex strolled between vendors' tents under a cornflower-blue sky on the day of the Newberry Wine Fest. With her kids in the care of her parents, she had resolved to enjoy this rare chance to relax.

"What do you want me to say? I like it. It's nice."

Alex brooded into his wineglass.

"What do *you* think?"

He let the wine wash over his palate, then held up his glass and studied the legs. "It's smooth yet restrained. Like there's something important beneath the surface, but it needs to be thoroughly explored to really get it."

She smiled tightly and scratched the back of her neck.

"What?"

"Nothing."

"What are you thinking?"

"You want to know? I'll tell you. I grew up hearing all these fancy descriptions of wine ever since I can remember, and I still haven't, as you so eloquently put it, 'got' it."

He blinked. "Are you saying you're not a fan of wine? Because that's what you were drinking the night I first saw you, at the Turning Point."

"Wine is, and always has been, part of my life. I like wine the way I like the smell of lasagna in the oven, huddling in my team sweatshirt at football games in the fall, and little girls in pastel Easter dresses. Life would be less rich without all those things. I just don't worship at the wine altar like some people do."

"I thought—"

"That because I'm from the Willamette Valley and related to the Friestatts, I must be some kind of wine snob who knows everything about it? I know. That's what everybody thinks."

"No, it's just that . . . okay, maybe I did make that assumption. But you have to admit, it's an easy one to make." He took another sip.

This was turning out to be the worst waste of a babysitter ever. It had been so long since Kerry had been on a date, she didn't even know how to behave on one. She almost felt sorry for Alex, even if he was a cop. "But that doesn't mean I hold anything against those who do. I don't judge. So. Tell me what it is you like about wine."

Alex made a huffing sound. "That question's about as broad as a barn door."

"Well, obviously wine means something to you, something profound. I can tell by the way you drink it. Plus, you brought me here," she said with a nod to the rows of white tents that filled up the town green.

Alex considered. "I like that wine is a living, breathing thing. That it's sensitive to its environment and the kind of handling it receives . . . how long it's allowed to rest on the lees, whether it's aged in oak or steel. The mystery of how grapes grown in exactly the same spot turn out different from year to year, depending on the weather. That it continues to change all the time, even after its bottled. For instance, this wine we're drinking today would have tasted different if we'd opened it last week, and it'll taste different again next week. Next month. Next year."

She shrugged. "Maybe it's just that I've never had that so-called wine epiphany. When you try something and it hits you between the eyes like *pow*, that's it. You want to know what I really think?"

"I have a feeling you're going to tell me."

"I'm not sure there's really any such thing as a wine epiphany."

She studied Alex's hand, cupping the bowl of his glass. They weren't like Danny's hands, slim and white and aristocratic; hands suited to an artist. Come to think of it, winemakers *were* artists, in a way.

Nobody in Newberry understood why Kerry had broken up with Danny Wilson. She knew that for a fact because for years after she had left town, her old friends and acquaintances still had quizzed her mother and brothers about it. Even now that she'd moved back home, they asked her, point-blank. It was almost as if the town took their breakup personally, and still held it against her.

Sometimes not even Kerry herself knew why. She'd always liked Danny well enough. But when he kissed her, and even the first time he had tenderly made love to her, the night before he went off to UC Davis to learn about wine and she went to the U of O, it was rather . . . clinical, as if her soul had left her body and was hovering above it, observing. Not that it was unpleasant. She had found the physiological aspects mildly interesting, if that counted. She just felt a little . . . *cheated* after all the fuss and frenzy she had heard and read about sex ended up falling flat.

The day after, Danny bought her flowers. If there had been such a thing as a Thanks for Having Sex with Me card, she was sure he would have bought her one of those, too.

She glanced at Alex's hands again. They were larger than Danny's. Broader, squarer, with a fine dusting of golden hair on their backs.

"Have you ever knocked a man out?"

His eyes darted to hers and away again. He took a slug of wine. "That's a strange question."

She took that as a yes.

She bet Danny had never punched anyone in his life.

Alex had hands that could flatten a man as adeptly as they handled fine crystal. She wondered what other talents they had. A shiver zigzagged through her. She averted her gaze to the safety of the horizon.

"Sorry. Occupational hazard of dating an attorney."

"Is that what this is? A date?"

"Oh." She felt her face grow warm. "I just assumed—"

"As for that epiphany, I'm still hunting for mine, too," said Alex. "They say when you find that special one, there's fireworks. Men have given up their careers, their families, their entire lives to pursue their epiphany. I've read so much about wine, sampled so many kinds ... even tried my hand at a wine blog."

Kerry pictured those hands dwarfing a keyboard and grinned. "How's that working out for you?"

"Not so good."

She laughed.

"It's still a mystery. I feel like I've unearthed every stone. Truth? At times I think I've given up on finding my epiphany, too. When it comes right down to it, how many of us are lucky enough to find 'the one'?"

A couple of young women rose from a park bench right in front of Alex and Kerry's path. They were lovely, talking and smiling together, their foreheads smooth as a sheet and their upper arms still tight.

A twinge of regret for the past shot through Kerry. Once, she had looked like that. She had thought it would last forever.

She glanced at Alex, expecting to find him

ogling them, but he didn't even seem to notice them.

Instead, he lowered himself onto the bench they had just vacated and patted the seat next to him.

"Did you ever think you'd come back here, to the valley?" he asked when she had sat down beside him.

She shook back her hair. "Hadn't planned anything, actually. I had no preconceived notion as to how my life would turn out. It wasn't till I interned for a judge in Portland the summer after I got my bachelor's degree that I figured out I wanted to be an attorney like my dad and Ryan. Then I found out I was pregnant with Shay."

"The statie. The one who ruined you for cops."

"The *first* cop who ruined me for cops." She laughed. "Yes, the trooper. When he bailed on me, I had no choice but to come home with my tail tucked between my legs and tell my family what was going on."

"What about ol' Danny Boy?"

She whipped her head around. "What about him?"

"Where's he fit into the picture?"

"How did you know about Danny and me?"

"Small town."

She gazed into her glass. "Danny's a nice guy. You'd be hard-pressed to find anyone in Newberry who would say anything bad about him."

"The nicest," drawled Alex, draining his drink.

"He *is* nice."

A part of her still felt guilty about letting Danny down. That must be what compelled her to defend him. "Okay. You want to know how nice? When that trooper abandoned me, Danny offered to marry me and raise my baby as his own."

"If he's so nice, why didn't you take him up on it?"

She'd lost count of the times she wished she had done exactly that. Her life would have been so much easier. Shay wouldn't have grown up fatherless. And she would have appeased her parents, instead of making them worry all these years.

But she wasn't about to tell Alex that.

"What about you? Is there someone pining over you back in Portland?"

"At least a dozen of them."

"I'm serious. Do you have any long-lost loves?"

He thought for a moment. "I think about love the way you think about wine epiphanies," he said, rising, slipping his hands into his pockets, jingling his change, and looking anywhere and at anything but Kerry.

Behind him, Kerry stood, too, and they continued their slow stroll in the dappled sunlight.

"Shay's a great kid," said Alex, changing the subject.

"She's the light of my life. Things are a little bumpy right now. But adolescence is always hard with mothers and daughters. Lord knows I was a pain."

"*Was?*"

She made a wry face.

They stopped at a corner of the green. "Want to keep going?" Alex asked.

For the first time, she noticed how, when he smiled, the fine lines leading from the corners of his eyes to his temples fanned out and down, almost meeting the lines that formed parentheses around his grin, and that the deep bow in his upper lip remained intact.

"Sure," she replied. "Who knows? Maybe we'll find that epiphany yet."

"On to the next tent," he said.

She thought she might have felt the brush of his hand on her lower back as he moved to offer her his elbow, but maybe it was just because she had become acutely aware of his smallest gesture.

Chapter Fourteen

Kerry stared at the bill for three months' day care for three children on her computer screen. Leaving that page open, she chewed her lip and pulled up her budget spreadsheet.

Monthly Income: fee from last month's embezzlement case

Monthly Expense: food, electricity, water, cable—Kerry had foresworn buying anything new for herself to preserve her kids' favorite shows—car payment, health insurance, college funds, summer day care, Chloé's flute lessons, Shay's boxing . . .

Luckily, she and her kids were included in her parents' family pool membership. It was a little thing, but every penny counted.

This called for more coffee. She got up from her desk and went to the law firm's reception area as she tried to think of nonessential budget items that might be candidates for the chopping block.

Ryan, hearing the gurgle of the coffeemaker,

popped his head out of his office, looking sharp in his white shirt and gray suit. "Hey, come look at these new pictures from the weekend."

"As soon as my coffee's done."

They were shoulder to shoulder, scrolling through the photos of his kids, when his phone rang. "Not in my contact list," he said, frowning at his screen.

"Go ahead and answer it," said Kerry. "Could be a referral."

"I'll put it on speaker. Hello?"

"I need an attorney. But not just any attorney. A ruthless, relentless bastard."

"Hold on." With a grin, Ryan handed it to Kerry. "It's for you."

She stuck out her tongue at him like when she was six years old and he was fourteen and he'd locked her out of the house and stood behind the screen door, grinning, until Kerry's hollering brought their mother running to scold him.

"This is Kerry O'Hearn," she said into the phone in her most professional voice, heading for her own office.

The caller explained that he had just been released from the hospital to learn he had been charged with reckless endangerment and second-degree disorderly conduct, was out on bond, and wanted her to plead his case.

It would be far easier to practice family law or work for civil liberties or environmental justice. But everyone deserved a fair and robust defense.

"How soon can we meet?" she asked.

* * *

School let out for the summer, but the boxing lessons continued.

Kerry's kids went to day care at the Community Center. On the Thursday after the wine fest when she arrived to pick up Shay, Alex pulled her aside while Shay finished stretching with the others. "Is there a good time when we could talk?"

She gave him a confused look.

"About Shay."

"Chloé," said Kerry, "could you roll that ball around with Ella for a minute while Coach and I talk?"

"Come on, Ellabella," said Chloé, headed for a blue rubber ball lying on the gym floor.

"She's a good kid," said Alex, watching them.

"What's wrong?" asked Kerry.

"Calm down. Nothing's wrong. You've heard about the exhibit we're preparing for."

Kerry's posture relaxed. "It's all she's been talking about, ever since you first mentioned it. What's there to talk abou—"

"Waaaaah!"

"Oh! Sorry, Ella!" Chloé ran toward where her little sister cupped her nose and cried, while the ball continued to roll a short distance before stopping.

Alex watched as Kerry went over and consoled both girls.

"Sorry," Kerry said, returning to Alex with Ella on her hip. The child's thumb was in her mouth, she was fingering a raggedy-looking, well, *rag*, and there were streaks running down her fat cheeks.

Amazing how, that time he was partnered with light heavyweight champ Manuel "The Razor" Martinez in a sparring match, he hadn't so much as winced, but a scowling, downy-haired little girl made his knees feel like jelly. "What's wrong, Ella-bella?" he cooed, wiping away a tear with the back of a scarred knuckle.

"Nnnn." Ella frowned even harder and hid her head in Kerry's shoulder.

"Shot down by a two-year-old," he said, grinning. "Way to bruise a guy's ego."

"What's this about, Shay?" asked Kerry, patting Ella's back, gently bouncing her, her body engaged in comforting one child while her mind focused on another. She seemed to have forgotten about Chloé, peering up at him, wide-eyed, listening. Then again, how thin could a person's attention be spread?

If she had managed to pry herself away from her kids once, maybe she could do it again. He forged ahead while trying to keep his voice casual. "I have off tomorrow. Is there a chance we could talk, without . . ." He jerked his head and rolled his eyes ceilingward.

"Tomorrow?" Kerry gazed at a spot on the wall over his shoulder and blew a stray lock of hair out of her eye. "Let me think . . ."

"I thought we could run by my house. There's that bottle of chardonnay I bought at the wine fest you liked. It was no epiphany, but it wasn't too shabby."

He pictured himself showing Kerry around his place and wondered if she liked birds.

"I'm afraid I can't. I have a new case I'm working on. Can't we just discuss whatever it is right now?"

Alex immediately berated himself for getting

his hopes up. To think she would actually go home with him, so soon after they'd met! Kerry O'Hearn, uber-successful Portland lawyer and now, as he'd recently learned, close relation of wine royalty. He was such an idiot. No wonder he was still alone at the advanced age of forty.

But then, they *hadn't* just met. He'd been obsessing about her for years—though, admittedly, not in a good way.

"Gene—Coach Lovatt—and I had the idea to stage a series of demos to get more kids to sign up for next fall. No big deal, just to introduce some techniques, show them it's nothing to be afraid of. We tossed around some ideas for a venue and came up with the pool. With the day care taking them there twice a week, we have a built-in audience." He went over to a desk and came back with a form on a clipboard. "I just need your signature on this permission slip."

He started to hand it to her, but her arms were still filled with thirty pounds of child.

"Would you mind holding it for me?" she asked, craning her neck to look at the paper.

Alex angled his body and stepped to within an inch of Kerry's side while sliding the clipboard before her eyes. All the other parents had barely skimmed the form before scribbling their signatures. But then, none of them were lawyers.

While he waited for her to scrutinize every word, he could feel the heat emanating from her body.

"I guess it looks okay," said Kerry after a minute. "Chloé, grab my pen from my bag, would you?"

"You're welcome to come watch," said Alex.

"I'll try to get to one of them," she replied around Ella's barrette, clamped between her teeth while she smoothed Ella's hair.

On the day of the first boxing demonstration, Kerry arrived at the pool ten minutes early. She slipped out of her suit jacket and draped it over the headrest in her car before she entered the packed pool area, fanning herself.

She needn't have hurried. Not only was she the first parent there, she might well be the only one, considering there were fewer than a half-dozen kids in the boxing class and most workers didn't have the flexibility to skip out of work midafternoon.

She shielded her eyes from the sun and looked for Alex or Coach Lovatt. Okay, she admitted to herself: *Alex.*

Over in the deep end, a man's head emerged from the water. He flattened his palms on the side of the pool and easily hoisted himself out, then strode toward the diving board, water sluicing off his glistening body in sheets. *Alex.* His board shorts rode low on his hips, even lower in the center front, revealing a snail trail of hair and washboard abs.

He rounded up his students one by one, laughing and joking with them, and herded them over to the squared off "ring" staked out in the grass with yellow crime scene tape. It struck Kerry that outside here, with the kids, he was in his element. His usual frown was nowhere to be seen.

Holding the demo here at the pool had turned

out to be a great idea. The fun, casual setting and shiny red-leather headgear and boxing gloves made for quite a spectacle.

Even Gerald Garrett, Newberry's chief of police, stood off to the side in a wide-legged stance, arms folded, watching.

And there, standing next to him, were Kerry's parents.

Kerry waved to them as Coach Lovatt gave a hand signal and the pop music blaring from the pool speakers cut off midsong, replaced by the theme from *Rocky*. That was enough to bring whoever hadn't already left the water or their beach towel over to the ring, until more than a hundred people, mostly kids, waited to see what all the commotion was about.

The song faded out and Coach Lovatt's amplified voice opened the event with his usual emphasis on respect, camaraderie, and honor. Then he talked about conditioning, using the bags, jumping rope, and running.

Meanwhile, Kerry's parents made their way over to where she stood, watching.

"What are you doing way back here?" her mother asked. "Wouldn't you be able to see Shay better if you stood farther forward?"

"I'm good."

The kids lined up to demonstrate the defensive technique of punch avoidance by taking turns throwing rights to the mitts on Alex's hands, two jabs apiece, ducking in between to avoid Alex's sideswipes to their heads, while Coach Lovatt narrated. "As you develop greater skill, you may be allowed to spar—that is, when, and only when, Coach

Walker or I deem you're ready. Given the short time since our program has started, today we have only one athlete who has earned that right, and that's Shay. She'll be paired with Coach Walker."

Kerry's father raised his chin and peered out through lowered lids.

Her mother put her fingertips to her lips. "They always used to say a girl's face was her future. And you know how much Shay likes to play with makeup and that sort of thing."

"Shay wants to do this. She doesn't see any connection between her appearance and boxing. Her coach's emphasis on values has really sunk in. Those were exactly the kind of things she needed to hear."

The truth was, the reason Kerry had found a place at the back of the crowd was so Shay wouldn't see her apprehension.

She swallowed hard when Shay and Alex came into the ring wearing headgear exposing only their eyes and nose. Alex had to squat down to Shay's height. The first time Alex swung at Shay, Kerry held her breath. But Shay didn't blink before slugging him back, tit for tat.

For the next minute, they practiced trading punches before a rapt audience, Shay giving it all she had. Alex, of course, held back, letting Shay be the star.

Afterward, there was a smattering of applause and even a few hoots from the boys.

Several kids crowded around Shay, wanting to try on the gloves, opening and closing the Velcro straps again and again just to hear the loud ripping sound, and fake shadowboxing in the slant-

ing rays of the afternoon sun. Granted, they were
mostly boys, but a couple of girls stayed, too, edging ever closer to Shay.

Kerry skirted the action, trying not to let her
heels sink into the grass, and made her way to Alex
and Coach Lovatt.

"You okay, Mom?" asked Alex, tossing a towel
around his neck. "You look a little woozy."

"I'll be fine." She fanned her hot cheeks.

"We're proud of the progress they're making,"
said Coach Lovatt. "But the Community Center said
we need to bring up our numbers to justify keeping
the program running next year. Hopefully, these ex-
hibitions will get more kids to sign up."

"There will be more?" asked Kerry's father, who
had also ambled up.

"Hopefully, word will get around and we'll get
even better attendance at the next one."

Kerry's parents waved and sought Shay's eye to
signal they were leaving, but Shay was preoccupied
with helping another girl try on her headgear,
while a second looked on, waiting impatiently for
her turn. They asked Kerry to tell her good-bye for
them and then left.

"Well," Kerry said, looking wistfully at Coach
and Alex's suntans, "looks like Shay's tied up.
Much as I'd like to hang out here the rest of the afternoon, I have to get back to the office."

"I'll walk you out," said Alex.

On their way, Kerry said, "Did you see those
girls clustered around Shay? Maybe she'll finally
make some friends."

"Shay's a coach's dream. Motivated, and with a
heart of gold. She's got *it*, whatever *it* is. I wouldn't

mind seeing more kids just like her sign up for fall."

Alex didn't stop at the gate but continued to Kerry's car, where he held her door for her. After she slid in, he stood bent over in the opening with one hand on the roof, giving her a great close-up of those rock-hard abs. "Just to let you know, I still have that chardonnay we liked in the fridge. It's waiting for you, whenever you're ready."

If his compliments for Shay were meant to soften her, they were working. But no. Kerry knew how to read people. That perpetual earnestness etched on Alex's forehead was the opposite of manipulative. He might have that tough cop persona, but at least, unlike most of the people she dealt with in her job, there wasn't a fake bone in his body. She hadn't forgotten how he'd virtually ignored those young chippies at the wine fest. That was no put-on for her benefit. He truly wasn't interested in them.

"Like I said before, I really don't date."

"Neither do I."

She smirked. "With three kids, it's not easy for me to get away."

"That makes it all the more worthwhile." He smiled down at her, something people did a million times every day, but when Alex did it, it qualified as an event.

The timbre of his voice had her body playing tug-of-war with her resolve.

He's a cop, she reminded herself. Then again, was she such a bargain? A thirty-eight-year-old mother of three?

"All my brothers have kids. Maybe I can swap babysitting services."

"I'll leave the timing up to you. Outside duty hours, I'm at your beck and call."

He slapped the roof of the car, making her jump in her skin, slammed the door, and stalked back to the pool.

She had driven a couple of blocks before she was able to bite back her smile.

Chapter Fifteen

A lex was giving Kerry a tour of his rental house. He was neat, she had to give him that. You could practically eat off his kitchen floor. His smoke-gray sheets were tucked beneath the mattress with hospital corners and his shoes were lined up in his closet. Now he opened the door for her to step into his minuscule backyard.

"Here's what sold me. When it's nice out, I can bring my glass of wine out here to the back patio and watch the birds at my feeders."

Kerry looked around at a slightly dented iron-work table with matching chairs she suspected had come with the property. Here and there along the edge of yard where it met the woods, bird feeders hung at staggered lengths from tree branches. The only thing moving on this sultry summer evening was a sparrow flitting from branch to branch on an ash tree.

"What do you think?" he asked.

At Kerry's farmhouse, there was no escape from the three very active and unique kids vying for her attention, and no matter how hard she tried to keep up, there were always toys and shoes scattered from one end of the house to the other. Sometimes, it seemed as though no time had passed since the days when she shared the house with three older brothers who were always talking too loud, having farting contests at the dinner table, or clamoring down the front porch steps, late for practice, with baseball mitts, hockey sticks, or footballs tucked under their arms, depending on the season. Though it might lack privacy, Kerry loved the chaos of a big family. There was no place she would rather be, no place she would rather raise her brood.

In comparison, Alex's house seemed positively funereal.

"Quiet, isn't it?"

"*Peaceful*," he corrected, proudly surveying the area. "When I'm in the mood to spice things up, I might even bring my laptop out here and watch a movie or work on my blog."

She lifted a brow. "Wow."

"I'll go open the wine. Be right back."

Kerry wandered out into the yard. This was Alex's idea of paradise? He wouldn't last one day at her noisy, unkempt house, coping with her girls' mood swings, having to scoop up after her wayward dog.

Whatever made her think she and Alex would be compatible?

Well, she was already out now. She had hosted

Marcus and Paige's kids for a sleepover last night in exchange for her freedom tonight, telling everyone she was going shopping. Free for the entire evening. Might as well make the most of it. She'd be decent to Alex. Polite and appreciative. After all, he'd made an effort, and he deserved that. But she would have to think of a tactful way to turn down any future requests for the pleasure of her company.

No dating. That was her unofficial rule, and she'd do well to stick to it. But sometimes, late at night, she imagined a future when her kids had flown the nest, and she pictured herself finishing out her life alone and lonely. That's when she started berating herself all over again for the mistakes that had put her into this position.

"Here you go." Alex returned to find Kerry seated at the wrought-iron table. He handed her the promised glass of chardonnay.

She sipped from it and lightly smacked her lips. "Ah, yes. I remember this one."

"I'm thinking of blogging about it," Alex said, holding it up to the light to judge its honey-gold color. "But lately, whenever I sit down to type, I—"

He caught himself.

"You what?"

He lowered his glass. "Remember that night at the Turning Point, when you called me out for being grammatically challenged?"

"In response to your insulting lawyer joke?" Just like that, the edge was back in her voice.

"Probably not the smartest thing to bring up on a date, huh?"

"A little late to think of that now. Where did that come from anyway?"

Alex rubbed his finger across the incised pattern of the tabletop. Their shared history had to come out eventually. He hadn't planned on it being tonight, but he supposed now was as good a time as any. "You really don't remember?"

She blinked and shook her head. "Remember what?"

"The Sullivan case."

Her eyes got a faraway look, then widened in recognition. "Officer Walker. You testified for the prosecution. That was you."

"I could never forget if I lived to be a hundred."

He could almost see her computer brain flipping rapid-fire through a catalog of memories thick as the stack of case files that had lain on the defense's table . . . the aha moment when she came to that page in the proceedings when he'd been called to testify.

"How long have you—" She cut herself off. "You knew that was me that first night, at the Turning Point, didn't you?"

You're hard to forget. And yet, she had apparently had no trouble forgetting *him.*

He huffed a laugh to cover the chasm of emptiness inside. "If seeing you in person wasn't enough, your name and face were on TV. Guess you're used to that."

"Not so much anymore. The embezzlement trial got a lot of press here in Newberry, but you know how it was back in the city. There was always plenty of fodder for the media. Only the biggest stories had legs."

She cocked her head. "What are you really doing in Newberry?"

He paused. "Looking for something better. You?"

"I already told you. Looking for a place to raise my kids."

She sounded like a different person than she had a minute earlier. Like the woman who had grilled him on the stand, lighting a spark of anger that had added to the chain events leading to him quitting his job, moving to Newberry, and finally to this moment.

"We're both professionals with jobs to do. I hope you didn't take it personally."

"That an attempted murderer walked?"

"It's moot, now. There's no point in rehashing it."

The anger that still burned invisibly beneath Alex's surface like a mine fire in one of those hapless, deserted coal towns erupted. "At least I can sleep at night, knowing I make an honest living."

Kerry rose from her chair and slung her bag over her shoulder. "Is this what you do for fun when you're not conducting illegal searches? Ask women out on dates and then ruin their night?"

Back when they were investigating the crime scene, Alex had heard his partner secure the verbal permission of the defendant's roommate to search for the weapon. Under the law, this permission only extended to the apartment's common areas—the kitchen, bathroom, and living room. Not the defendant's bedroom, where the gun had ultimately been found.

It was Alex's word against the roommate's. But he had told the truth and paid the price. Not only had the bad guy walked on the grounds of illegal search and seizure, Alex had lost his longtime partner and friend when the guy asked to be transferred. None of which would have happened were it not for his stubborn need to help people. That's why he became a cop in the first place. Even as a kid, helping others was all he'd ever wanted to do. But it always seemed to go sideways.

"Kerry—" She'd just got here, and he'd blown it.

"For your information, *Officer Walker,* I happen to like certain aspects of being a defense attorney. Maybe I *get* people who are flawed and complicated. Most of my clients have the same hopes and fears, aspirations and despairs you and I do. They might have made mistakes, but they're not evil.

"I don't look at my job as just asking for bond reduction, investigating the evidence, and filing motions. I take a bigger view. My work is upholding the Bill of Rights. Making sure peoples' constitutional rights are protected.

"And with three kids to support, I'd like to know what other choice I have. Maybe if their fathers, who happen to be—oh, that's right, *cops*—would step up to the plate, I would have opted to stay in the prosecutor's office. But kids have this annoying need for things like lunch money and braces and . . . boxing lessons. Not that you would know anything about that."

She was already striding around the side of the house to the driveway where her car was parked when Alex caught up with her.

"Kerry. Wait."

She arched a brow at his fingers gripping her arm, and his hand sprang away as if scalded.

"Don't leave. We have a whole bottle of chardonnay to drink."

"What's the point?" she huffed, now almost to the driveway. "This could never work. We're too different."

"No, we're not."

She halted at her car, giving him a scathing look. "Name one thing we have in common."

She was the eloquent one. When it came to words, he stunk. He planted his feet in front of her and his tongue battled for the right response, his lips forming around first one and then another attempt, discarding each in turn.

Kerry huffed with impatience and reached for her car door.

By some stroke of luck, he'd gotten Kerry O'Hearn—the woman whose image was tattooed on his mind—here, and now she was slipping right through his fingers.

Alex had always been better with his hands than words. He grabbed her upper arms and positioned her against her car.

"We're both as stubborn as—as two . . . pigheaded . . . *mules*," he finally spat, with a tightly controlled jolt for good measure.

Kerry's forehead scowled above eyes flaring with self-righteousness, her breath rushing in and out of parted lips.

Those lips. He had never been able to forget them. And now they were only inches away, so temptingly close he couldn't tear his eyes away from them.

He gulped. Chances like this didn't come along

twice in a lifetime. He leaned forward, wanting to taste them, to revel in their plump fullness.

He dipped his head and crushed them against his.

In the onslaught of Alex's kiss, Kerry forgot all the reasons why the two of them were so wrong for each other. Forgot to think, period. Her brain flew off to a tropical island, put up its feet, and sipped a margarita through a straw, leaving behind only pure, unadulterated *feelings* in charge. And as anyone old enough to have sworn off dating well knew, feelings were the most unreliable basis on which to make decisions. Feelings were treacherous, sneaky, and lacking good judgment. If feelings were a person, they'd be your barefoot, eight-months-pregnant second cousin wearing a skintight T-shirt that shouts KISS MY BASS with a cigarette dangling from her lips.

Kerry's world zoomed in small . . . smaller, until all that remained was the feel of Alex's wet, warm mouth on hers, her blood pulsing through her veins, her breasts pressed against his hard chest. His hands on her arms held her up so her heels had left the ground, only her toes in tenuous touch with reality.

The truth was, the moment Alex mentioned the Sullivan trial, her recollection came rushing back like a tsunami. She *did* remember him. At the time of the trial she was practically a newlywed, and Chloé a colicky infant. Kerry was strained to the breaking point from lack of sleep and preparing for the biggest trial of her career. If there was ever a wrong time to be attracted to a man, let alone an opponent, that was it. So why did she flush and get a buzzing in her head whenever he entered the courtroom? *Post-pregnancy hormones running amok,* she had scolded herself.

It all came back to her now. The very air between them shimmered like heat waves on a country road in August. That disconcerting, syrupy feeling low in her belly when she paced the floor, roasting him on the witness stand. Those stormy eyes, searing through her tough business suit to the woman she was inside . . . she had the sneaking suspicion he knew the color of her lingerie. At the time, she'd chalked it up to a cop's self-righteous anger. But even then, she knew she was in denial. The primal connection they shared was unanticipated, unwelcome, downright disturbing, and just plain wrong. She had no choice but to deny, deny, deny. Apparently, she'd done an exemplary job of it. Until now.

Dinga-dong-dong-dinga-ding-dong.

As suddenly as he'd grabbed her, Alex let her go. Her heels hit the ground, her breath came out in a whoosh, and she staggered to stay upright. But only for a second, because now he was embracing her, his hands everywhere, grasping, adoring, now cupping the back of her head, now slipping deftly under her shirt to span her lower back, and he was kissing her again, only this time her own traitorous arms were snaking around his waist and his neck, and now her tongue was meeting his, thrust for thrust.

Dinga-dong-dong-dinga-ding-dong. Louder, this time.

"Mmmm*wwwa*!" She managed to wrest her head to the side, breaking the suction. "My phone," she gasped, her lips feeling bruised and swollen.

With a sigh, her brain set down its frozen concoction and asked, *What now? Can't you manage without me for one instant?*

She fumbled in her bag as the phone rang yet a third time, jangling nerves that were already shot to hell.

Paige, her sister-in-law. Automatically, scenes of medics running with stretchers and red lights flashing in the background sprang to mind.

"What's wrong?" she blurted breathlessly.

"*Tsk,*" Paige clucked her disapproval.

Kerry felt as transparent as Saran Wrap. She imagined Paige frowning at her smeared mascara and lips that felt like fat, overripe strawberries.

"Nothing's wrong with me," Paige continued, sounding a touch miffed. "What's wrong with *you*? Can't you trust your own sister-in-law to watch your kids for an evening?" She chuckled then. "Anyhoo, sorry to interrupt, but Marcus and I were thinking of taking the kids for a drive to the river, but that'll mean we probably won't be back by the time you get home. I figured you wouldn't mind. More shopping time for you, right? But if you—"

"No," snapped Kerry, slipping a thumb under a bra strap and yanking it up, the skin on her lower back still humming with the touch of Alex's hand, her insides feeling dangerously liquid. "I'm coming home."

"What? You've only been gone an hour. You don't have to—"

"I said I'm coming home now. I'll pick up the kids at your place, and then you and Marcus and your kids can go on ahead to the river."

While poor Paige tried to make sense of Kerry's sudden change of plans, Alex backed up just far enough for Kerry to open her car door and slip behind the wheel.

"Okayyyy," said Paige finally.

Kerry had but one goal—to escape from Alex's tempting kisses, the intoxicating feel of his hands on her body. She tossed her phone onto the passenger seat, turned the key in the ignition, and shoved the gearshift into reverse.

Alex leaned on the ledge of the window that had been left open because of the heat. "Something else we have in common . . ."

The intensity in his face was almost more than she could bear, but she couldn't back up with him halfway in her car. She averted her eyes and stared, unseeing, out the windshield.

He reached in, cupped her chin, and kissed her yet again, and damned if she didn't surrender to him again, so hungry for his lips that she shifted into park so she didn't accidentally jam her foot on the gas and drag him backward along with the car.

Just when she was seriously considering going back inside with him and tearing apart his carefully made bed, he withdrew, leaving her feeling inexplicably bereft.

". . . passion," he finished.

Confusion reigned in her. She could never fall for another cop. So then how could she explain these feelings? She needed time, that's all. Time to think. Time to come back to her usually logical senses.

She shifted into reverse yet again.

Alex took a step backward.

But in her peripheral vision she couldn't help but see him standing there watching her until she was out of sight.

Chapter Sixteen

Two days after Kerry O'Hearn's visit, Alex's head was still back in his driveway, savoring her lush kisses, while his body lounged at a table with his first cup of sludge from the office pot, half listening to Chief Garrett's morning briefing.

No sooner had he moved to Newberry than Kerry had rocked his world on its axis. He felt the need to re-evaluate, restore his lost sense of balance. Instead of taking notes on Chief's briefing, he was taking notes on his life.

Fact #1. His life was here now, in Newberry, and so was Kerry's.

Fact #2. The boxing lessons were turning out to be his favorite part of his week. After all these years, maybe Chief had seen something in him that he never had. Maybe you *could* teach an old dog new tricks.

And Shay was his star pupil, vulnerable, talented, and anxious to please. As for him, there wasn't much he wouldn't do for her either.

Fact #3. Kerry was right—they would never work. She was far and away the most intriguing woman he had ever known. They had both come to Newberry for the same reason: a fresh start. Yet despite the fact that it almost killed him to admit she was right and he was wrong, they were both too headstrong, too volatile. Like oil and water. Fire and ice.

Something Chief was saying about having to pay a visit to a lone wolf who lived by the river caught Alex's attention.

"What about Curtis Wallace?"

"You *are* listening. Glad to see you got your head out of the clouds, Walker. Aw, forget it. Doesn't matter anyway. I'll go myself. I'm the only one that's got a snowball's chance in hell of getting through to the old curmudgeon."

"What's Curtis's crime?"

"Insists on burning his own trash, despite the no-burning ordinance. Lady who lives downwind who claims to have bad allergies calls to complain about the smoke every blessed week, without fail. I got no choice but to file a report, at least some of the time."

"Let me go," said Alex.

"A CAP guy? I couldn't ask you to stoop so low," he kidded, to the amusement of the other officers.

"Yet you were willing? Seriously, Chief, I can stop out there right before dark, before I head home."

Later that evening, Alex drove slowly along the river road, looking for Curtis Wallace's hand-lettered sign that Chief Garrett and the other members of the force at this morning's briefing had har-harred about.

He slowed when he saw a sign up ahead, next to a clearing.

PRIVATE SIGN—DO NOT READ.

Smiling at the old goat's sense of humor, he turned the Taurus right and braced himself for the ruts in the unpaved road.

Another sign fifty yards farther on warned trespassers to KEEP OUT.

Undeterred, Alex stuck a toothpick between his teeth and kept going until he saw the rust-colored logs of an A-frame cottage and a pickup truck parked alongside a shoulder-high stack of firewood. From the few slowly rotting stumps, he deduced the wood had come from trees felled to make the clearing for the house. In the Willamette's maritime climate, it wasn't that unusual for some rugged folks to rely solely on wood fires for heat.

Alex got out and hopped up the porch steps to where a lonely Adirondack chair sat. He flattened his back along the exterior wall, turned his head, and peeked into the window.

As it turned out, the neatly stacked wood was no indication of the house's interior. On a couch positioned for the best viewing angle to the TV were a balled-up blanket and a bed pillow, still with the indentation of a head scooped into it.

Alex turned away from the window and went to the front door. Considering yet another sign tacked onto it, this one reading, COME BACK WITH A WARRANT, the WELCOME doormat was an ironic touch.

"Curtis! It's Alex Walker. Answer the door."

When no one came, he followed the aroma of grilling meat to the back of the cabin, where a stretch of riverfront had been cleared to give a view of the water. There, beneath a beat-up camo ball cap with a pair of shades propped on its bill he found Curtis standing over a charcoal grill jerry-rigged out of a barrel, wielding a long fork.

"Can't you read? Get the hell off my property." He raised his fork in a threatening manner.

"It's me," said Alex without breaking stride. "Walker. From the Turning Point."

Curtis lowered his weapon halfway.

"Killing two birds with one stone, I see," said Alex with a nod to the fishing rod balanced across two sawhorses, its line pulled taut at an angle by the river's current.

Curtis tipped his head back and polished off the last of the clear liquid in his Mason jar, then disappeared into a ramshackle garage with a NOTICE: AUTHORIZED PERSONNEL ONLY tacked at an angle above the door. A moment later, he reappeared holding his own refilled jar plus another. "This summer's gonna be a hot one, I can feel it. You came all the way down here, might as well join me," he told Alex.

Even this late in the evening, the air outside Alex's air-conditioned car was sweltering. Gnats buzzed around his head. He tossed away his toothpick, took the jar Curtis offered, and lowered his nose to the rim.

"Woowhee!" It smelled like Granny Smith apples soaked in gasoline. "If I didn't know any bet-

ter, I'd say that's moonshine. But then, that'd be illegal."

"Taste it. Tell me what you think."

Alex hesitated, then threw caution to the wind.

At first, nothing. Then came the flame, like a
blowtorch burning a hole in the back of his throat,
making his knees threaten to buckle.

"One ninety proof," said Curtis proudly.

Alex held the jar up to the light. "That stuff
packs a potent punch."

Curtis grinned, the gap in his teeth showing.
"Take another sip."

He knew he shouldn't. But there was something
contagious about Curtis's devil-may-care attitude.

"Holy shit." He shook his head like a wet dog.
"Feels like my face is melting off. But not in a bad
way."

"Ha! If likker's too much for you, there's beer
over there in the cooler."

"Maybe. Just to cleanse my palate." Alex set the
jar on the table and grabbed a cold can of De-
schutes.

"You draw the short straw? That what brought
you here?" asked Curtis as he took a fearless swig
of 'shine and then used his fork to flip the slab of
meat on the grill.

"Volunteered," replied Alex, looking beyond
the evidential burn barrel to a trash heap consist-
ing of cans, bottles, and other noncombustibles
that gradually disappeared into the thick brush
surrounding the riverbank. "Don't you have trash
collection out here?"

"What do I need to pay someone to haul my

trash for? It's my property, my trash. I can do what I want with it."

Now Curtis was tearing up slices of bread and tossing the pieces onto the ground in the direction of the riverbank.

"Just sayin'. You might get more people stopping by if you tidied up around the place a little."

"What do I need company for? I like livin' off the grid."

"Aw, come on, Curtis. Don't tell me you don't get lonely out here all by yourself."

You're a good one to talk, thought Alex.

"Bull. Why would I get lonely? I got everything I need, don't I? Roof over my head, bed to sleep in—"

By the looks of his couch, Alex bet there weren't many nights Curtis made it to the bed.

"—coho and steelheads straight from the river. I go to town to cash my check and buy more beer. That's all I need. Steak's about done. Got plenty of it. More than I can eat. Hand me one of those plates, wouldja?" He carried the meat to the picnic table, sawed it in two, and forked half onto a second plate lying there.

"That's all right," replied Alex. The sizzling beef smelled amazing, but this wasn't a social call.

"Have a seat," Curtis ordered. He climbed over the bench attached to the table and, without ceremony, began to eat.

Alex stared uncertainly at the extra steak, still glistening from the grill. It's outside was nice and charred, and the inside was the perfect shade of pink, just the way he liked it.

He could eat here, sit at Ruddock's by himself,

or go home and cobble something together and hope it tasted halfway edible.

He took a seat on the bench across from Curtis in the shade of a tall tree, reached for the extra knife and fork, and tucked in.

For someone who didn't like company, Curtis sure did like to talk. Once he got started, Alex could barely get a word in edgewise. Curtis rambled on and on about everything under the sun, from his cranky neighbor with her so-called, made-up allergies who was always complaining about him to the species of fish in the river and the best baits to catch each, and then back to the weather.

"How long've you lived out here?" Alex managed to slip in when he got an opening.

"Nine years, ever since I lost my wife and son. Couldn't go back to our house. Too many memories. I'd be thinking about them every time I looked around."

"What happened, if you don't mind my asking?"

"Driver ran a stop sign. They never knew what hit them."

"That how you got your leg hurt?"

"Shattered my femur. Was in the hospital four months. Still full of pins. They said I'll probably never get through a metal detector again."

"Five years is a long time. How old are you?"

"Forty-two on the Ides of March. That's the fifteenth, in case you didn't know."

Only forty-two? Alex almost choked on his beer. "Plenty of time left to meet someone new."

Again—he was a good one to talk.

Curtis set down his steak bone, wiped his hands on a blue bandanna, and pushed his plate to the side. "If I had to go through that again, I couldn't take it."

"I don't mean to downplay what happened. Not by any means. But isn't that what life's about? Taking risks?"

"I was taking a risk when I got out of bed that morning, wasn't I? And look what happened. No, thanks. I'm through with that. Nothing but heartache comes from getting close to people."

Alex heard quacking and watched as a raft of ducks climbed out of the water upriver from Curtis's fishing line and began pecking at the bread he had thrown there.

"Something tells me this isn't the first time those ducks have found a meal up here."

"Yeah, I can count on them to come visit me just about every night."

"What about the rest of your family? Any brothers or sisters?"

"A sister, but we had it out a few years back. She's called a couple of times. Left messages. Haven't gotten around to answering them yet." He got up and headed toward the cooler.

"No, thanks," said Alex with a chopping motion across his throat when Curtis started back holding two more cans. He'd barely made a dent in the first one. "I'm technically at work."

"One more. Who's gonna know? I'm sure as hell not gonna tell 'em."

Alex rose and picked up his plate, intending to carry it inside.

"Don't worry about that." Curtis waved it away impatiently. "I'll get it. Did I tell you the story about—"

"I got to go," said Alex, leaving his unfinished

beer on the table. "Thanks for the hospitality. Call the trash company and get them to come out here and take care of your trash for you. Otherwise we have no choice but to keep bothering you."

"No bother," Curtis said and kept on talking as he accompanied Alex to his car.

As Alex drove away, he could see Curtis in his rearview mirror, still talking to himself.

Chapter Seventeen

A lex hadn't even made it back to the main road when he heard Dispatch call to Patrol about an incident at the Thrifty Market. Two young boys had been caught shoplifting and were being held by the manager.

It wasn't Alex's call. His shift officially ended in less than an hour, at ten p.m. But he had to drive through town anyway to get home, and he'd never met an officer who didn't appreciate backup. He sped toward the market.

When he got there, he found Myers's patrol car sitting parallel to the store's entrance.

Alex flashed his badge to a store clerk and was pointed toward the manager's office. He entered to find two skinny boys with shaved heads slumped in chairs. Myers, listening intently to the manager's account of what had happened, acknowledged Alex's presence with a nod.

The boys sat up straighter when they saw Alex.

When his eyes met their green ones, his suspicions were confirmed.

"What's going on?" he asked the boys in a low voice.

Neither responded.

A package of hotdogs, moisture condensing on the plastic, lay on the manager's desk.

"Okay," said Myers, walking over to Alex and the boys. "You already apologized. The manager's not going to press charges. Time to go home."

"A word?" Alex led Myers outside of the office.

"These are the same boys I caught out after curfew and then trying to break into the school cafeteria. They were crawling with lice. That explains the shaved heads. The parents have been fined twice for neglect."

Myers shifted his feet. "The Pelletiers are good customers. The owner doesn't want to make a stink. It's his store. His call."

"Those boys are stealing food for one reason: they're hungry. If not for food, then for"—he'd been about to say *love*, but that sounded so sappy—"attention."

"You're new here. You don't know what you're up against."

"Let me take this one. I'll owe you."

Myers looked over his shoulder at the store-owner.

"Chief was there before when I brought them in," said Alex. "He talked to the social worker. He knows what's what."

"Well . . ."

"Come on, boys," said Alex.

"Where are you taking them?" asked Myers.

Alex pretended not to hear. Because he didn't know yet where they were going to end up. All he knew for sure was that he needed to witness these kids eat a good, hot meal with his own eyes.

He took them to a diner along the highway outside of town and asked for a booth toward the back.

The aromas of frying bacon, toast, and fresh coffee hit them as they walked through the door.

"What's your favorite thing to eat?" he asked the boys sitting across from him as he cracked open the menu.

It was the first time he'd ever seen them grin.

"Pancaketh," said Travis.

"Hotdogs," said Tyler, not surprisingly.

Alex ordered a burger for himself. He added applesauce for the boys, because it sounded healthy, and milkshakes to put some fat on their bones.

He had a ton of questions for them, but first things first. He ate his burger while watching them shovel food into their mouths as fast as they could.

"Slow down," he told Tyler. "You're barely even chewing that hotdog."

Tyler frowned and tongued one of his back teeth. "Hurts when I chew."

Once the boys' medical and dental problems were diagnosed, Alex had simply assumed they would be attended to. Apparently, he had assumed wrong. The lice, yes. School rules required that be treated. But the cavity was less obvious.

He clenched his hands in his lap. "Any plans to get that fixed?"

Tyler shook his head. Then, to cover for his parents, he added, "Sometime."

"Your folks know where you are?"

Their smiles disappeared and they clammed up.

"Be real with me, now. I want what's best for you. Don't you know that by now?"

Travis stabbed another forkful of the pancakes Alex had cut into bite-sized pieces for him and left a trail of maple syrup across the Formica while Tyler used his finger to wipe up what was left of the catsup on his plate and lick it off.

Dejection rose from the boys like the steam from the hot coffee the server had just poured into Alex's china mug.

"Let me put it this way. Is your dad home?" Beneath his calm demeanor, Alex could feel the vein throbbing in his neck. He'd about had it with the mom. What he wouldn't give to have a good, old-fashioned mano a mano with the dad—better yet, go a couple of rounds in the ring with him.

Travis shook his head.

"Travis!" scolded Tyler. "You're not supposed to tell."

"I don't care." Travis frowned. "They went on a trip," he told Alex.

"To where? Where'd they go?" The longer he kept firing questions at them, the greater the likelihood they'd drop the pretense.

Travis eyed his brother warily.

"They had to go away for a while," Tyler said, sucking his milkshake through his straw.

"Who's watching you while they're gone?"

"Nobody," said Travis.

"We can take care of ourselves," added Tyler with a hint of boastfulness in his tone that only wrenched

at Alex's heart more. Tyler couldn't fight his way
out of a paper bag. But the kid had his pride.

"You must have a babysitter. A grandparent?
Neighbor looking in on you?"

Tyler shook his head.

"When are they coming back?"

Travis shrugged.

"Don't know," said Tyler.

"How long do they usually go away for?"

"Last time, about ten days," replied Tyler before
he thought the better of it.

Alex massaged his chin. If he hadn't met Mrs.
Pelletier himself, seen that stone-cold face, that
blatant lack of remorse, he wouldn't believe what
he was hearing. But he had. And he did.

He pulled out his cell phone and, in coded language, advised Dispatch that he was on his way in
with two juveniles and to have CPS standing by.

It was midnight when a caseworker finally left
the station with the Pelletier brothers in tow.

"Did you tell her about Tyler's tooth? He's already gone too long without getting that cavity
filled."

"I told her," said Ms. Bartoli, watching Alex stare
after the van's receding taillights.

"What kind of people would actually go out of
state and leave kids that age alone, unsupervised?"

"At least the dad gave the kids a cell phone."
When she reached Greg Pelletier on the number
programmed into it, he claimed he and his wife
were already on their way back to Newberry.

But the boys were too young to be taken directly home without an adult present, and there were no nearby relatives.

"What will happen next?"

"Abuse and neglect cases tend to move very quickly. If the boys aren't returned to the parents or some other arrangement isn't made within seventy-two hours, the case will have to go before the court. My recommendation will carry some weight, but ultimately it's going to be up to the judge."

"If the parents are deemed unfit, what'll happen to the boys?"

"Their case will be reviewed by a special multidisciplinary team. Almost without exception, the objective of CPS is to reunite the family unit, even when that unit is less than perfect. The children will remain in temporary protective custody. If that happens, cross your fingers we'll be able to keep the boys together."

Until then, it hadn't occurred to Alex they'd be separated. But of course, she was right. "Where I'm from, it seemed like there were never enough foster families to meet the need."

"It's the same everywhere, I'm afraid."

At the prospect of the boys losing first their parents and then each other, a fresh anger rose in him. He pictured Travis with no big brother to look up to, and Tyler with no reason to keep from bowing to peer pressure and getting into progressively deeper trouble.

He'd seen it for himself. Well-adjusted adults didn't randomly start stealing cars and committing

robberies. The seeds of criminal behavior were
planted early. Children who were neglected by
their primary caregivers sought human connections wherever they could find them. Too often,
that meant the dregs of society.

He dug his roll of TUMS out of his pocket and
peeled back the wrapper. "What'll happen to the
parents?" he asked, tossing a handful of tablets
into his mouth.

"That's up to law enforcement. But you said the
storeowner doesn't want to press charges for theft,
so the only thing we have is another misdemeanor
neglect charge. My guess is that the parents will be
given a plan they'll have to comply with to get the
kids back. Typically, what that looks like is manda-
tory family counseling and psychological evaluations.

"Now, I'm going home to get some sleep, and I
suggest you do the same. Tomorrow's another day."

They exited the station together, the sound of
their footsteps echoing in the quiet night.

"Where's your car?"

"This is Newberry, Detective Walker," Ms. Bartoli said with an indulgent smile. "I'll be fine."

"Call me Alex. That's what I thought, too, when
I moved to the Willamette. Now, this."

"I'm Olivia, or just Livvie, if you like. We don't
often see abuse of this type around here, but that
doesn't mean it doesn't happen. It's just hidden in
plain sight. Newberry is mostly middle class, with
pockets of real poverty, especially in the rural areas
outside town. But in my line of work you find out
that affluence is no guarantee against child neglect

or abuse. The problems are just different. The rich often use food as a means of control . . . for punishment and reward."

Alex paused next to her car while she climbed in. "When I came to Newberry, I hoped I'd left the worst sort of humanity behind. Should've known."

"Don't give up on people," Livvie said, her face partially hidden in the minivan's shadowy interior. The buckle on her seat belt clicked and he heard the soft *thunk* of shifting gears. "There's still a lot of goodness in the world," she said just before she pulled away. "You just have to stay open to it. Keep trying to help, in hopes that one day, you'll find someone who appreciates what you're trying to do."

Chapter Eighteen

"**A**ddison invited me to the mall tomorrow with her and Mia! Can I go? Please?"

"They did?" Through the phone, Kerry could almost see Shay there in the Community Center, jumping up and down with excitement.

A breakthrough, praise God.

"Good news?" Ryan sat at the conference table where he and Kerry had been going over the Lewandusky case.

Kerry covered the receiver and whispered, "Shay made a friend!" She was almost as excited as her daughter. But the logistics were going to be tough.

"How are we going to work it with day care?" Surely Addison's mom wasn't planning to be gone the whole day.

"I can just stay home by myself tomorrow. She can pick me up and drop me off at the house."

"I don't know . . ."

"Mom, please? When are you going to start trusting me?"

"I do trust you." It was other people she didn't trust.

"Then why won't you let me do this?"

"Addison's mom can pick you up and drop you off at the Community Center."

"Great. Addison and Mia will see me at day care. Do you know how embarrassing that is? They'll totally drop me as a friend. Please, Mom?"

The desperation in her daughter's voice tore at Kerry's heartstrings. The mall was an hour away. The Community Center was in the opposite direction. Not that Shay would know that, but Addison's mom would. It would add time and fuel to the trip.

They would probably stay at least a couple of hours to make the drive worthwhile. That meant Shay would only be at home alone for half the day at the most.

"I suppose I could have Grandma check on you while you're there."

"Really?"

At her *squeeee*, Kerry winced and moved the phone away from her ear.

"I gotta go call Addison back."

Kerry punched End and perched atop the conference table facing her brother. "It's been a long time coming, but it finally happened. Couple of girls Shay met at the pool asked her to go to the mall tomorrow."

"Good for her. By the way, how's the boxing coming along?"

"Actually, Shay was just part of a demo at the pool. You should have seen her fancy footwork. Alex—"

At the memory of their kisses, Kerry felt her face redden.

"—her coach even let her take a few swings at him. That was how she got to know Addison and Mia. They came up to her after the exhibition and they've been talking ever since."

"Sounds like Coach Alex has been good for Shay. What about for you?"

Kerry took her seat across the table and began sifting through the papers spread before them. "Alex Walker's a cop. 'Nuff said."

"I call foul. Would you like it if people called you 'just a lawyer'?"

"That's about all I am anymore. That, and a mother." The sensual, feminine side of her was fast becoming a memory.

"Is that enough for you?"

Kerry let her hand filled with papers drop to the table. "We're supposed to be reviewing the Lewandusky case."

"No wonder they call you Cutthroat O'Hearn," teased Ryan, retrieving the papers he'd set down when Shay had called. He frowned. "Looks like we can't get away from Detective Walker. Were you aware he was the Lewandusky arresting officer?"

So far, Kerry had only spoken briefly with the prosecutor. She reached across the table, snatched the paper from Ryan's hand, and skimmed down the page.

Ryan said, "If this goes to trial, Walker is going to have to testify."

"Oh, Lord." Kerry closed her eyes and rubbed her temples.

"Now what?"

She rose yet again with a sigh and looked out the window.

"Ker. What's wrong?"

She turned around and sat on the windowsill to face her brother. "Do you remember the Sullivan case?"

"My baby sister's first murder trial. I'm not likely to forget it."

"I wasn't the lead."

"You never would have known it from the media coverage. The press loved you. Hot young twenty-something as opposed to crusty, ol' Donowitz? It's a given."

"First, ew, you're my brother and you're not allowed to talk about me like that, and second, crusty ol' Alan Donowitz happens to have been my mentor. He taught me everything I know, and I'll be forever grateful to him.

"Alex Walker ratted out his own partner rather than lie under oath," Kerry reminded him.

Ryan whistled. "That's right. The illegal search and seizure of the shotgun, resulting in an acquittal." He angled his chair away from the table, crossed his ankle over his knee, and massaged his lower lip. "You haven't known that Coach Walker was the same guy you butted heads with in the Sullivan trial for long or you would have mentioned it. When did you put two and two together?"

"Saturday night."

"Wait—the night Marcus and Paige watched your kids? You said you were going shopping."

"Jeez, Ry. I'm a grown woman. Aren't I entitled to a little privacy?"

Ryan leaned forward. "You were out with Walker?"

She sighed and rolled her eyes.

"Like, *out* out? On a *date*?"

"For lack of a better word."

Ryan put his fingertips together and grinned salaciously.

"Don't give me that look. It was no biggie. Alex invited me over for a drink. That's it. I knew if Dad found out, he would make noises, and you and Marcus and Keith would waste no time torturing me—"

"If I didn't give you a hard time, I wouldn't be doing my job as a brother."

"Trust me, you've got that covered. Seriously, Ryan, I was protecting the girls. If I ever *do* start dating—and that's a big *if*—I won't drag them into it till I'm absolutely certain it's the real deal."

"The Sullivan trial was ten years ago. How'd it happen to come up on Saturday?"

"I didn't remember Alex. *He* remembered *me*."

"Shocker."

Kerry made a face and was immediately annoyed with herself for taking her brother's bait. "How is it you can still sucker me into acting like I'm four years old?"

"Okay, I won't insist on all the details. Just tell me how you left things with him."

She hesitated, deciding how much information to reveal.

"Ker?"

When she still didn't answer, his provocative demeanor switched to one of concern, satisfying Kerry that no matter how mercilessly he taunted her, if anyone *else* so much as harmed a hair on her head, he would come at them with guns blazing.

"Did things get . . . heated?"

Interesting choice of words.

"Everything's fine."

"You're lying."

"I'm not a kid anymore. You don't have to worry about me."

"You? I'm worried about *him.*"

"Ha." She almost preferred his joking to making him worry.

"You both need to realize that now that you're in Newberry, you're bound to go head-to-head again. Even though the vast majority of defendants plead rather than chance a jury trial, eventually, you're going to be in another courtroom show-down. It's inevitable." He scooted in to the table again to get back to business. "Just Alex's luck, it looks like it's going to be sooner rather than later."

"Yes," she said thoughtfully as she perused the document more closely. "It looks like Lewandusky has no intentions of pleading."

"You can't discuss the case, obviously, but if I were you, I would make nice with Walker. He seemed like a half-decent guy at the Policeman's Benefit. Word around town is he's going to work out, despite some initial concern about his advanced age."

Kerry's mouth dropped open. "Says the guy who's older than he is."

"Oooh, right in the heart," said Ryan, clutching his chest, falling sideways in his chair.

"This is a small town, Ker. You're going to have to get used to that. You don't want to make enemies right off the bat, especially within the system. And look what Walker's doing for the community, particularly for Shay. You said it yourself. It's because of him that Shay's finally making friends."

Kerry considered. "If I'm going to meet with Alex again, then you're going to have to watch my kids for me."

Ryan sighed heavily and his eyes rolled to the ceiling. "Those brats? If I must."

She pressed her lips together and reached across the table to take a swat at him, but he was too quick.

"Whoa." He laughed. "I can see where Shay gets her gift for boxing. That right hook has real potential."

Chapter Nineteen

The day after Shay went to the mall, Kerry showed up to get her from boxing practice a few minutes early, hoping to have a word with Alex.

She told herself that she was only following her brother's advice to establish a civil relationship with Alex, given the likelihood of them facing each other again in a court of law. But she couldn't deny a certain tingle of anticipation at seeing him again.

When she arrived, Alex and Shay were intent on demonstrating her jabs to his mitts to some fascinated onlookers, a clutch of other kids she recognized from day care.

Alex finally looked up to see Kerry standing in the doorway. The two locked eyes.

There went that flutter in her lower abdomen again.

Alex set his hand on Shay's shoulder. "I'm going

to talk to your mom a minute. Why don't you ask your classmates if they have any questions?"

"Me?" she mouthed, putting her gloved hand to her chest. But she was grinning ear to ear as she skipped over to the kids, who immediately closed in around her, regarding her with equal measures of respect and awe.

Kerry warmed inside. She was supposed to be the one with the silver tongue. But everything *she* said irritated Shay, whereas Alex had this knack of making her feel good about herself.

His usual frown back in place, Alex strode over to Kerry, ripping apart the Velcro on his glove with the loud ripping noise she had grown accustomed to. "Something I can do for you?"

"Stand down. I come in peace."

Alex looked at Kerry askance. "What's the catch?" he asked, turning a blind eye to her to observe Shay's interaction with his potential new students.

"There is no catch."

"Kerry O'Hearn doesn't make a move without a reason."

"We have to talk."

It was hot in the gym. "So, talk," he said, wiping his forehead with the back of his arm. "I'm listening."

"Not here."

"Then where?"

"The Turning Point. Tonight. Seven o'clock."

"Eight."

"Seven. I have story time at eight thirty."

"Seven thirty. A pair of house finches are build-

ing a nest in my gutter and my feeders need filling." He'd just spotted the birds that morning,
when it was too late to do anything about it.

"Fine," she said tightly, "seven thirty, then."

At seven thirty-five, Kerry and Alex sat next to
each other at the bar, looking straight ahead at rows
of spirits on display.

Both were thinking of the last time they'd been
there, when they'd tormented each other with bad
jokes.

"I trust you got your feeders filled," said Kerry,
stubbornly refusing to make eye contact.

"Did you know that only twenty-five percent of
songbirds survive the first year of life? A reliable
food source year after year can make all the difference."

"This is your first year in the Willamette. The
birds don't even know you're here yet. Should I assume that means you'll be staying?"

He took a long drink. "Never know what the future holds."

Even though she was the one who had called
this meeting, she wasn't going to be the savior this
time. He was going to have to contribute something to the conversation. She clammed up.

"I apologize again for the other night. I don't
know what came over me."

Kerry looked at him in surprise. Did wonders
never cease?

"I'm sure it's not easy to forget losing a case like
that," she conceded.

"It's been ten years. More than enough time for me to have moved on."

"You are moving on. You came here, didn't you? And now, here we are, stuck with each other. That's why we needed to have this talk. I'll admit, it was my brother Ryan's idea. He says it's not good for us to be on the wrong side of each other, and he's my big brother, so it must be true."

Alex grinned into his wine. "Your brother's right. You and I already know too many people in common."

"It's only going to get worse. You know that, don't you? We're going to be running into each other on the reg."

He shrugged. "Can't be helped. We're in the same line of work."

"You're my daughter's coach."

"Shay's my little rock star."

Alex's words unlocked a side door to Kerry's heart she hadn't even known existed.

Shay's my little rock star. Kerry repeated his words in her head so she could experience again the burst of warmth they elicited in her.

Shay, whose own father had rejected her, and whose stepdad never called or visited. Kerry loved all her girls equally, but not in the same way. She'd always felt Shay needed special protection. Now that her marriage to Dick was over, she could finally admit that even when he had shared their Portland home, he'd never really tried to form a close bond with Shay. He didn't roughhouse with her or chase her, laughing, through the yard the way Marcus and Ryan did. He treated her more like the child of a friend whom he forgot the moment she was out of sight.

True, Shay had Ella and Chloé and too many cousins to count, along with aunts, uncles, and grandparents. But to them, she was just another child among many. Precious but not unique.

"Think about it," Alex was saying. "I'm surrounded all day by bad actors who are damaged, compromised in some way. Then along comes your daughter, and she's overflowing with all this pure, unadulterated . . . *joy*. Guess you could say Shay restored my faith in people."

Now Kerry looked straight at him. "I love her more than the sun and the moon and the stars, but lately I'm lucky if she gives me the time of day. The truth is, sometimes when it comes to Shay, I feel like an abject failure."

He snorted. "You want to talk about parental failure? Hop in the car. I'll show you a prime example within a mile of where we sit."

That made her feel a tiny bit better. "You're forgiven, as long as you cease and desist with the lawyer jokes.

"What about you?"

"What about me?"

"You know all about me. I know nothing about you."

"Not much to tell."

"Were you ever married?"

He peered down into his wineglass. "For about five minutes. It's hardly worth mentioning."

"My brother also reminded me that, just like all defense attorneys aren't bad, neither are all cops."

"I'm liking this brother of yours more and more all the time."

She smiled and her face softened. "He's very special. And if you ever tell him I said that, I'll deny it to my dying breath.

"Well, well, look who's here?" Laurel the bartender arrived for the start of her shift and started in with her usual friendly banter.

"How have you been?" she asked Kerry.

"Fine."

"I can see that." Eyeing Alex sitting next to her, Laurel's eyes twinkled.

"Don't see something where there's nothing," warned Kerry.

"Whatever you say," Laurel replied in a singsong voice. "How're your drinks?" she asked, peering down her nose into their glasses.

When both Kerry and Alex said they were good, she made her way down the bar to check on the other patrons.

"How do you know Laurel?" asked Alex.

"She and I go way back. Looks like she's still spring-loaded to fix people up. That's always been her thing."

"It's good you set her straight where we're concerned. We've both got our hands full."

"For sure."

"You with your family, and me with"——He scrambled to compile all the reasons——"my blog and my birds. Not to mention work, of course. Work keeps me slammed."

"Work, work, work," she said cheerfully. "It never ends."

"Glad we got this straightened out."

"Me too," said Kerry, finishing her drink. "Well. I'd better get back and put Ella to bed."

"I'll see you after boxing practice." He held out his hand in friendship. The gesture couldn't have been more different from the way he'd clutched her arms in his driveway.

Kerry looked at it, then her eyes rose to his as, automatically, she placed her hand in his.

Despite her skill at maintaining a straight face under pressure, Alex thought he saw a flicker of emotion in her eyes.

But this was all they were destined to have. Like she'd told the bartender, it just wouldn't work.

And like Curtis had said, *Women. Can't live with 'em, can't shoot 'em.*

Chapter Twenty

"Have you heard? Lewandusky's lawyered up."
Alex had learned to remain standing when he was called into the chief's office rather than subject his oversize frame to one of those cruel yellow plastic chairs.

"Can't wait to hear his excuse for laying by the roadside with a hunting rifle."

"Maybe he thought it was deer season. At any rate, the DA will be in touch to go over your testimony."

"Who's defending Lewandusky?"

Compared with the number of felony cases that went to trial in Portland annually, Alex had told himself it might be years before he was forced to butt heads with Kerry O'Hearn in court again.

"Kerry O'Hearn. That was her daughter in the boxing exhibit at the pool, wasn't it?"

It was a rhetorical question. No response was needed.

"I think I remember telling you that Newberry's the kind of place where everybody knows your name." The chief eyed Alex closely.

Alex wondered if Chief Garrett had been aware of the Sullivan trial, back when it was going on. Even if he had been, the chances he still recalled it after ten years, let alone knew of Alex and Kerry's joint involvement, were slim. Not that it mattered. Kerry couldn't be expected to recuse herself—and lose out on a hefty fee—on the grounds that she and Alex had been on opposite sides of the courtroom once before.

It was just a good thing they had backstepped before things had gotten out of control.

"Next item of business. How did you find Curtis when you were out there at his place?"

"Seemed okay. A little toasted, but okay. Why?"

"He's back at it."

"You said this is a habit with him. What do you want me to do?"

"I never minded taking a break now and then, sneaking a sip of 'shine in the shade while the wife was at choir practice, but now that the spring concert's over, she's home more in the evenings."

Alex didn't get what Chief's wife's chorale practice had to do with Curtis.

"Why not just fine Curtis again and be done with it?"

"Curtis doesn't give a hoot about the fines. Just pays 'em, and then the next week, he's burning his trash again. He knows his neighbor'll call us and then someone'll come out and see him about it."

Realization dawned. That explained why there

were two plates out. Curtis was counting on company from law enforcement.

"If companionship's what he wants, why doesn't he ask you straight out?"

"That's not how he operates. Curtis was once a fully functioning member of society. Did you know he's a certified public accountant? Hell, I trusted him to do my taxes for years."

"From his appearance, I had him pegged as a guy who'd spent his life working outside, maybe as part of a road crew." So much for his astute powers of observation.

"After his wife left him, he secluded himself to the point where he can't admit he needs people, even to himself. He'd rather break the law and pay repeated fines than concede that he's lonesome."

"I thought his wife died in an accident."

"That's the story he convinced himself of to deal with her leaving him and taking their child. No sense arguing with him at this point."

"His leg?"

"Fell off a ladder working on his roof. Too stubborn to ask for help."

"How long has this been going on?"

Chief sat back in his chair. "Since around the time my wife joined the chorale. Going on ten years."

Alex's head jerked back in surprise.

"You might see it as a little unorthodox, but it's making the best of a sorry situation. Curtis gets his company, the town coffers get a regular injection of capital, and whoever takes the complaint gets some grilled salmon or a sirloin—done to perfection, I might add."

Alex shrugged. "I won't dispute that." When he thought of that steak, his mouth watered all over again.

"Didn't think so. So, what do you say? You want to hop on down there again for me, or should I ask Zangrilli or Myers?"

Put like that, what choice did he have? Both Zangrilli and Myers had kids. "No need to take married officers away from their families at suppertime."

But that evening, when Alex walked around back of the log house expecting to find Curtis standing behind his grill with his barbeque fork in hand, he found him instead lying faceup on the ground, his long fork next to his open palm.

Alex jogged over to feel for a pulse in his neck, but by the time he saw his face up close, he already knew he wouldn't find one.

Immediately, he alerted Dispatch, then took stock. There was no blood, no sign of trauma. Nothing suspicious. Other than Curtis, everything was the same as the last time he'd been there. There was the remainder of the charred white contents of the burn barrel, the smoky petroleum smell of charcoal in the grill. A raw steak lay on a plate, waiting to be cooked. It appeared Curtis had died of natural causes the same way he'd lived, all alone.

"Rest in peace, Curtis," he said softly, to the sound of approaching sirens in the distance.

Scarcely a handful of mourners showed up at the Newberry Memorial Park in a fine drizzle for

Curtis Wallace's simple service. Among them were Alex, Chief Garrett and Olivia Bartoli.

Somewhere in his eulogy, the minister admitted he had never met Curtis. Alex tuned out his generic platitudes, thinking instead about how Curtis had cast off society, thrown away his money, and, ultimately, his life.

During a pause in the service, Livvie came up to him.

"The chief told me you'd been out to see Curtis. Thank you for being a friend to him." Tears glistened in Livvie's eyes.

"How did you know Curtis?" asked Alex, thinking perhaps their connection had something to do with her profession as a counselor.

"He was my brother."

The sister Curtis was on the outs with. That was this woman standing before him holding an umbrella over her head? That was Olivia?

He wondered if she knew about the still Curtis kept hidden in the garage.

"He had been suffering from liver disease secondary to alcoholism for a while. Basically, he drank himself to death. It tore me apart, him keeping me and our mom and everyone else who could have helped him at arm's length for so long. But ultimately, only he could make the decision to become a hermit."

Alex searched the detached faces surrounding them, but they were mostly other middle-aged men like himself. "Are your parents . . . ?"

"Our mom died last year and our dad lives on the East Coast somewhere. He"—she looked down, embarrassed—"couldn't be here."

He fumbled for words that expressed his regret without sounding too clichéd. "Maybe Curtis felt he had no other option."

"As long as there's breath, there are options. His choice to isolate himself ended up costing him a small fortune in fines and dragging more people under with him."

"Sorry about your loss." So much for not resorting to clichés.

Heads bowed for the benediction. From where Chief Garrett stood, Alex heard snuffling. He opened one eye to catch the chief wiping his nose with his handkerchief. Unobserved, his gaze traveled over the others, and it struck him that for the most part, everyone present stood slightly apart, inside his own personal space. By and large, they were all a bunch of solitaries.

He gazed beyond the people at the rain-soaked tombstones planted in the lawn and wondered if, now that he was a citizen of Newberry, this would be his own final resting spot. This was as good as any, he supposed. His parents had divorced before their passing, their ashes buried miles apart. And there was no room next to his paternal grandparents' graves. If he wanted to be buried in their cemetery, he'd have to purchase a separate plot, alone among strangers.

He'd never been to his maternal grandparents' gravesites. He didn't even know what town they were in.

That being the case, who did he think was going to visit *his* grave? Easy: *no one.*

A trickle of rainwater ran down his collar and he shivered.

Chapter Twenty-one

Alex poured an ounce of the same wine from each of two successive vintages into glasses and sat down to compare them with his laptop nearby, prepared to take notes on differences in color, aroma, and taste.

He turned his focus to his blog notes. What he needed was a third vintage to compare with the other two. Most wineries released the same label wines around the same time every year, often in the springtime.

A quick search of the Net revealed he was in luck—May was the release month. And this year, rather than purchasing it at his regular shop in Portland, he could practically walk to the winery where it had been bottled.

That's what he needed to elevate his blog—a visit to the winery, complete with his own photos. Even better would be if he could somehow get a behind-the-scenes tour, obtain exclusive shots that would scoop all those other wine bloggers competing with him for readership.

He carried his wineglass out back and crept stealthily to a spot beneath the roofline where he'd seen the purple finches carrying wisps of dried grass, to check on the progress of the nest.

But it was nowhere to be found. The half-built nest had been so fragile . . . it must have blown away in the wind.

He looked around, but the birds themselves had disappeared, too.

As usual, whenever he was perplexed or disappointed, his thoughts defaulted to Kerry O'Hearn. Why, after so many years, did she still occupy such a disproportionately large space in his mind?

Around the time of the Sullivan trial, Alex had completed advanced, science-based training designed to optimize his powers of observation. By viewing a series of objects flashing in progressively faster microseconds, he'd learned to rapidly distinguish between, for example, a wallet, a cell phone, and a handgun.

Back then, he'd viewed Kerry as a frigid shrew with a heart of stone.

But maybe he'd been overconfident in his powers of perception. Now that he'd gotten to know her, doubts had begun to poke holes in his original assessment. No longer did anger threaten to swamp him every time he thought of her. He'd seen a gentler side of her, like the way she'd rescued Ella without panicking when she'd fallen face forward in the pool so that she wouldn't develop a fear of water. How she made sure her middle child always felt included.

She could be a tiger mom, like the time she'd set aside her misgivings and brought Shay to find out about boxing so she could learn to defend herself.

Then there were those passionate kisses in his driveway, the way her eyes burned hot and intense. Alone at night in bed, he'd replayed the scene in his head so many times, he knew each kiss by heart.

In the corner of his eye he saw a flash of magenta feathers and followed one of the finches carrying a twig in its beak to his gutter.

Maybe he and Kerry could never be lovers. But where was the law against a cop and a defense attorney being—dare he even think something so radical?—*friends?*

Without friends, Alex was more like Curtis than he cared to admit.

His pulse began to pound, bringing on a rush of second thoughts. He must be crazy. Keeping his eye on the nesting birds, he pulled out his phone and punched in Kerry's number before he came to his senses.

When Kerry saw who was calling, she set down the coffee she'd made to get herself through her afternoon slump and picked up her phone, almost dropping it in her haste. Why was Alex Walker contacting her? This was no social call. Probably he wanted to talk about Shay being in another boxing exhibition.

Ignoring the fluttering of her heart, she cleared her throat. "Kerry O'Hearn."

"How are you?"

They hadn't had many phone conversations. The technology made his voice sound even deeper.

"I'm fine." Blindly pacing the carpet in her office, she clutched her phone tightly and forced her breathing to remain even. "You?"

"Good. I, ah . . . I was calling to ask a favor."

Kerry froze in her tracks. The embezzlement case suddenly seemed like it was eons ago. Ella had been resisting her naps lately at day care, making her cranky and easily frustrated in the hours between dinner and bedtime, and Chloé had dropped Hobo's leash and gotten poison ivy chasing him through the hedgerows surrounding the vineyard. The lotion Kerry applied to Chloé's rash at bedtime didn't last through the night, so she'd been showing up next to Kerry's bed in the wee hours, scratching and miserable. When Kerry's alarm clock went off at five thirty, she dragged herself to the bathroom sink, splashed cold water on her face, and groaned at the dark circles under her eyes.

But Alex's call had reawakened her senses like a brisk slap in the face.

"Do you think you could introduce me to Hank Friestatt?"

Hopes she didn't know she possessed plummeted. What had she been expecting? That out of the blue, Alex was calling to take her out to a relaxing, grown-up dinner, someplace with white tablecloths and real napkins, where she didn't have to referee two kids' constant taunting and hold the third over the restroom potty to keep her from falling in?

Not a chance. This was about his wine blog.

"I'll call the Sweet Spot and see when Hank will be around."

What was she doing?

"After that, I can text you my work schedule for the next week," said Alex coolly.

She wished she felt as serene as his voice sounded, and that she didn't have to fist the phone so tight to keep her hand from trembling. Well, she could act cool, too. She'd done it a thousand times in court. "And then I'll have to find a sitter."

"Sorry. Sounds like a lot of trouble for you. Maybe we should just forget it."

"No!" She winced. "I mean, no. You brought it up. Now I'm holding you to it." Her heart thudded against her ribs. Far from sounding cool, she sounded desperate. Blame it on that part of her that wouldn't give up—the part that would scratch and claw for her clients until the bitter end. The same part that couldn't stop thinking about his kisses.

"Is that right?"

Was that a smile she heard in his voice? Was he on to her? Her face burned, but she had come this far. She wasn't backing down now. "That's right."

"What do you think *you're* going to get out of this?"

"I'll *tell* you what. A few precious hours of adult

conversation without fighting anyone to eat their broccoli and no mention of either My Little Pony or the Powerpuff Girls."

"Fair enough. But I got to warn you . . . I'm not big on broccoli either."

Chapter Twenty-two

W hen Alex asked Kerry for an introduction to Hank Friestatt, he hadn't figured on her coming along. Then again, he hadn't thought it through at all, merely acted on impulse.

Now, here he was, waiting for her in the parking lot of the Sweet Spot. When he saw her 4Runner pull up, he walked over to meet her.

"Hope it wasn't too much trouble getting away," he said as he tried not to stare at her slender calf emerging from the SUV.

"My parents live right next door. When I have to run out unexpectedly, I can rely on them to watch the kids. But they drove to the coast for a couple of days. And even if they were around, they don't have as much energy as they used to. Whenever I'm going to be gone longer than an hour, I usually ask one of my brothers and their wives."

"Which one drew the ace card this time?" he

asked as they took their time strolling under the oak trees toward the tasting room entrance.

"Marcus is out of town on business. That means Paige is already shorthanded with her two, so I asked Ryan and Indra. They have three kids of their own. They were taking all six to the big playground in the park, in two cars so they had enough seat belts. You can imagine what their day is going to be like." She grinned and rolled her eyes.

"Actually," said Alex, looking at his feet as they walked, "I have no idea. But it sounds kind of fun."

Kerry looked at him from the corner of her eye. "You really think so?"

He shrugged.

"Tell me. Have you ever changed a diaper? Stayed up all night with a puking kid when you yourself have the worst flu of your life?"

He shook his head. "I wouldn't know the first thing about it. Got to admit, though, the boxing has been going better than I thought."

"It's been the best thing that's happened to Shay since we moved back to Newberry."

Alex shot Kerry a look of gratitude. "I said it before. Shay's a special kid."

Kerry hesitated, weighing her next words. "She thinks you walk on water."

Tears stung the back of Alex's eyes. He shouldn't have invited Kerry O'Hearn into his off-duty life. She stirred up a barrage of emotions he didn't know how to deal with. They weren't even inside the winery yet and here he, Alex Walker, veteran detective, witness of countless despicable, violent crimes without so much as batting an eye, was on the verge of crying over—of all things—a child.

He cleared his throat and switched his focus to the reason they were there: meeting the owner of one the valley's premier wineries and taking a ton of notes for what was sure to be his best blog posting ever.

"Is your cousin meeting us in the tasting room?"

"He said he'd be here around two. It's a quarter of."

"Gives us a few minutes' head start."

Kerry squinted up at the sun shining through the dense canopy of green and sighed with obvious pleasure. "It's so nice to have an afternoon off, without rushing."

Maybe I'm overanalyzing, thought Alex. *Maybe it's good Kerry came along after all.*

As they reached the tasting room and ascended the first step, Kerry's phone rang. She frowned and paused at the top of the steps. "My phone's on Do Not Disturb except for family." She glanced at the screen. "It's my brother. The one who's watching my kids.

"Hello?"

Alex stopped along with her, his cop's sixth sense going haywire.

"Oh, no." Her eyes, full of concern, flew to Alex's. "How bad is it? Of course." She paced across the porch, rubbing her forehead. "Um, let me see . . . no, how about you stay with Indra and I'll come get the kids . . . yes, all six of them! . . . I can manage. She does? That's insane . . . hold on."

She lowered the phone and took a deep breath

before addressing Alex. "I really hate to ask you this, but my sister-in-law injured her eye at the park and she needs to go to the emergency room. Her own family's in India and we're more like real sisters than sisters-in-law. We've gotten super close, and she's asking for me . . ."

Alex cupped Kerry's elbow and was struck to realize she was trembling. *She, the invincible Kerry O'Hearn.* "Whatever you need. Name it."

"It's all so confusing, but young Seamus has a ball game at four, and if Ryan has all six kids, there's no way he can legally get them all into the same car—"

"Calm down. Get to the point."

"Can you follow me to the hospital in your car and then take my kids back to the farmhouse and watch them till we know what's going on with Indra's eye?"

"Let's go." Alex's hand slid down Kerry's forearm, grasping her hand in his and, together, they skipped down the steps and made a beeline back to the parking lot, his excitement at meeting the Sweet Spot's owner already gone.

"Are you okay to drive?" he asked as they walked briskly to their cars. They hadn't had so much as a drop to drink, but she was clearly shaken.

She nodded.

"We'll need to transfer Ella's car seat." She pulled up short. "I just thought of something. What if you get called out on a case?"

"I'm not on call."

"But—" Worried sapphire eyes ground into him.

"For God's sake, Kerry. Just trust me."

"Right," she said, starting off again.

Alex wasn't fooled. She was only relying on him because it was an emergency. It stung a little. But this wasn't about him. It was about three little girls who needed his protection.

Chapter Twenty-three

Ella's whimpering at leaving her mother with a stranger turned into a full-fledged meltdown the moment she, Alex, and her sisters exited the ER's sliding glass doors into the bright haze of the July day.

"Mommy!" she howled, arms outstretched over Shay's shoulder, her face distorted in anguish.

Ignoring the spectacle of her screaming baby sister's hands grasping pitifully at thin air, Chloé calmly latched onto Alex's hand and gazed up at him through impossibly long, pale lashes with a look of complete and utter trust.

So, this was what it felt like to be an all-powerful god. He resolved to slay dragons for Chloé from that moment forward. Or at least until her mother got home.

"Coach Walker? Is Aunt Indra going to be blind like Helen Keller?"

"Helen Keller was blind, deaf, and dumb," said

Shay in a superior tone. She adjusted the bawling Ella on her hip. "Aunt Indra will probably just have to wear one of those black eye patches for the rest of her life, like in *Pirates of the Caribbean*."

"The doctors are taking good care of your aunt." Indra was, indeed, in good hands. The girls, not so much. In his entire life, Alex had never so much as babysat one kid, let alone three. He had no idea what he was in for.

"Mommeeeeeee!"

Alex cringed. How could a scream that spine-tingling originate from lungs that small?

A matronly woman on her way into the hospital gave him a bland smile, and Alex was sorely tempted to offer her half his weekly salary on the spot to accompany them back to the farmhouse until Kerry got home.

But another part of him had the urge to prove to Kerry—and her girls—that he was perfectly capable of being a substitute parent.

He lengthened his strides, swinging open the back door of his vehicle and putting Ella's special seat in, then, satisfied that it was secure, moved aside for Shay to deposit Ella in it, and slid into his own seat up front.

But then he immediately felt bad that he'd left Chloé to open her door for herself. It was his first glimpse of what it was like to be a middle child.

He was shifting out of park when he looked in his rearview mirror and saw Shay, still leaning over Ella. "Pile in, Shay. This ship is sailing."

"I can't just sit her in there. I have to buckle her *in!*"

Of course. "I meant, after you're done."

In the rearview mirror, he watched Shay buckle the squirming, screaming child in so tight it was a wonder she could still breathe, then slam the door and scramble around to the front.

"I want"—sob—"Mommeee," cried Ella, plucking at some random heartstring Alex hadn't known he had. At least she had stopped howling. Now there were occasional breaks between sobs.

They'd only been outside of the air-conditioning for a few minutes and already Alex was perspiring.

"What's that?" asked Shay the minute she got in, reaching for a switch on the dashboard.

"Don't touch that!"

At the wail of the siren, Shay jumped.

In the parking lot, people stared.

Alex flipped the siren off and pointed his finger in her face. "Don't. Touch. Anything."

Shay withdrew from him and huddled up against her door. "All *right.*"

"Hungry," sobbed Ella.

"What does she eat?" asked Alex, pulling onto the road.

"It sounds like you're talking about a dog or something," said Chloé.

Shay was already absorbed in browsing the pictures on her phone screen. "Huh? Who?"

He frowned. "Is that thing connected to the Internet?"

"Uh, *yeah.* How else could I play my games?"

"Shut it down."

"But—"

It wouldn't kill her to do without her phone for a couple of hours. "I'm going to need your help, okay? You're the oldest. You know what to do."

"Hungry," cried Ella again.

Shay whipped her head around. "Mom usually keeps some animal crackers in her purse for her."

"Animal crackers?" His foot let off the gas. "Where do you buy those?"

"Any store," said Chloé.

"Thrifty Market," said Shay simultaneously.

"Thrifty Market's not on our way."

"Waaaaaa! Mommy!" wailed Ella.

Recalculating.

"Keep your eye out for any kind of food store, men."

"Aye, aye, captain." In the rearview, he saw Chloé salute.

God love her.

Shay raised a brow. "I *could* look it up on my phone, if I was allowed to."

Alex pressed his lips together. In the short time he'd lived in Newberry, he had never driven the stretch of road between the hospital and the farmhouse.

"Waaaaa!"

"Do it."

Since when were twelve-year-olds able to shop online and navigate using GPS? Alex raised and lowered his eyebrows in the rearview, checking out his wrinkles to reassure himself he wasn't *quite* as old as he felt.

In the backseat, Chloé began singing to Ella, which, thankfully for his blood pressure, quieted her a little.

A few miles down the road, when they pulled into the store, Alex automatically hopped out and headed toward the entrance before spinning on the ball of his foot when he remembered his precious cargo.

Back inside the car, he pulled out his wallet and handed Shay a twenty. "You go. I'll stay here with"—He nodded toward the back—"the prisoners. Oh, and if you see something you and Chloé like, get that, too."

"I hope she gets me a Snickers," murmured Chloé a moment later as they watched Shay disappear through the glass door of the store.

"What would you say the odds of that are?" He found he couldn't take his eyes off the door, in case someone attempted to kidnap Shay.

"What are *odds*?"

He couldn't have Chloé feeling slighted again. "Go in and tell her you want a Snickers." He sighed.

Left alone in the back, Ella started screaming again.

"Hey, little baby," he cooed in the rearview. Who knew he was capable of such a high pitch? He did a quick reconnoiter of the parking lot to make sure no one was eavesdropping. "Don't cry. Your sisters are coming right back."

He might as well have recited the Pledge of Allegiance for all the good it did.

"El-la," he sang, his voice cracking. He wished he knew the song Chloé had been singing. If only he had one song from his childhood he could draw on, but his mother had been too busy to sing to him.

Wait. He knew one, from a book.

" 'The itsy bitsy spider went up the water spout—' "

"Waaaa!"

"Come on, girls," he muttered. "Let's get a move on."

But they still didn't come.

Finally, he got out, opened the back door, and fumbled around with the latch on Ella's car seat. When it finally snapped open, the buckle smacked her in the face, her new screams making her earlier cries pale in comparison.

"Oooh! I'm so sorry, baby! I'm sorry!"

At last, she was freed from the contraption and in his arms, and he found himself gently bouncing her as he cuddled her warm, damp body against his chest.

"Shhh. On your wedding day, you won't even remember this. I promise."

He was dying to get a look at her forehead, hoping against hope there was no mark. That was just what he needed—returning Kerry's kid to her with a welt on her face and no witnesses to back up his story—but he couldn't risk changing position for fear of her getting hysterical again.

"Hey, baby," he cooed for what seemed like the hundredth time, stroking the back of her head where the soft, fine angel hair stuck to her scalp. "What's the matter? What's so bad that you have to carry on like that?"

Ella frowned hard at him. But at least she had stopped screaming.

"Your momma's going to be back soon." He made up a tune to accompany those words and began waltzing her around the parking lot, while still keeping an eye peeled on the door of the store.

"Yes, she will."

Fingering a button she'd found on his shirt, Ella heaved a great sob.

A moment later, to Alex's great relief, the girls finally reemerged, Chloé biting off a chunk of a giant-size Snickers and Shay holding a bulging plastic bag in one hand and a fountain drink large enough to use as a vase in the other.

"About time," said Alex, putting Ella back into her seat, only to have her start to cry again. "Sorry, baby, but it has to be this way," he said, all thumbs at snapping her in. Finally, he climbed back into the front. It seemed like they'd been on the road for hours.

Shay sat down beside him, pulled a Hershey Bar out of the bag and, using her teeth, ripped the paper off the end.

Alex held out his hand, whereupon Shay gave him a puzzled look.

"Change?"

"Oh," said Shay, digging in her shorts pocket and dropping a few sticky coins into his palm.

"That's it?"

"You said get whatever we want."

He peered into the bag to find it filled with candy and snack food, and his head fell back and hit the headrest.

So be it. He told Kerry he'd watch them. He never claimed to be able to feed them properly.

"Wait." He stirred around in the bag's contents. 'Where are the animal crackers?"

Shay's eyes got big and her lips came unglued from the straw stuck in her drink. "Oh."

"Don't tell me—"

"We forgot," said Chloé.

"Jesus Christ Almighty."

"I'll run back in," said Shay brightly.

"No!" Alex's hand clamped down on her shoulder. "Do not get out of this car, or—" In the nick of time, he caught himself before he threatened to cuff her. He dug in the bag again. "Is there *something* in here Ella can eat?"

"A Pop-Tart," suggested Chloé.

"Yeah, a Pop-Tart. They're soft." Shay opened the box and passed a foil packet backward.

"Can you give her a hand with it, Chlo?" asked Alex.

"My name's not Chlo. It's Chlo-*ée*."

"Chlo-*ée*. Can you please help your sister?"

"Sure."

After what seemed like a year, they finally drove down a tree-lined lane until they came to an old, white clapboard house with additions extending off the main structure indicative of the diverse eras in which they'd been built. It was a great example of an early Oregon farmhouse—if you were into that sort of thing. It was also a maintenance nightmare. Alex pitied the poor soul responsible for keeping it up.

Scattered in the driveway were a pink tricycle, a two-wheeler lying on its side, and assorted dog toys.

Alex and Shay got out. "We're here," said Alex, looking around with his hands on his hips. It seemed like a minor miracle.

He went to unbuckle Ella yet again and he almost choked. "What in the world—"

Seeing his wrinkled-up nose, Chloé leaned into Ella and sniffed. "Ella go poopy?" she asked in a singsong voice.

Ella grinned happily and nodded her head.

"Don't tell me that toxic odor is coming from that little cherub. It smells like the entire Sonics offense took a crap in a bucket back here."

"Ommmm." Chloé clapped a hand over her mouth.

"I said, crap. Crap's not a bad word."

"Mommy says it's not nice to say—"

"Don't *you* say it." Alex pointed his finger at Chloé, and in the voice he used with the most hardened felons growled, "Not a word to your mother. Do you understand?"

"Mommy said if a grown-up tells us to keep a secret we're supposed to tell her right awa—"

"Do you understand?"

She nodded slowly, blue eyes as round as marbles.

"Let's go in.

"What time's bedtime?" he asked Shay.

"Nine o'clock on a school night. But in the summer, we're allowed to stay up later."

Alex wasn't sure he would make it.

"Can you walk, Ella?" he asked, trying not to inhale as he freed her from the confines of her car seat. The prospect of handling her in her present state was daunting. There must be a knack to carrying a kid with a full diaper, but in all his forty years, he had yet to learn it.

"Nnn." Ella reached for his neck in a stranglehold and buried her face in his shoulder, giving him no choice but to gather her into his arms.

"Whew-eee!" exclaimed Alex as he carried her down the crooked walk paved with bluestones toward the house, her butt resting heavily on his forearm.

Swinging her plastic bag full of goodies nonchalantly, Shay looked over her shoulder and said, "Sometimes she still has accidents."

His eye paused on an inflatable pool in the front yard filled with water, and he got an idea. He halted and looked around. *Bingo.* A garden hose, coiled up against the house.

Alex fished in his pocket. "Come here and get the house keys, Shay," said Alex, dangling them toward her. "Now go inside and empty that bag of candy and bring me back the bag."

Shay opened the door, and when she did, a dog of medium-size and indeterminate breed sprang out past her into the yard.

"Hobo! Come back here!" Shay dropped her bag on the porch and tore off after him.

"Don't ask me to help chase him. Last time, I got poison," deadpanned Chloé, strolling up behind Alex, gnawing at her second, or maybe it was her third, candy bar. There was a ring of chocolate around her mouth and a smudge on her top with the cartoon pony on the front.

"How far will he run?" asked Alex, watching Shay canter pell-mell down the overgrown meadow leading to the vineyards beyond.

Chloé shrugged, unconcerned.

Meanwhile, his arm was growing warm with Ella's well-padded underpants molding around it, taking on its shape.

"Go over and empty out that bag on the porch and bring it to me."

Thank God someone did as she was told.

"Now, go in the house and bring me out a roll of toilet paper."

"Seriously?"

"Do I look like I'm kidding?"

Must he overemphasize everything he said to get results?

Off Chloé trotted, while gingerly, Alex set Ella on her feet. He pointed at her and said, "Stay." He waited a few seconds. When he realized she wasn't likely to go far, he dipped a hand into the pool water to find it nicely warmed by the sun. Then he backed over to the house, turned on the spigot, and held his hand under the trickle of water. "Brace yourself, kiddo. This might be a little chilly, but better a few goose bumps than having to call a trauma response team for a biohazard clean-up of your bathroom."

Chloé bounced down the porch steps and held out the empty bag. "Here you go."

"Look away," Alex warned her. "This ain't going to be pretty."

Apparently ten-year-olds were in to gross, though. From the light in Chloé's eyes, he might as well have given her an engraved invitation.

"I've watched Mommy change Ella lots of times."

"Well, this might not be how Mommy does it. But it'll get 'er done.

"Come here, Ella." He stripped her dress over her head, tossed it aside, and turned her around. With the water now flowing from the hose and the bag handy, he held his breath and hooked his thumbs in the elastic waistband of her padded pants.

"She's supposed to be lying down!" giggled Chloé.

"I knew that." He picked Ella up by her waist and gently lay her faceup on the grass.

She looked up at him with a puzzled expression. Hopefully that little red mark on her forehead would fade by tomorrow and Kerry would never know the difference.

And then, time stood still. Alex felt like he was having an out-of-body experience. Nobody would believe this—not that he would ever tell them. Or maybe he was on one of those hidden camera shows, and next week his fellow officers would be sitting around the briefing room watching him on TV, pointing at him and cracking up at his expense.

"Here goes nothing." He held his breath, turned his head askance, and squinted. Down came Ella's disposable britches in a series of tugs, until they slipped off her feet and Alex whisked them into the bag.

"That wasn't so bad, was it? Up you go." He rose, and with his arm extended, he dangled Ella by her arm like a rag doll as far away from himself as possible while, with the other, he held his thumb over the hose, spraying her entire body in an up and down, sweeping motion.

"Ahahahaha!" Chloé laughed, holding on to her sides to keep from falling over.

"Now. How about a dip?" He sat the naked Ella down in the water and stood back. "Feel better? I know I do." He sucked in a lungful of country air. "I can breathe again."

Ella had the vacant stare of a shock victim—

until her palms smacked the surface of the water, splashing her face. Then she blinked and gazed up at Alex with eyes the frosty turquoise of sea glass, water droplets decorating her face, and a toothless grin, and his heart turned into that porridge the hipsters ate down at the coffee shop.

"She caught him," said Chloé, peering past Alex to the meadow. "Shay caught Hobo."

Alex followed Chloé's gaze to where the mutt bounded toward them like an eager sled dog, his tongue hanging out, dragging Shay behind him at an awkward run.

They were headed straight toward the baby pool.

Alex threw up his hands and yelled, "Stop!"

There was a great splash. Chloé clapped her own cheeks. "Hobo! Get out!"

Ella blinked rapidly, her little hands waving in front of her droplet-spattered face like a tightrope walker balancing on a wire.

"Hobo!" scolded Shay.

Standing in the pool, Hobo cocked his head at Shay. Then at Chloé. Then, in his confusion, he licked Ella's face.

"Out you go, mutt." Kneeling, Alex took hold of Hobo's collar and led him out of the pool and into Shay's waiting hands, but not before Hobo's toenail sank into the side.

There was a *pflop* and, before their eyes, the pool began to melt.

"He ruined it!" whined Chloé. "Hobo broke our pool!"

Just in time, Alex stepped out of the way of the water rushing toward his shoes.

He sighed and rubbed a hand over his face. "I imagine he needs to be fed, too," he said to no one in particular.

"I'll do it," said Chloé, heading into the house, calling Hobo's name.

His head spun. One minute these kids were driving him crazy and the next they were surprising him with their sweet natures.

The whole thing was a wonder.

Chapter Twenty-four

It was after ten p.m. when Kerry made it home. Inside the screen door, Hobo wagged his tail in greeting.

No way would she have imposed on Alex Walker to watch the girls if she hadn't been with him when the crisis struck. At least she knew he'd been thoroughly vetted. Not only that, if he messed up, not just she but her father would have his head on a post.

The whole way home, she had steeled herself for mayhem. She imagined Alex would have one foot out the door, chomping at the bit to leave. Ella would be red-faced from bawling, Chloé would be begging her for the Calamine Lotion, and Shay would start in complaining about her lengthy absence. It would be an hour before she could fall into bed herself.

Instead, she entered a quiet, dimly lit kitchen. This morning's cereal bowls, which she'd left stacked in the sink, were drying upside down in the dish drainer, and the tea towels were neatly folded on their racks.

"Girls?"

She tiptoed into the living room to find Alex softly snoring on the couch with Ella sound asleep in his arms and Shay and Chloé in sleeping bags on the floor, eyes closed, hair still wound up in towels from their showers. The faint smell of shampoo lingered in the air. On the TV, Cinderella's prince twirled her around the ballroom floor with the sound muted.

For a second, she wondered if she was in the right house.

She touched Chloé and Shay's heads. "Go up to bed," she whispered. "I'll be up in a minute to tuck you in."

While they stumbled off, clutching their pillows to their chests, she gathered Ella into her arms and, with some difficulty, carried her upstairs, followed by Hobo, and lay her gently in her crib. *My last baby*, she thought, brushing Ella's hair off her brow. For despite all her career success, her babies had brought her more joy than any legal triumph. After she whispered a quick prayer over her, Hobo circled and lay down on the rug.

Kerry stopped by Shay and Chloé's rooms before going back down the creaky stairs. She touched Alex's shoulder and said, "I'm home. You can go."

When he woke to find his arms empty, he sat up in a panic.

"It's okay. Everyone's in bed."

He sank back into the couch with his arm across his brow, his feet still on the floor. "What time is it?"

"Going on eleven."

"There was a day when I'd be getting ready to go out clubbing at eleven."

She chuckled softly and fell onto the foot of the couch next to him. "Me too. You still can, if you want."

"Think I'll pass." He yawned and sat up, rubbing a hand over his head. "How's your sister-in-law?"

"They were able to save her eye, though they said she has more surgeries ahead of her."

"What happened exactly?"

"It was one of those weird things. She was chasing the kids down a path through the woods surrounding the park when she ran into a tree branch."

"Oooh. Not good. The girls were concerned for her."

She winced. "They didn't give you too much trouble, did they?"

"Naw. No trouble at all."

"I was amazed to find Ella's Pull-Ups still dry. Did she go potty?"

"If by *go potty*, you mean did LeBron James somehow sneak past me and take a dump in her diaper, then yes."

Kerry's head fell back in laughter.

"What about Chloé? Did she have you put some Calamine on her poison ivy?"

"She didn't mention it."

"Hm. It has been a week since she got it. Maybe it's almost better.

"Thanks again for stepping up to the plate. I don't know what I would have done without you."

Kerry had always had some kind of hold on Alex, but he'd never been able to pinpoint exactly what it was.

Now, even after the long day she'd had, everything about her looked beautiful . . . the arch of her brow, the curve of her jaw, every fine line sweeping out from the corners of her eyes.

"Can I get you anything? Glass of wine . . . cup of coffee?"

His body was reacting in unsettling ways, making him recall kissing her against her will in his driveway.

"I should go." He rose to his feet.

"Don't go. Not yet."

At the touch of her hand on his arm, he sat back down, elbows resting on spread knees.

"Sitting with Indra all afternoon, her hand squeezing mine so tight I thought the bones might break, gave me lots of time to think. Life is so fragile, you know? You can wake up in the morning and look out at the leaves shimmering in the wind and see the faces of your loved ones, and the next thing you know—*poof*—it's all gone, just like that. It reminded me of how lucky I am."

"I went to a funeral the other day," he said.

"Someone around here?"

"I know what you're thinking—that I haven't been here long enough to make friends."

"Not at all."

"Couldn't blame you. Tell you the truth, I'm not sure why I went, given the short time I'd known Curtis. That was his name. Curtis Wallace."

"Curtis Wallace died?"

She sounded genuinely moved.

"How?"

"He . . . let's just say his heart gave out."

"That's such a shame," she said, slowly shaking her head. "Curtis was closer to my brothers' ages. I wonder if they know. I remember them saying what a fun guy he was back in school. Then, after his divorce, he just shut down and wouldn't let anyone in."

Alex studied her, breasts gently rising and falling with each breath. Hard to believe she was the same imperious Kerry O'Hearn he thought he knew. After all these years, he finally saw her as a whole woman, not just the strong, competent side she presented in public but her soft, vulnerable side, too. Never could he have imagined that one day she would entrust him with her children, her most precious possessions, and that they'd be curled up next to each other on her couch in her dimly lit living room.

He reached over and picked up a lock of her hair, rubbing it between his thumb and finger. "It's like you said. Sometimes you don't know what you've got till it's gone.

"Let's start over," he said quietly.

She gazed up at him, her eyes sparkling in the lamplight. "Yes. Let's."

She looked so fetching. So approachable.

"Is it okay if I kiss you?"

She smiled the smile he had thought of a thousand times since he'd first passed her in the hallway at Pioneer Courthouse. Only this time, it was for him and him alone.

Then she nodded and they came together, and

he did his best to obliterate that smile with his mouth.

Following their disastrous first kisses, the careful consideration each gave the other was almost comical. But it wasn't long before their breathing became urgent, her decorative throw pillows were flying through the air, and they were falling back together on her family-size couch, so wrapped up in each other they hardly knew where one ended and the other began.

Alex's palm was luxuriating in the soft flesh of her outer thigh beneath her skirt when a small voice came from the vicinity of the staircase.

"Mommy? Where are you? My mosquito bites are itching."

He broke their kiss, his eyes looking down into Kerry's round ones staring up at him.

Getting caught in the act had never once crossed his mind. But then, except for his brief, disastrous marriage, he'd never shared his time . . . his home . . . his life. It had always just been *him*.

"The Calamine's in the bathroom cabinet, Chloé," Kerry said calmly. "I'll be up in a minute."

They lay perfectly still, listening to Chloé's receding footfalls as their pounding hearts subsided.

"Sorry." Kerry made a wry face. "Comes with the territory."

Alex released his held breath, then braced his arms on either side of where she lay and put one foot on the floor. But before he stood up, he paused and gazed down at her face, surrounded by the halo of her hair spread across the cushion.

God, he wanted her. It took everything he had

not to scoop her into his arms and carry her up the stairs and ravage her, damn the consequences.

But there was more to it than lust. Now that he'd walked in her shoes, he thought he might burst with a newfound respect and admiration. Upstairs, three little people—at times smelly, at times maddening, but always sweet—depended on her for their every need. For a magical moment in time she had entrusted him with that awesome responsibility.

Only now that he was getting ready to leave did it occur to him that he was reluctant to give it up. He had an insane yet undeniable urge to shoulder some of that burden himself, in part to lessen her load but also for the richness it would give to his own empty life.

"I'll let you get to it," he said.

"See you Thursday when I come to pick up Shay," she said as she walked him to the door.

Before he left, he kissed her one more time, sliding his hand under her shirt and rubbing her lower back. "Want to take the girls for tacos afterward?"

She smiled. "That would be nice."

Several days later, Alex followed Kerry and her brood to a taqueria on Main where the grown-ups ordered at the counter and the kids piled into a table topped with red plastic.

"I have a question for you," said Chloé with a frown, setting down her half-finished flauta and licking her fingers. "How come you were with Mom

when she showed up at the hospital the other day
when Aunt Indra hurt her eye?"

Alex's burrito stopped in midair, halfway to his
mouth. He thought he was home free after the
close call on the couch, later that same night. His
thoughts flew back to the way Kerry had looked
and felt in his arms. It had been years since he'd
wanted a woman so much. Thank God for bug
bites. That was the only thing that had stopped
him.

It wasn't that simple. Kerry wasn't just Kerry.
She was a package deal. She came with awesome
responsibilities—responsibilities Alex had vowed
he never wanted.

"I'll let your mother answer that."

"That's easy," replied Kerry. "Coach Walker is
interested in wine. Naturally, he wanted to meet
Uncle Hank, and I told him I would introduce
them. That's where we were when Uncle Ry called
me—at the Sweet Spot."

Her acting was Oscar-worthy. But then, come to
think of it, the courtroom was a lot like a stage,
wasn't it?

"Oh." Chloé raised a brow, cocked her head as if
that made perfect sense, and picked up her flauta
again.

But as Shay studied Alex and Kerry, realization
dawned on her face.

Shay had begun to morph before Alex's eyes,
her legs lengthening like a colt's, her face narrowing. These days it seemed like every time he turned
around she was brushing her hair or checking out
her appearance in her phone screen. There would
be no fooling her for long.

The food was mostly gone, the table strewn with wadded-up napkins and remnants of tortilla. Kerry pulled a pack of wet wipes from her seemingly bottomless bag and began wiping Ella's hands and face. "Why don't you girls go back to the restroom and wash your hands before we leave?" she said to Shay.

"Well played," said Alex, watching Chloé follow Shay down a hallway.

"All week, I've been debating bringing this up. It's so soon. We have no idea where this—whatever it is we're doing—is going. But . . ." She whipped her head around to make sure the girls were out of earshot. "I have to put my kids first."

"Whatever it is, just say it."

It might feel soon to her, but he'd been riveted by her for ages.

Ella began to whine.

"Sorry, baby. Are you tired of sitting? Here." Kerry set her on her feet, and she toddled over and planted her palms against the glass door, in the path of customers coming and going.

"Ella . . ." Kerry sighed heavily and began to rise to fetch her.

"Sit down. I'll get her," said Alex. In one giant stride, he caught Ella by the waist and swooped her into the air, making her giggle, before bringing her back to the table, sitting her on his knee, and giving her his car keys to play with.

Kerry glanced toward the ladies' room. "They'll be out in a sec."

When had he become so highly attuned to her slightest sign of discomfort? Even more absurd, why did he feel the urgent need to fix whatever it was that needed fixing?

"I'm past the age where dating is a game to me, Alex. This is real life. As real as it gets. I can't let Shay and Chloé get attached to another man and then . . ."

The restroom door swung open and Shay and Chloé emerged, arguing whether the color of the stalls was rose or magenta.

Alex made a decision. "I don't know where this is going either. But I promise you, I won't let anyone get hurt."

They exited the restaurant, and Alex watched them pile into Kerry's car. He bid Kerry a chaste farewell, then held up a hand in response to all the fluttering waves good-bye coming out of the car windows as he watched her pull into traffic.

What had gotten into him? He had no business making promises he couldn't keep.

Nothing of great consequence had happened yet. It would be best for everyone concerned if he nipped this in the bud.

Tomorrow. Maybe.

But the next day, he ended up in a foot chase with a guy who'd robbed the pharmacy, resulting in a sprained ankle and an X-Ray, and the day after that, he'd been forced to detain both the husband and wife involved in a domestic dispute. By the end of the week, he found himself wishing for another simple supper with a decent woman and her sweet girls, the kind eaten with your hands and paper napkins.

Chapter Twenty-five

Kerry called Hank to explain why she and Alex had stood him up. He had already heard about Indra's accident, of course, and he waved away her apology. But when he asked if Alex wanted to reschedule, Kerry didn't know what to say. They had parted outside the taqueria without making any more plans.

Then came the heat wave.

Most older homes in the Willamette didn't have air-conditioning. But not even her parents had requested it in their new place. Historically, it simply wasn't needed. The average summer temperatures hovered around the seventies during the day and the nights were delightfully cool.

This summer was turning out to be an exception. The day care took the kids to the pool during the day while Kerry was at work in her air-conditioned office, but the evenings felt more like Florida than Oregon. Her girls were too listless to play with their toys. They stripped down to their swimsuits and watched movies on TV in the path of a box fan cranked on high.

As Kerry rinsed the supper dishes, she could hear Hobo panting, lying on the kitchen floor behind her. She glanced at the old thermometer outside her kitchen window. Still eighty-six degrees.

That's it. The dishes only half done, she dried her hands. "Girls, put your shoes on. We're going to town to get a new pool."

Ella, deeply into *The Little Mermaid,* didn't budge. "'K," said Chloé.

Kerry went upstairs and pulled a gauzy caftan on over her suit. On her way back downstairs, Shay finally sighed and got up off the floor and slid into her flip-flops.

Kerry grabbed the remote, clicked the TV off, and lifted Ella into her arms.

But as they were piling into her SUV, her hand paused on the door handle when she heard a car.

Shay and Chloé followed Kerry's gaze down the lane until a white Taurus came into view.

"Coach Walker," Shay murmured. "Wonder what he wants?"

A kaleidoscope of butterflies danced in Kerry's midsection as she watched him come closer and closer.

He parked and hopped out with a wave and a grin. "Hey, girls." He went around to his trunk and retrieved a large box, which he carried toward the circle in the yard where the grass was still yellowish and matted down. "Got you something."

"A present!" shouted Chloé. She and Shay were out of the SUV in a flash, tailing after him.

"I want out," cried Ella.

Kerry carried her over to where Alex was dismantling the box and set her on her feet.

The pictures on it were a dead giveaway.

"A pool! He got us a new pool!" The girls skipped around him, forgetting that they were sweaty and drained from the heat. Apparently, a pool brought by Alex warranted way more excitement than any pool Kerry had ever bought them.

Ella looked up at Kerry with her toothless grin and said, "Poowl."

"We were just on our way to get one. How did you know?" asked Chloé.

"Figured you were probably missing the old one in this heat."

He pulled the pool from the box and unfolded it, frowning. "Where do you suppose the thing is to blow it up?"

"That's a lot bigger than our old pool," breathed Shay, duly impressed.

Kerry set Ella down and carried two folding lawn chairs over from another part of the yard and sat them at an angle to each other.

"Thanks." There was an unmistakable twinkle in Alex's eyes when he glanced at her before lowering himself into one of the chairs. He found the inflation valve and blew a mighty breath into it. And then another, and another.

"Nothing's happening," said Chloé.

Kerry grinned and sat down in the other chair while the girls ran to where the hose was coiled up alongside the house and began bickering over who was going to drag it to the pool.

"That's going to take forever."

"Thank you, Ms. Genius. How'd you get your old one blown up?"

"Same way. Good old-fashioned lung power."

"Any time you want to take a turn, it's all yours."

She laughed. "No one said you had to get one twice the size of the old one."

The girls ended up each grabbing a length of hose and walking it over.

"I wasn't thinking, or believe me, I wouldn't have. Either that or I would've bought a pump."

"I didn't mean to sound ungrateful. It was a very thoughtful gesture. You saved me a trip."

"Should've done it sooner."

"Here," she said, reaching for the pool. "I'll take a turn. Your face is red as a beet."

Alex and Kerry alternated blowing for a quarter of an hour, while the girls tried to be patient, giving Hobo drinks from the hose, squealing with laughter when he bit at the stream of water.

"What kind of dog is he?" asked Alex. He had never had a dog himself.

"The guy at the shelter said his mother was mostly Sheltie, and judging from the puppies, they thought the father might be some sort of terrier."

Finally, Alex and Kerry sat back in their chairs and Hobo lay down in the shade of the house, all three of them exhausted, while the girls alternately sat in the spacious, empty oval and held the hose over it. They were delighted to find it was large enough to hold all three of them, with room to spare.

Kerry and Alex talked and watched the girls play until the sun went down and a silver moon sailed into view and the bats swooped low overhead, making the girls duck and shriek in mock terror.

"Keep an eye on them a minute?" Kerry went into the house and returned carrying a tray laden with Mason jars, a small plate of cheese and crackers, and two glasses of red wine.

The girls cavorted after fireflies in the dense night air, their long hair flying as they pounced in the grass, yelling, "I caught one! I caught one!" until Ella, whose jar was still empty, began to cry and Chloé gave her some of hers.

Finally, Kerry stood and drifted over to them. "It's that time, girls." Over the usual protests—though tonight they were weaker than usual, thanks to the heat and the exercise—she said, "Tell Coach Walker good night, and don't forget to thank him for the pool."

She warmed inside as she watched Alex close his eyes with each child-size hug, savoring it.

"Guess that's my cue to go, too," he said, rising on stiff legs.

"Sit here and enjoy the quiet, why don't you?" said Kerry. "They're worn out, thanks to you. I shouldn't be long."

There it was again, that spark of something that looked like hope in his eyes. It made Kerry rush through her bedtime routine with the girls, making her feel guilty. A little.

A few minutes later, she returned and collapsed into her chair next to him, letting her head fall back. "Ahhhh."

Alex tipped his wineglass. "After you left, I wasn't sure if I should have offered to help or what."

"The girls passed out the second their heads hit

the pillow." Kerry's head lolled toward him. "How's the wine?"

He smacked his lips in satisfaction. "I'm already writing my blog entry in my head. It's going to say, 'best enjoyed in a camp chair on a hot summer night, when the stars look close enough to touch.'"

Kerry raised her glass to him. "And you claim you don't have a way with words."

For a few minutes, the only sound was the drone of insects in the meadow beyond the lawn.

Kerry gathered her hair together and held it in a bunch at the back of her head, letting the air cool the nape of her neck.

"I'm hot." It wasn't just the climate. Alex had awakened something that had long lay sleeping, something she thought she would never feel again. She was suddenly very aware of him. She imagined she could feel his breath on her skin, hear his heart beating in his chest. She had to get away from him. She rose, pulled her caftan over her head, tossed it onto her chair, and stepped into the pool. There she wedged her wineglass among the tall blades of grass, sat back, and swirled the water with her hands.

What was she doing? *He's a cop*, whispered a small, inner voice. *You can't trust cops*. But lately, that voice seemed to come from farther and farther away. And hadn't she just finished telling him he was a decent man—and meant it?

Maybe it was the heat, or maybe it was because it had been a very long time since she had simply sat in the moonlight with a man. Any man, but especially a man whose relaxed demeanor couldn't hide the power she sensed he was capable of unleashing at the slightest provocation.

Chapter Twenty-six

Alex narrowed his eyes and watched Kerry bask in the dark water, her wet skin glistening in the moonlight.

You sure are, he thought with admiration. *Hot, that is.*

Until he'd moved to Newberry, his life had been a meaningless sequence of unrelated events on a timeline leading nowhere. Just like Curtis Wallace, one day he would die, and that would be that. He had come to accept it. What else could he do? He was too old to believe in happily ever after—if indeed, he ever had. He and his ex had only gotten engaged because all their friends were doing it, and look how that had turned out. After growing up being passed back and forth by his own parents, he should've known better.

But recently, he was seeing connections everywhere he looked. A certain momentum was gathering force. Like a storm cloud, or a snowball rolling downhill, growing larger as it went. A vibration hummed in him that made him feel like he was teetering on the cusp of something big. Something earth-shattering.

Kerry shook back her hair. "Come on in, the water's fine."

"I didn't bring a swimsuit."

She looked around. "Who's going to see you?"

He gulped. *She* was, that's who. The thought of *the* Kerry O'Hearn viewing him buck naked for the first time was disconcerting enough, but to stride over there blatantly displaying the erection that was currently safely tucked away in his shorts?

His pulse began to thrum at the potential. "You sure?" he asked, buying time while he worked up his nerve.

"If I weren't," she said wantonly, "I wouldn't have asked."

Alex had never been one to back down from a challenge. He downed his wine in one gulp. "Ready or not, here I come." He stood, whisked off his shirt and stepped out of his shorts, and headed toward the pool with his head high and his shoulders back like Poseidon, his trident proudly leading the way.

As he drew nearer, Kerry blinked, quite unprepared for the sight of *that*.

He stepped into the shallow water in front of her and planted his feet in a wide-legged stance. Two things were clear: *one,* there was no way he could hide his towering arousal, and *two,* she couldn't hide *from* it. It was the proverbial elephant in the room, seeming to take up the entire space between them.

He spread his arms. "Where am I supposed to sit?"

"The pool seemed a lot roomier before—" She giggled without finishing, hugging her knees to her chest.

He lowered himself with control, ab muscles contracting and water sloshing over the side when he finally sat down with his legs on either side of hers, their coarse hair brushing up against her smoothness.

He looked around, suddenly at a loss. "Should've got more wine first."

"We can share." She took a sip and leaned forward, meeting his lips with hers, letting the wine drain from her mouth into his.

His arms went around her and he pulled her close, kissing her again the way he had kissed her in his driveway, kisses she relived every time she closed her eyes. But this—this was so much more. She arched against him, throwing all caution to the night wind.

Alex scooted her closer still, lifting her feet up over his thighs until she could feel his warm, insistent arousal pressed up against her abdomen.

"This was a bad idea." He frowned down at her, sucking in a much-needed breath between kisses.

"Why is that?" she panted.

"Because now I'm going to have to buy another damn pool."

With that, he positioned her across the pool's inflated edge and balanced himself above her on his thick forearms.

A short time later, a *pfuff* affirmed Alex's prediction. Kerry's lower back sank softly onto the earth, while his hands cupped beneath her lifted her entire pelvis off the ground to meet each powerful thrust of his hips, and she gazed over his shoulder at the stars winking down on them, gasping as her pleasure built and built until she shattered into a million pieces.

Alex lay facing the sky, half on the flattened pool and half on the grass, waiting for his breathing to return to normal.

Ever since his father died of a heart attack at forty-two, he took for granted that he was doomed to the same fate. If this was what a heart attack felt like, bring it on. It was insane. For a decade he had told himself that he detested Kerry O'Hearn. So why was he sprawled out in a kiddie pool with her next to a vineyard at eleven o'clock at night, when he should be in bed alone with his copy of *Birds of America*? Yet here he was, lying in her backyard. Behind the tough trial lawyer façade was a deliciously sensuous woman and, God help him, he couldn't get enough of her.

He thought back to all those times when merely observing her across the courtroom had driven him to distraction, to the point where he couldn't tear himself away. Throughout the remainder of the trial, he'd gone back again and again. He'd told himself that his obsession was normal. After all, it was his case. His offender. His dignity, if not his reputation, on the line. Only now did he understand the deeper meaning of his actions. He had fallen in love with Kerry way back then. How could he have not recognized it? Was he that out of touch with his own feelings? His own needs?

After all this time, he was *still* in love with her. It explained everything. His anger at her besting him in court. He winced at the memory. He'd been young then, young and cocky and hot-tempered. Unprepared for a lioness like her in his life.

It explained why he had never found another woman who sent all his senses reeling the way she did—not that he hadn't tried. Once the trial was over, he was at loose ends. There was a period in which he'd gone out every night with the intention of never going home alone. Usually, he succeeded. But he soon gave that up when he realized that being with women he felt nothing for only made him lonelier.

But this . . . he looked over at Kerry, lying on her side with her cheek resting demurely on her hands, and his heart melted like warm caramel. Here, with this woman, and her girls nestled safely upstairs in the old farmhouse, he had never felt so whole . . . so complete. It was the closest he'd ever come to being *happy*.

Chapter Twenty-seven

A lex began spending more and more of his free time at Kerry's place.

He didn't plan on taking charge of Hobo. It started one cool evening when he got there after dinner but before the kids' bedtime.

"Hi, girls," he said, tossing his keys in the usual place on the foyer table. "Where's your mom?"

"She just went upstairs to give Ella her bath," said Shay, watching a music video on her phone. One earbud was lodged in her ear, while the other swung back and forth as she wiped the supper dishes.

Hobo sat panting at the back door, tail wagging, an anxious look on his face.

"Whatsamatter, boy? You need to go out?"

The dog whined softly but urgently and wagged his entire rear end. Alex wondered how long he'd been patiently waiting there.

"Where's his leash?" he called to the girls.

Shay had put in the other earbud and was singing along.

Chloé's head was buried in a book. "I dunno," she said without looking up.

Alex searched through the pegs crowded with hoodies and jackets next to the back door, retrieving the items he knocked onto the floor until he finally found the leash buried beneath a fuzzy pink vest.

The dog barely made it down the porch steps before lifting his leg on the first bush he came to. *Poor fella.* There was no mistaking the gratitude in his eyes when he looked up at him.

"Must be tough being the only testosterone in a houseful of estrogen."

Hobo pulled the leash taut and gazed out at the meadow with longing, then back at Alex, his tongue hanging out of his mouth, exuding pent-up energy like a spring.

He'd seen him pull the girls around on his leash. Walking him had become a real challenge for them.

"I could use a good run, too, bud." Kerry would be busy upstairs for a while yet. "Let's do it."

Thirty minutes later, they returned to find Kerry matching the socks in a laundry basket. Hobo ran to her, while Alex hung up his leash and filled his water dish at the sink. He was still on a high from his run and that feeling he got from doing something good for someone else, even if that someone was only a dog.

"Where have you been?" Kerry looked at Alex, ruffling the fur on Hobo's neck.

"The dog wanted to run. So, I took him."

Kerry walked over, took the water dish from Alex, and set it on the floor, where Hobo began loudly lapping it up.

Then she rose to her full height and folded her arms. "I don't need your help."

Alex was struck speechless.

At the dining table, Chloé looked up from her book. Over on the couch, Shay turned her head.

"I never said you did."

"I'm perfectly capable of taking my own dog for a walk."

"No offense, but a dog that size needs more than an occasional stroll around the yard. He needs regular exercise. How would you feel if you were cooped up in a house all day?"

Kerry took a step closer, so close she had to tilt her head to look up at him. "Did I ask for your help? I've been taking care of myself and my kids for years. I don't need a man to do it for me!"

Alex held out his hands. "Okay. Fine. Message received loud and clear." He would have said a lot more, but Chloé and Shay were watching. Instead, he backed up until he bumped into the door, snatched his keys from the spot that less than an hour ago he'd thought of as his, and left.

Striding down the path to where his car was parked, his hands jammed in his pockets, he glanced over his shoulder, hoping Kerry would come after him. But by the time he was buckled in, a watchful eye still on the house, she still hadn't come. Even when he got to the end of the lane and looked in his rearview, all he saw was the yellow light in the windows of the cozy, familial kitchen.

He drove off alone as all around him, darkness fell.

"Why'd you do that?" Chloé asked Kerry, after Alex had gone.

"Do what?" Kerry snatched another shirt from the laundry basket and attempted to fold it, but when she dropped it onto the couch cushion it landed messier than before.

"Yell at Coach Walker."

"I didn't *yell* at him." She shook a pair of jeans in the air with a loud crack.

"Yes, you did."

"No, I didn't. I simply reminded him that we're a self-contained, fully functioning family unit that doesn't need any interference from the outside. Have I ever failed you before? Was there ever a time when we didn't have a roof over our heads?"

Chloé got up from the table and walked into the living room. "No, but—"

"Food to eat?"

"No."

"I admit, things haven't always been perfect," Kerry said, hating the rising hysteria in her voice. "Maybe I don't know how to install a dishwasher or what questions to ask the roofers for an estimate, and maybe the dog doesn't get walked as often as he should. But what parent is perfect, I ask you?"

"Mom," warned Shay.

"No one, that's who. We just do the best we can using what we've got. Luckily for us, I have a marketable skill. The farmhouse. A brother willing to create a place for me at his firm—"

"*Mom*," said Shay. "Stop it. You're scaring Chloé."

"I am not," Kerry said shrilly. "Are you scared, Chloé?"

Chloé, looking pale, swallowed.

"Even if she's not, you're going to wake Ella," said Shay.

Kerry's bottom plopped onto the couch. She balled up the shirt she'd been wrestling with and tossed it across the room. Then she dropped her elbow on her hand. "Ow," she cried, forgetting it was bruised from when she'd banged it against the wall dragging a heavy chair up the steps the day before.

Gingerly, Chloé lowered herself beside her at an angle. "Why are you picking on Coach Walker? What'd he do?"

Why, indeed. What was wrong with her?

"All he did was walk Hobo," she added, her forehead wrinkled in a frown.

On Kerry's other side, Shay slid her foot beneath her so that now both girls flanked her.

"You're right."

"Then how come you're so mad?" asked Chloé.

Kerry whisked away a tear.

"I'm scared, girls." Her lower lip trembled.

"Scared of what?"

She brushed some imaginary lint off her jeans. They were too young for this. She couldn't dump her fear of failure on them. It wasn't fair. It wasn't right.

"Well," she said shakily, "just scared, you know. Everyone gets scared sometimes." This was untrodden ground. She had never admitted any sort of weakness to her daughters before.

She was a crappy mom.

Chloé reached her little arms around Kerry and buried her head in her shoulder. "Don't be scared, Mom. You've got us. We'll take care of you."

That was it. Kerry hid her face in her hands, but she couldn't hide the sound of her sobbing.

Shay dashed to the kitchen and came back holding out a tissue, which Kerry took and blew her nose into. "It's not your job to take care of me."

Shay sat down again, and this time, both girls wrapped their arms around Kerry. "It doesn't matter whose job it is. So what? What if we *feel like* taking care of you sometimes?"

When had her children become so wise?

For a terrifying minute, Kerry thought her sobs might never stop. She'd been strong for so long. She didn't even admit her doubts and apprehensions to her own mother. After all, Rose was a dynamo in her own right, having raised not three but four children. Yes, she had Kerry's father by her side, but he wasn't the easiest man to live with.

But Kerry was so tired. And after all, she was only human.

She dabbed her eyes with the crumpled tissue. "I'm okay," she said. "I'll be all right." Just admitting she was overwhelmed made her feel lighter.

"We know you will," said Chloé, giving her another squeeze that almost started her going again.

"Honest. I'm fine," she said, drying her eyes yet again, forcing a small laugh. "I just lost it there for a minute."

Chloé sat back on the couch. "You hurt Coach Walker's feelings," she said. "I could tell by his face."

That's right. Alex. He had no one to comfort him.

"You should call him and apologize."

Kerry laughed again, authentically this time. "That sounds just like something I would say to you."

"Where do you think we got it from?" asked Shay, attempting her own smile.

The question was, where had she gotten these amazing . . . resilient . . . kind kids?

Kerry got to her feet, turning to straighten the afghan on the back of the couch.

"You know what?" she asked, wiping her tearstained hands on her seat. "You're right. I will call him. Just as soon as I finish this laundry and sweep the kitchen and pack up my work bag for tomorrow morning and . . ."

Chloé stood on spindly legs. "I only got one more chapter to go. Think I'll read it in bed."

"I'll finish folding clothes for you and carry them upstairs," said Shay, reaching into the laundry basket.

Kerry pressed her lips together, reached around Shay's shoulder, and grabbed Chloé's shirtsleeve before she got away, almost knocking her off balance in the process. She folded her daughters into her embrace. "I love you guys," she mumbled into their hair. "I don't know what I'd do without you."

"We love you, too," they murmured.

Alex was nursing a glass of pinot noir when Kerry's name lit up his phone screen.

"Hello."

"Hi."

Pause.

"This is your controlling, uptight, asshole girl-friend."

"I thought I recognized that voice."

"The girls said I needed to apologize to you."

Pause.

"Okay. Is that the only reason you called me?"

"No."

"Then why else?"

"Because *I* thought I should apologize, too."

Alex looked up at the night sky and exhaled. "I was only trying to help you out. Not just you, the dog."

"I know. You were right and I was wrong. It's just that it's hard for me to accept help. Anyone's help. Not just yours. I've been trying to prove to myself that I can do it all on my own for so long, I don't know how to do it any other way."

Another pause.

Alex sipped his wine. "Do you think you could try?"

"I could try."

"Try to try?"

She giggled. "Yes. Try to try."

"Well, I guess that's all I can ask for."

"Then I will." She sniffed. "That's what I intend to do."

Alex started. "Were you—"

"No. Just allergies."

He relaxed again. Not that he believed her. But whatever tears she'd shed must have acted as a re-lease valve.

"I'm warning you, once I put my intention on something, it usually works."

"That's good to know."

"So, I hope you're ready for things to change."

Pause.

"All I can do is try," he said.

"Okay, then. It's settled. We're both going to try."

Alex smiled and looked in to his glass, seeing not the bloodred wine but Kerry's face, relieved that now, he would be able to sleep that night after all.

Chapter Twenty-eight

The next week, when Alex was absentmindedly yanking out the weeds around the garage on his way into the house, he used his elbow to polish a circle in a grimy window and glimpsed something inside. He leaned closer, cupping his hands around his eyes to get a better look.

He waited until after supper, while the kids splashed in the pool and Hobo lay at his feet, tired from his run, to bring it up.

"How often does the meadow need to be cut?"

She followed his gaze to the waist-high swath of native grasses and wildflowers.

"You're asking me?"

"I could ask your father, but you're sitting right next to me."

"Now that you mention it, back in the spring Dad told me to remind him to hire someone to mow it, come fall. His new house doesn't have the view of the meadow. Plus, I have a sneaking suspicion his memory isn't what it used to be."

"That riding mower in the garage," he started out. "When was the last time it saw action?"

"I've never been on it, if that's what you're asking. Don't know the first thing about lawn tractors. Before that, I don't know. I haven't been here."

"Is the garage locked? I'd like to check it out. That is, if it's okay with you."

Kerry opened her mouth to object, then remembered their pact. "I, ah, um . . ."

He lifted a brow. "Tell you what. I'll mow in whatever pattern you want. Horizontal, vertical, plaid . . ."

"The garage is unlocked. Have at it."

Within minutes, he had the tractor gassed up and was driving out to mow the meadow, as if the property belonged to him and he had some stake in its upkeep.

Awesome. The O'Hearn property was like his rental on steroids—spacious, serene.

In the distance, Kerry waved to him.

He liked being out here, where he could keep an eye on her and her brood, eavesdropping on the frequent yelps of laughter and occasional howl of complaint.

It was dusk when he putt-putted back to the garage, full of satisfaction.

Kerry waltzed over with Ella on her hip and a lazy grin on her face. She sneezed. "Look at you." She laughed, picking a straw out of his hair. "You're covered in grass clippings and pollen."

He brushed his hands against the sides of his threadbare jeans with the hole in the thigh where a patch of hairy leg peeked through. "Man's work," he said, feeling even more macho in her Madonna like presence.

"I have to admit, letting go feels very freeing. One less thing for me—and my dad—to worry about."

"I wanted to do it," said Alex. All he had ever wanted was to be of help. Not for the accolades. Because it made him feel like a part of something bigger. Like he belonged. Now he soaked up her appreciation like an old, dried-up sponge.

Kerry, Ella in her arms, watched until he finished tinkering with the machine and put it away. When he came out of the garage, without warning Ella reached for him.

"Awex."

It was the first time Ella had ever uttered his name. He almost melted into his boots. Without thinking, he lifted his hands to take her into his arms. That's when he saw the grease stains, smelled the gasoline and engine oil and sweat. His eyes flew to Kerry's in a silent plea for her consent.

Without a word, Kerry's body angled sideways to ease the transition.

He gathered the child into his arms. "Hey, Ella," he cooed softly. There, on a broken concrete slab outside the garage in the summer twilight, with the humming of insects in the background, a chubby hand reached up and touched the stubble on his chin with the delicacy of butterfly wings. Her eyelashes were pale and fine as a spiderweb.

That he had once dangled this child by the arm and sprayed her with a garden hose was inconceiv-

able. That was before he'd gotten to know her as
the infinitely precious creature she was.

Kerry moved into them, ignoring his sweat-
soaked shirt. She gazed up at his dirt-speckled
face, her eyes sparkling wetly, and brushed his lips
with hers.

When the kiss ended, Alex slung his free arm
over Kerry's shoulder and the three of them slowly
ascended the porch steps as the sun set behind
them.

In the coming weeks, Alex took the girls for
walks through the vineyards and showed them
how the grapes were growing fatter and turning
from green to purple, and drove to town to pick
up ice cream or laundry detergent—whatever
Kerry needed.

He and Kerry made furtive love every chance
they got. But Kerry always woke him up before it
got too late. She made it clear she couldn't afford
to have one of the kids wander into the living
room or backyard in the middle of the night and
find him there.

One evening, after Ella was in bed when they
were sitting on the porch talking, Shay ran to
Kerry with her phone in her hand to ask permission to go over to a friend's house the following
night.

"She's changed a lot this summer," said Alex as
they watched her skip away, chattering animatedly
into her phone.

"It's such a relief to know she'll be going back to
school having friends this year."

"Do you ever let her babysit?"

"No," she replied sharply. "We live too far out. I'd worry too much."

"She'll be a teenager, right?" Lately, all Shay could talk about was her birthday. "How old is old enough?"

Kerry sighed. "I know. I just hate thinking about it."

"She's not going to be a little girl forever." Alex measured his words. "I'm not saying I don't like coming over here, but I wouldn't mind taking you out on a real date once in a while. Your parents are right next door. You could even ask one of them to drop by unannounced, to, say, borrow a cup of salt."

Kerry chuckled. "First person in history to need an emergency cup of salt."

"Sugar. Whatever. Has Shay ever asked if she could babysit her sisters?"

"Last year, all the time. She really resented being in day care."

"I remember," said Alex, peering out over the vineyards. Never before had he actually spent a summer watching a crop ripen before his very eyes. It would be a couple of years before the wine from this year's fruit was ready to drink, but he had already made a mental note to mark his calendar.

"You do?"

"It's hardly a secret."

Kerry rubbed at a torn cuticle.

"What are you going to do with her this year?"

She shrugged. "I have no choice. She'll be too old for the Community Center. She'll have to come home from school on the bus. I'll ask my parents to check on her from time to time."

The system was forcing change on Kerry, whether she was ready or not.

"In that case, what do you think about giving her some practice? We could start out slow. Say, leave for an hour. Then work our way up to two. Don't get me wrong. The girls are amazing. Call me selfish, but I want you all to myself now and then, no"—he rubbed her bare foot with his—"interruptions."

Following a glance behind him through the window where Chloé lay on the couch reading, he leaned over and kissed her, letting his fingertip trail along the edge of her halter top. "Have I told you lately that I love you?" he murmured.

Kerry shivered and felt her nipples tighten. "Not since this morning, when you were whispering naughty things to me on the phone, knowing full well I was on my way into a deposition."

He gave her a wolfish grin. "And that there's no other woman who can make me feel like you do?"

"You may have mentioned it a couple hundred times."

"Think of it, Ker. You and me, at that out-of-the-way corner table at Ruddock's. No spilled sodas, no endless arguing over whether or not catsup is a vegetable . . ."

"Mmn," said Kerry, smiling and ducking her chin where he tickled her neck. "You make a good case."

In the end, Alex won.

Shay considered it a win for her, too. She was secretly thrilled to occasionally be able to complain to Mia and Addison with a heavy sigh that she "had to babysit."

One evening in late July, when Alex pulled in to the farmhouse, Shay came running out to meet his car.

"Can you come to my birthday party?" she panted.

"Party?" he asked, retrieving a bag of groceries from the backseat. "What party?"

"It's at Grandma and Grandpa's house," Shay said as they walked to the house. "Grandma's making my favorite supper, lasagna, and *everybody's* going to be there."

With Shay glued to his side, Alex gazed up to the porch, where Kerry stood with her hand resting on the railing.

"Did you check with your mom?" He could tell by Kerry's wary expression she hadn't.

"Mom, can Coach Walker come to my party? Please? He *has* to. It won't be any fun without him."

Chapter Twenty-nine

Alex had spent the first twenty years of his life learning how to fend for himself and the second twenty witnessing the most depraved acts human beings could inflict on one another. Not much intimidated him. But being impressed was different than being intimidated, and there were two things that impressed him: strong families and fine wine.

The tight-knit O'Hearn clan was the closest thing wine country had to royalty. Walking onto their classy, pergola-covered patio to shake hands with Kerry's privileged older brothers and regal father, he felt like a commoner invited to the palace, wary of placing a foot wrong.

But it was clear that Rose was the real power behind the throne, and she wouldn't tolerate anything less than perfect hospitality on the part of her progeny. As she served him another helping of lasagna, Alex felt his shoulders relaxing.

That second glass of wine probably helped, too.

When the enormous silver casserole dish was empty, the kids were set free to run on the manicured lawn and the women went inside to put the finishing touches on the ritual cake and presents.

Shay remained at the table with the men.

"Don't you want to go play with your cousins?" asked her grandfather.

"Nah. Too babyish."

The judge pushed back his director's chair from the table, revealing a comfortable paunch, and crossed one leg. "Why don't you run inside and see if your mother and your grandmother need any help."

"They told me to stay out here so it'll be a surprise," she countered, thumbing her cell phone.

For a few awkward moments, the only sound was the shouting of the youngsters in the background. Alex fingered the fringe on his cloth napkin, left behind when Paige had swooped his plate away. The bond between him and Shay had grown even stronger since he'd started spending time at the farmhouse. When they'd arrived at the party, Shay made it clear to everyone within hearing that she wanted Coach Walker to sit next to her. Her wish had been granted, ostensibly because it was her birthday. Now, she peered up at him. "Do I have to?"

The air thickened while the O'Hearn men waited for Alex's response.

He tossed his head toward the house. "Do as your grandfather said."

She got up slowly, rolling her eyes. "Oh-kaaay."

When she was gone, four pairs of eyes regarded him evenly.

"Why do I feel like I'm here to take Kerry to the prom, and any second one of you is going to set a thirty-aught-six across your knee and start cleaning it?"

"Now, what in the world would make you think that?" asked the judge, brushing a crumb off the table.

"Kerry told me about her past. That I'm her third cop."

"We have nothing against cops, per se," said Ryan mildly.

"Just the ones that hurt our sister," said Marcus, fiddling with his dinner knife.

"I have no intentions of hurting her."

"Just what are your intentions, if you don't mind me asking?" asked the judge.

Had someone turned back the calendar a hundred years when Alex wasn't looking? Whatever the future had in store for him and Kerry, this night would set the tone with her family. He bit back the urge to tell them his feelings for her had nothing to do with his profession. "Right now, we're just getting to know each other. Enjoying each other's company."

"Kerry can't afford to be recusing herself from cases on a regular basis."

After the second time they had made love, Kerry had handed the Lewandusky case over to Ryan. What Ryan said was true. Right now, she was still living off the income from the embezzlement case, but that wouldn't last forever.

"I know how significant that was." He might not be a lawyer, but he was neither stupid nor insensitive.

"That's exactly why I retired early," added the judge. "The county only has four municipal judges. Given that two of my offspring followed me into the practice of law, my being one of them would have muddled up the system like a feather in a whirlwind."

"I'm not the only cop in town. Last I counted, there were twenty of us making arrests. That leaves plenty of opportunities for Kerry."

"It's not just Kerry," said Marcus. "Those kids of hers have been through the wringer. Last thing they need's another 'Walkaway Joe.'"

"*Walkaway Joe*"? Alex's hands clamped down on the arms of his chair. But he'd barely risen from his seat when the others looked toward the house, smiling broadly at the approach of their women singing the birthday song.

Out in the yard, the kids' ears perked up, and seeing thirteen candles ablaze in the twilight, they came racing back, joining the others in song.

"'Happy birthday to you, happy birthday to you. Happy birthday dear Shay, happy birthday to you. And many more. . . .'"

"Make a wish," said Kerry.

Shay looked at Alex, eyes sparkling. Then she unleashed a lungful on her candles.

"You got them all on the first try!" exclaimed Chloé. "That means your wish'll come true. What did you wish for?"

Shay reached her arm around Alex as far as it would go.

"Don't tell—" Kerry started to say, but too late.

"I wished Coach Alex would be part of our family."

"Awesome!" yelled Chloé, bouncing on her chair.

Alex thought his heart might burst. He returned Shay's side hug, but she was already intent on her grandmother's pearl-handled knife sinking into the soft cake, depositing the first slice onto her plate.

There, beneath the pergola, Alex watched the firelit faces of the other kids gathered around, jockeying for their own piece. Kerry and the girls were squarely on his side. But where the men were concerned, he still had a ways to go.

He rubbed his beard. Some things never changed. Who did he think he was, to believe for one night that he would fit into this exclusive bunch?

Would he ever truly belong anywhere?

Chapter Thirty

Alex was leaving the hardware store with a brown paper bag containing a replacement bulb for the light in Kerry's porch ceiling when, across a side street in an alley, he saw a kid standing on a box peering into a dumpster while another kept watch.

He jogged across the street as the lookout anxiously tugged a warning on the hem of the dumpster diver's shorts.

"Travis?" exclaimed Alex. The boys were supposed to be safely ensconced in a foster home.

Travis hung his head. He was barefoot. His feet were filthy and there were dark circles under his eyes.

Alex knelt before Travis, uncomprehending. "What are you *doing* here?"

Hearing Alex's voice, Tyler's head appeared from inside the dumpster, his eyes like two holes burned in a sheet.

For the first time since he'd been going to Kerry's house, Alex got that old, burning sensation in his chest.

"What's going on? Tell me! Why are you—" He searched up and down the alley for a clue that would explain away the dread that was creeping over him—"*here?*"

He reached for Tyler's hand and helped him off the cardboard box. "Where's your shirt?"

He pointed to Travis's feet and scowled with disapproval. "What happened to your shoes?" As if Travis *liked* going around barefoot on the hot August pavement.

When Travis finally met Alex's eyes his dirt-streaked face crumpled. Instead of running, as Alex was conditioned to expect, Travis stunned him by throwing his puny arms around Alex's legs and sobbing without making a sound, as if his tears were all dried up and there was nothing left inside.

Alex automatically shielded the boy's back, his shoulder blades sharp beneath his fingers.

"Please don't make us go back," pleaded Tyler.

Rage bubbled up in Alex's throat, threatening to boil over.

But first, the boys.

He swept up Travis, his skeletal build bringing to mind the hollow bones of a sparrow, took Tyler by the wrist, and turned toward his car.

Tyler yanked free of Alex's grip and stood his ground. "Are you going to make us go back?" The very prospect threatened to collapse his brave yet fragile façade . . . the façade he put on for his brother's sake. It was the gesture of a much older boy, and it redoubled Alex's determination to do right by them.

"No," he ground out. "You have my word."

Still, Tyler vacillated, his face mirroring his uncertainty.

When he finally took a step forward, relief washed over Alex.

He drove straight back to the taco place and ordered the same dishes he had seen Kerry get for her girls. Then he sat across from the boys and watched with some small satisfaction until they'd eaten their fill, while silently, he chewed half a roll of TUMS and weighed his options.

At least Tyler's cavity had been taken care of.

This was his fault. He was the one responsible for putting the Pelletier boys into evil hands. If he'd never picked them up in the first place, they might still be underfed, but at least they would still be in their intact family, their home.

There was only one thing to do. He would probably get an official reprimand; a permanent mark on his record that would make it impossible for him to get another job in law enforcement. Maybe even get fired and have to resort to making a living as a laborer. But none of that mattered in the light of the injustices that had been done to two lost boys.

"You have to call CPS. There's no getting around it," said Kerry over the phone.

Alex paced his back patio in the dark. Travis and Tyler had bathed and were sleeping soundly in his own bed, relegating Alex to the couch.

"I won't allow them to go back to foster care. I promised them, Ker. They *trust* me. I'm the only one they trust."

"There's evidence of physical abuse?"

"Could be just from living on the streets, but I would be surprised if they hadn't been pushed around."

"You've got to have them checked out by a doctor."

"They've already been through all that."

"That was when they were with their natural parents. Now that they've been in a foster home, they need to be reexamined."

"It seems so . . . punitive for the victims. Why do they need to go through all that again? They're just kids, Ker."

"That's the way it is. You know that. You must. All those years on the force?"

He knew. He just didn't want to hear it. Because now it was personal.

"Let me put it another way. If the foster parents have committed a crime, don't you want evidence so you can prosecute?"

Abuse fell squarely under Alex's purview of Crimes Against Persons. But at the moment, he cared more about the boys—*his* boys—getting a decent night's sleep. "I can't call CPS tonight."

"You have to, Alex. The longer you wait, the more trouble you're going to be in. The fosters may have already reported them missing."

"If there was a missing child report, I'd be the first one to know."

She considered that. "The longer they wait, the worse they're going to look, so it's probably just a matter of time," she said. "You don't have rights to them. I know you're a loving, caring person. I've seen it in the way you act around my kids. But as much as you might care about them, those boys don't belong to you. They're not yours."

Alex gazed up at the stars. There was something he was dying to tell Kerry. Something he had never told anyone. He began to pace again, clenching the phone in his fist, then halted.

"I've always wanted kids."

There was a long pause.

Finally, in that supremely confident voice that had first made him notice her, she said, "Even more reason to do this right."

She supported him. She believed in him.

His heart soared. Suddenly, anything was possible.

"All right. I'll call them."

"Call me back then. I'll wait up."

Heart thudding against his chest, he punched in the number for CPS and asked for Olivia Bartoli.

Chapter Thirty-one

Chief Garrett wasn't gung ho on the idea of Alex fostering the Pelletier boys, even after he heard the parents had fled town.

"It's a blatant conflict of interest. Your job is to go after the offenders, not succor the victims. Let CPS do it. That's what they're there for."

"The Pelletiers were charged with a misdemeanor for neglect and fined. Granger can take over the case against the foster parents, assuming there is one."

Chief swiveled his chair back and forth, tapping the armrests with his fingertips. "What do you know about being a parent?"

"I'll learn. I know good parenting when I see it." By now, everyone in town knew he and Kerry were dating.

"The judge and I go way back," said Chief. "I know for a fact Kerry had a solid upbringing. And her oldest has definitely taken a shine to you."

Chief had been to the boxing exhibit at the pool. He had seen the special bond that had developed between Alex and Shay.

"All three of Kerry's kids are great."

"I distinctly recall a day last spring when you sat right there in that chair and told me all you wanted was peace and quiet."

"That was then. This is now."

"You're about to go from recluse to family man with a stroke of a pen." Behind his desk, Chief studied the form he held between his hands. "Are you sure?"

"Never been surer of anything in my life."

Alex needed just one more signature. His toes curled inside his boots.

"Who's going to watch them while you're at work till school starts, and then after school?"

"The day care at the Community Center."

After another endless pause, Chief sighed and scribbled his name, then tossed his pen and thrust the paper across his desk to Alex. "Good luck."

But the chief's apprehensions had got to him. By the time he got to Livvie's office to deliver what was left of his paperwork, he was thinking about everything the chief had said, and thinking that maybe he was right.

"How are you?" asked Livvie, once they were behind her closed office door.

Alex opened his arms. "Look at me. Do I look like a daddy to you?"

She laughed, eyeing him up and down. "In my experience, no two dads have ever looked alike. The question is, do you want to be one?"

He tried to swallow, but the sides of his throat stuck together.

Livvie went to a minifridge in the corner and pulled out two bottles. "Tell me what it is you're most concerned about."

He cracked open his water and downed half of it in one swig. "Do you have kids?"

She looked at her hands, devoid of jewelry. "I haven't been so blessed. But I try to look on the bright side. In my line of work, it's nice to be able to go home to my peaceful apartment and sit down and have a quiet glass of wine."

"What am I doing? What if one of them gets sick? Falls off his bike and breaks his arm . . . his *femur*? What happens if—down the road—some girl breaks his *heart*?"

Livvie perched on the edge of her desk. "If they get sick, you'll take them to the doctor. As far as the broken heart, the best I can tell you is just to be there, in the good times and the bad. That's all kids like Travis and Tyler want. Not money. Not a big house. Just someone who cares about them. Someone they can depend on, no matter what. A feeling of belonging is as basic a human need as food and shelter."

Alex set down his empty bottle and ran a hand across his head. "Maybe I should give this some more thought."

"You treated my brother like a person instead of an outcast. And I've seen your concern for those boys from the get-go. You're going to be fine. Will there be problems from time to time? Absolutely. You'll handle them as they come up.

"As for the approval, you passed the basic requirements with flying colors. You already had the background check under your belt. When it comes to your references . . . I mean, the chief of police? Come *on*." She grinned and waved the long white envelope Alex had handed her.

"I was able to expedite your approval, but be forewarned that someone will be out to check that you've installed separate beds for the boys in the second bedroom, as the law requires."

There went his home office.

"And later on, to confirm that you've completed the training series."

"I chose the online option. No sitter required."

"Okay. Other questions?"

"What are the Pelletiers chances for regaining custody?"

She sighed. "As I told you back when all this started, the system is geared toward family reunification. After they complete the assigned counseling sessions and psychological evaluations, CPS will take another look at the Pelletiers' parenting capabilities, the possibility of repetition of the pattern of neglect, and the degree of the boys' emotional attachment to their parents. Assuming they pass the psych evals and comply with the ruling, the children will most likely be returned to them."

"And if they don't?"

"At that point, the children typically remain in foster care for another six months."

Alex sighed and rubbed a hand over his face. "Then what?"

"The kids' welfare is paramount. Research shows that in most cases, reunification is usually best. After six months to a year—again, depending on all those factors I told you about—the court can proceed with terminating the parents' rights, making the children eligible for adoption."

Livvie hesitated. "Off the record? I would caution you to maintain your perspective through all this. Expect pushback. Especially from people like the Pelletiers, who can afford good lawyers." She gave him a meaningful look. "After all. They have their reputations to protect."

She went behind her desk, took her seat, and neatly slit Alex's envelope open. "I've informed the judge that this is a special case and he's agreed the boys can remain where they are while you're taking the classes."

"Thanks, Livvie. This wouldn't have happened without you."

Livvie looked at him straight on as she inserted the chief's recommendation into a thick yellow packet. "Remember what I said. You're going to have good days and bad days. Just like any family."

Alex held out his hand. *Just give me the papers.* By now he was itching to take possession of the packet with his name on it.

Finally, she extended the envelope to him. "Congratulations, Officer Walker. You're a foster dad."

Chapter Thirty-two

Kerry and Alex lounged at a table in the shade of an umbrella at the Community Pool, studying their respective broods.

No sooner did Tyler jump off the board than he climbed out and got right back in the continuously circulating line of kids to dive again.

Meanwhile, Travis zigged and zagged unselfconsciously in the grass, the toy plane Alex had bought him in his outstretched hand . . . a runtylooking kid, lost in his fantasy world, yet careful never to let Tyler out of his sight.

"Do they talk about their parents? Their foster parents?"

"If I ask about them. Otherwise, no. It's like that old song, you and me against the world. Like they're a family of two and have been for a while."

Alex didn't like thinking about before the boys were his. He was focused on the future. "It's amazing, isn't it? Look at how Ty and Trav are in constant motion. And there's Shay sitting cross-legged on her towel, talking nonstop with the other girls her age, and Chloé is so patient with Ella and her ball," said Alex.

"I bought toy trucks for Shay when she was little and she never touched them," mused Kerry, jaw resting in one hand, twirling her headband around on the index finger of the other. "By the time Chloé and Ella came along, I just stuck with the tried-and-true—My Little Pony and Dora."

Alex's hands worked the stiff leather of a brand-new baseball mitt. "I swear, those guys never run out of gas. Trying to keep up with them wears me out more than running ever did."

"They're two lucky little boys." Beneath the table edge, Kerry placed her hand on his thigh. "Don't get a big head, Detective, but fatherhood becomes you."

"You're one sexy mama, yourself," he said, setting the mitt aside, draping his arm around her shoulders and giving it a squeeze.

"Just one thing. When are we ever going to find another chance to . . . you know."

They'd become expert at stealing moments wherever and whenever they could. Standing up in the kitchen while the girls were outside playing. In Alex's unmarked police car. Once, even in Kerry's office in the middle of the day with the door locked.

He grinned. "What are you trying to say, Ms. Eloquent?"

She pursed her lips and elbowed him in the ribs.

"Have sexy time."

"Ohhhh," he said, tilting his nose to the sky. "You mean, go heels to Jesus?"

She grinned despite herself. "Is that what you call it?"

"Waka waka. Sweeping the chimney. Threading the needle. Whatever. We're going to have to come up with a code word."

"I vote thumbs-down to all of those." She laughed like confetti falling.

He squeezed her again. "There's always sign language." With his other hand, he reached around and pinched her rear, and she squealed and jumped.

"Hey." He nodded toward a fringe of shrubbery around the pool fence. "How about those bushes over there?"

"What? Now? Are you crazy?"

"Crazy about you," he said, and he kissed her.

"Hey. Look at that."

Alex followed Kerry's eyes, where little Travis hesitated on the end of the board.

"Can he swim?" asked Kerry.

"Like a fish," replied Alex with a ridiculous pride.

"But can he dive?"

"Looks like he's trying to. He'll do almost anything to be like his big brother."

Alex cupped his mouth with his hands. "Go for it, little buddy!"

Travis hurled himself into the air.

"Gaaa!" moaned Alex, blocking out the sight of Travis's Superman-in-flight pose with raised arms. "What was *that?*"

Kerry winced when Travis hit the water in a spectacular belly flop.

"That hurt," said Alex, getting up.

Kerry set her hand on his arm. "Don't."

"Didn't you see that belly flopper?"

"Wait and see how he is."

She could almost feel Alex's struggle to keep still while he watched Travis climb out of the pool, arms folded around his stomach, and head to his balled-up towel lying in the grass.

"He's hurting."

"Just wait and see before you run over."

Three girls Shay's age huddled on the pool deck, whispering and pointing at Travis.

Now Kerry rose, too. "That's Helena Young. The girl who was tormenting Shay last spring."

"This is bullshit." Alex took off with Kerry close on his heels.

But Shay beat them to it. Stomping over to Helena, she jammed her fists on her hips and thrust her face into the other girl's. "*Stop it!*"

On the other side of the pool, Kerry and Alex stopped in their tracks.

"What's your damage? You've been making fun of Travis since we got here. What kind of a person makes fun of a little kid? He can't help it he did a belly flop. Everyone's watching you, you know. *Everyone!* And they don't think you're cool at all, or funny. They think you're sad and pathetic and you have no life. So how 'bout next time you think about making fun of someone, think about *that*, why don't you?"

Alex's body surged forward, but Kerry stopped him with a hand on his biceps.

Helena looked around to see every pair of eyes on her. She smirked at Shay before turning to skulk off. But when she looked for her friends for support, they'd begun distancing themselves by degrees.

Shay went over to where Travis and now Tyler stood, and put her arm around the younger boy.

Alex told Kerry, "I'll let Shay bask in her glory. But I'm going to catch up with that Helena girl and tell her I have my eye on her."

Now more kids were gathering around Travis and Shay, offering their shy support.

"A chat with her parents from law enforcement is in order, too," said Alex.

Chapter Thirty-three

Travis and Tyler were practicing the boxing moves Alex had taught them.

"Guys!" he yelled. "Do you have to do that in the middle of the living room? I'm trying to concentrate."

They stopped what they were doing immediately. "Where else are we supposed to go?" Tyler panted.

Suddenly, he was filled with guilt. "I don't know," he said. "Go outside, why don't you?"

"It's raining," said Tyler.

He knew that.

Their bedroom was barely big enough to hold two twin beds.

Alex sighed and closed his laptop. The whole idea of blogging was to post regularly. To condition readers to expect interesting, fresh content. If you didn't, you risked losing them to those who did. He hadn't worked on his wine blog since he'd gotten the boys. At this rate, he might as well hang it up.

"Tell you what. Let's make something."

"Yeah!" Travis perked up in anticipation. "What are we going to make?"

"Birdhouses."

He stopped hopping around and looked at Tyler. "Birdhouses? How come?"

Alex could tell by their faces what they were thinking: *Who cares about birdhouses?*

"Birds need homes, just like people."

"Their nests are their homes," said Tyler.

"That's true. Some build their nests in trees. But others, like bluebirds, prefer the shelter of a birdhouse. It makes them feel safe, and protects them from predators. You can imagine what happens when a big wind comes up. The exposed nest might fall out of the tree. But the nest in a strong wooden box will never blow away.

"Let's go on out to the patio. There's a closet there for rakes and tools and things."

"Do we get to do it ourselves?" asked Tyler eagerly.

How old did you have to be to learn to hammer? Alex had no clue. All he knew was that he wanted to bond with the kids, and he wanted them to be happy.

"We'll take it step by step."

Alex showed them a diagram of the finished project and the dimensions. Then he sawed a three-quarter-inch length of cedar into thirds, giving each boy a piece of wood, a pencil, and a ruler, and told them to keep in mind the old adage, to measure twice and cut once. "Tomorrow, after they're finished, we'll go out in the woods and you can each pick a spot to hang yours."

Then he took his own piece of wood and, congratulating himself on his teaching skills, set to work.

The boys looked at each other. Then they studied Alex. Tyler took a stab at drawing a line the way Alex had.

A minute or so later, Alex happened to glance over at the hopelessly wavy lines he had attempted.

Travis's board was still blank.

"Don't you know how to use a ruler?" he joked.

Travis bit his lip and shrank behind Tyler.

And that's when Alex realized they didn't know any such thing.

He sighed. He was going to have to break this down into itty-bitty parts. That meant that no way would they be finished today. Or even, tomorrow. In fact, this was going to take forever.

So be it.

"I'll be right back," he said.

He went in and got the sheaf of paper he kept in his printer.

"Okay, men," he said when he returned, handing them each a few sheets. "Grab your pencils and your rulers and gather round. I'm going to show you how to draw a straight line."

Once they had gotten the hang of that, Alex showed them what each little line meant on the ruler. "I can't believe they didn't teach you this in school," he said.

Tyler shook his head. "We don't learn anything hands-on. It's all tests."

"Well, then, I guess you'll just have to learn here, at ho—"

Three pairs of eyes met.

Alex cleared his throat. "Home."

The boys grinned.

Alex frowned. "You lost a tooth."

Travis tongued the hole in his gum. "I know."

"When did that happen?"

"Last night."

"Why didn't you tell me?"

His smile vanished. "Am I in trouble?"

"No, you aren't in trouble. It's just that we have to put it under your pillow so the tooth fairy will come."

Ty and Trav exchanged looks.

"You're weird," said Travis, his tongue visible between the spaces in his teeth.

"I can't believe you don't know about the tooth fairy. How many—never mind. Did you keep it?"

"Keep what?"

"The tooth."

"No."

"What'd you do with it?"

"I swallowed it."

"Swallow—" Alex's head fell into his hand.

Travis giggled.

Tyler grinned.

Alex sighed and shook his head. "Good thing you guys came to live with me when you did. Where were we? Right. Looks like we're ready to saw. Travis, you go first. Just let me brace this plank—"

He should really have a vise. But back in what he now thought of as the old days, the idea of owning a complete set of tools had seemed somehow stifling. Besides, there wasn't much to sawing a short, straight cut.

"—and you hold the saw like *this*, and now just—"

"Ow!" Alex winced and shook his finger. "God-dammi—" He stuck it in his mouth to stanch the bleeding.

The boys grinned.

"Oh, it's hilarious. Is there anything you guys don't think is funny? Hold on. I'll be right back, as soon as I get a Band-Aid."

Saturday night, all seven of them—Alex, Ty, and Trav, and Kerry, Shay, Chloé, and Ella—prepared to gather around Kerry's antique dining room table.

Chaos reigned in the old farmhouse as Kerry passed out paper plates and yelled at Shay and Chloé for speed walking carrying glasses brimming with water from the sink to the dining room. Then Kerry lit the candles stuck in two wine bottles, their shoulders running with layers of multicolored wax.

"What happened to your finger?" Chloé asked.

He had wadded up tissue under the Band-Aid, making it appear worse than it was. He shook his head gravely. "Not sure you could handle it. It's pretty gross. A lot of blood."

"Ew!" Chloé leaned forward, fascinated. "Tell me."

"Men? What do you say? Do you think Chloé has the stomach for a tale of gore and guts?"

"No way!" laughed Travis and Tyler.

"Yes!" Chloé shouted.

All three girls began pounding on the table while chanting, "Tell *us!* Tell *us!* Tell *us!*"

Hobo started barking.

"All right, all right. It was like this . . ."

The kids couldn't stop howling as Alex described to Shay and Chloé in exaggerated detail the story of how Travis had savagely wounded him with a giant saw.

Kerry moved around in the background like the calm center of the storm. Alex was having so much fun being the center of a laughing tribe of monkeys, he scarcely took notice when she set a glass down in front of him.

"And that's when Travis, here, decided to saw my finger off—"

"No, I didn't!" shouted Travis, giggling, pizza falling out of his dentally challenged mouth onto the red-and-white-checked tablecloth. "I did not!"

Ella gazed around the table, not comprehending yet fascinated all the same.

Alex took a sip of wine. "And then, while I was on the floor writhing in agony, I screamed to Tyler to rip a sheet up into strips and told him how to tie on a tourniquet—" He stopped in midsentence, his brows knitted together, and held his wineglass up to the light. He took another small sip, letting it swirl around in his mouth.

"What?" pressed Chloé. "Tell us! What happened next?"

"Wow!"

Kerry, finally scooting in her chair across from Alex and placing her napkin on her lap, paused.

"Have you tasted this?" he asked her.

"Not yet. Hank only released it in May." She put her nose into her glass and sniffed, and her eyes grew round. "Lovely nose." She tasted it. "Balanced, with great length."

Alex took another drink. "It's a revelation." He picked up the bottle and read the label. Then he smelled his wine again and raised his free hand in frustration. "Damn! I wish I could describe the taste. I can pick out the separate components, but at the same time I can smell the blend. I've never tasted anything like this. It's fantastic. It's like—synergy! Greater than the sum of its parts. I finally get it! I can't wait to write about this in my blog."

Kerry's eyes danced. "Cheers!" She reached across the table and they touched glasses to the ringing of crystal.

Shay and Chloé clinked water glasses. "Cheers," they aped.

"Cheers," said Travis and Tyler, touching *their* glasses, grinning from ear to ear.

"Has everyone toasted?" said Alex. "It's bad luck to leave anyone out. Look each person in the eye, and don't cross anyone else's arm or it's seven years of bad sex—*luck.*"

Kerry tried to give Alex a stern look and failed miserably.

The clinking continued around the table with water sloshing, more giggles erupting.

"Not too hard, kids," said Kerry. "We don't want any more bloodshed today."

Amid the ruckus, Alex sipped his wine and rolled his eyes up into his head in pleasure. "Better than sex," he mouthed to Kerry.

Her face glowed in the candlelight. She lifted a brow, as if to say, *Really? We'll see about that.*

Chapter Thirty-four

Ella was already asleep, while the other kids were kicking a soccer ball around out in the yard. Alex disposed of the paper plates and shook the tablecloth, then came up behind Kerry as she was washing the glasses and encircled her waist with his hands and peered over her shoulder.

"No sooner do I think of something that needs to be done and the next thing I know, here you are, doing it."

"After all these years, I'm used to cleaning up after myself. Didn't your ex help out around the house?"

"When he did, he turned it into a main event. He thought he deserved a trophy."

"Not to ruin any inroads I've made, but you could use a dishwasher. A mechanical one, not a human."

Kerry remembered his surprise when he'd first found out the farmhouse didn't have one.

"Hurry up and finish that," he murmured as he gathered her hair from her neck and kissed her nape.

Her head fell forward and her hands stilled in the soapy water. The rambling house with its many additions had felt somehow hollow since she'd returned to it. But Alex's bold presence filled it up. Maybe it was pheromones . . . his utter maleness in her all-female household.

Or maybe, just maybe, Alex wasn't like the others. Maybe the third time really was the charm.

His hands slid around her waist, one cupping her breast, the other, the V where her thighs met.

Then he turned her around to face him.

Her wrists draped over his shoulders, dripping water.

"My hands are wet."

"Who cares? We're *alone*. Seize the moment." He folded her body into his and kissed her deeply.

Rapid footsteps, followed by the slam of the screen door, forced them apart.

"Tell Shay you have to have both feet on the ground when you do a throw-in," panted Tyler, crimson-faced and frowning.

"Arrrgh." Alex's head fell back in frustration. "Can't you guys figure it out for yourselves?"

"Shay *thinks* she knows the rules of soccer, but she doesn't."

"Go on back outside. We'll be out in a minute," said Kerry.

As Tyler skulked out, Kerry eyed Alex up and down, still trying to put a name to what it was that had every old wall and fixture in her childhood home feeling fresh and new, then tilted her chin up for another of his blazing-hot kisses.

"I wish these long summer nights never had to end," she said.

He didn't reply. He was too preoccupied with nuzzling her temple and getting his hands up into her shirt in the back, fumbling with the hooks of her bra.

She lowered her arms, effectively blocking him. "We can't do that right now."

"Who says?" he mouthed against her skin, trailing kisses down her neck.

"I says. Listen to me. There's something I want to talk to you about. School's going to start soon. Then there's going to be homework and bedtimes and cold weather coming."

"And . . . ?"

It struck her: He hadn't the slightest idea of how overwhelming the start of the new school year was going to be.

"You're going to have to take them shopping for clothes and school supplies and get them haircuts and checkups, all of that. And it will get—" Hands jerked her hips into his. "Oooh! Darker," she gasped, "earlier and earlier."

Now he was cupping her bottom.

But this was important. "Alex."

"Mmmm?"

She leaned back from the waist, her hands on his upper arms. "We're never going to get the chance to see each other."

He frowned. Finally, she had gotten through to him.

She scrutinized the strong jawline, the guarded

gray eyes. After months of him mowing her lawn and bringing pizza, he had become a part of this place. Part of *her.* She'd thought this over carefully. It had seemed so logical earlier today, before he arrived. Alex's lease was up at the end of the month. And tonight, the way he'd goofed with the kids was confirmation that the closed-up detective she'd spotted at the Turning Point last spring had opened up in a way she never would have thought possible.

But now a sudden attack of nerves made it feel like there was a weight on her chest, making it hard to breathe.

"You're not . . ." In a heartbeat, his suntanned face had turned ashen.

She shook her head. Yet more proof that inside the tough guy who fearlessly hunted down dangerous criminals beat a soft heart.

"No, no. I'm not breaking up with you."

He released his held breath.

"Just the opposite. I love how well you and the girls get along. It's so special. And making love with you, spending time just talking and hanging out, the way you take care of us . . ."

"I love taking care of you," he murmured into her shoulder as his hands roamed over her back.

"I haven't been this happy in a long time. Maybe ever."

"Me neither," he said in her hair.

"I can see us as a family."

"A family." Alex held her at arm's length and searched her face.

"So, I was thinking," said Kerry through swollen lips. "Why don't you move in with us?"

For a moment, confusion clouded his eyes. His mouth opened, but nothing came out. He turned from her and paced the kitchen, rubbing the back of his neck and then his jaw.

She flew to him, heart pounding. "I know it's kind of out of the blue and I'm not expecting an answer anytime soon, but it makes sense, don't you think?" she pleaded, turning him around to face her again. "We can spend every night together. You'd like that, wouldn't you?" She kissed the hollow at the base of his neck.

His eyes rolled back in pleasure and his lids closed.

"Alex. We can make this work. I know we can."

Still, he hesitated.

"Are you sure about this? What about the girls? Is it what they want? Getting used to a new man around? Sharing their mom with someone?"

"It'll be a huge adjustment. But we'll talk to them and make them feel like they're part of the decision. I know they'll be in agreement. They'll be thrilled."

"What role do you see me filling for them? I mean, do you see me as a father figure, or just a roommate who's hands off when it comes to the big stuff like grounding them when they come home late from a date and deciding which college to go to?"

Kerry laughed. "You really think ahead, don't you?"

"Seems like you're the one who's been thinking ahead."

"If you need more time, I understand. It'll be a

big change for someone who's never had kids. If it's too much too soon . . ."

He rubbed her arms with his thumbs. In his eyes was a faraway look. She could almost see the wheels turning in his head. See him dredging up all the reasons why this was a bad idea.

"Maybe you're right. Maybe I'm rushing things." What was she thinking? It had only been a couple of months, way too soon for such a huge step. "I'm not asking for an answer right now. Think about it. There's no deadline. No pressure. I just . . . it's just that you've shown me that I could be happy again."

He cradled her face in his hands. "Yes."

Her pulse leaped. "Yes?"

"*Yes.*"

"You'll move in here? With me and the girls?"

"There's no place I'd rather be." His mouth came down on hers in a celebratory kiss, and she threw herself into his arms, reveling in the sheer solidity of him.

Alex was going to be *hers.* All hers. Together with her in this house, nestled in the valley and her beautiful daughters, her life was finally going to be complete.

Now his hands on her body were an impatient blur of sensation as he tried to take all of her in at once. He walked her backward until she felt the sink hard against her butt, reached around to the back of her thigh and raised it to his waist. She hooked her leg around his hip, granting his hand access to her most sensitive place.

"Oh."

"Does that feel good?"

"Yes."

"Really good?" he murmured into her neck.

"Yes!" A carousel of angels was lifting her off her feet, making her feel light as air.

"Should I keep doing it?"

Bells clanged. "Yessss . . ." Trumpets rang out. "Yes! *Yes!*"

Kerry had barely caught her breath when Alex took her by the hand and started for the back door. "Let's go tell the gang the good news."

"Wait. Already? Don't you think—"

"Wait? For what? Don't you think the kids are going to be as thrilled as we are that we're moving in together?"

"Maybe we should talk first about how we're going to—"

But his enthusiasm was bubbling over.

And after almost giving up on romance, suddenly Kerry was glowing from within. How could she ruin this for him? For those poor boys? For all of them?

"Kids!" shouted Alex. "Come 'ere! We've got a surprise for you!"

Chapter Thirty-five

Travis came tearing out of his bedroom with his brother on his heels. He grabbed onto the back of Alex's recliner, where he sat with his laptop, spinning him halfway around.

Tyler picked up Travis and body-slammed him, then fell on top of him.

"No!" yelled Travis, laughing and kicking the back of Alex's chair.

"Can't you guys go outside and wrestle?"

Alex thought wistfully of the days when he could write in quiet solitude as he caught the empty bottle of wine on the end table before it fell over. It was his day off and he'd been struggling for the past hour to put his epiphany into words, but it was hard to concentrate with the TV blaring an action cartoon. Soon, when he moved in with Kerry, his household would double in size.

"It's raining," whined Travis.

"Come on," said Tyler, giving his brother a hand up. "It's not raining that hard."

Just before they exited out the back door, Alex caught a wary look in Tyler's eye, and his father's words came back to him. *"Can't you find anything constructive to do?"* Now, Alex was repeating the cycle.

Tyler knew he and Travis had dodged a bullet, and even though he no longer carried the burden of seeing that his little brother got enough to eat, he still had to make sure he didn't blow this new chance—for either of them.

Alex stuffed a load of dirty socks and underwear into the washer in the hall closet, then sighed and got back to work. Tyler was right. It wouldn't kill the boys to play in the rain for a while.

He turned off the TV and settled back into his chair, relieved to finally have some quiet.

A short time later, he heard the back door open.

"Travis fell out of a tree," said Tyler, his hair matted down, wet T-shirt clinging to his shoulders.

Alex *knew* he should have been more attentive. He leaped to his feet. "Where is he?" He followed Tyler back outside.

"We were trying to hang up the birdhouse to surprise you. Don't be mad."

"I'm not mad." Alex had been expecting to see Travis the moment they went out back. *"Where is he?"*

"In the woods," said Tyler, breaking into a trot.

Three hours later, Alex and the boys were finally getting back to the house, Travis proudly sporting a neon-blue cast on his arm.

"He's going to be all right," said Alex into the phone. "Turns out one out of a hundred kids breaks their forearm. Can you believe that?"

"I recall Marcus falling down the steps and breaking his arm when we were little," said Kerry on the other end. "What about foster dad? Are *you* all right?"

"Why wouldn't I be?" he replied, shutting the door behind the kids.

"When your child gets hurt, it hurts you, too."

"Ew," said Tyler, balancing on one foot on the carpet. Water dripped from the toe of the sneaker held aloft.

"All's well that ends—what the . . . Christ almighty."

"What?"

"The house is flooded."

"What?"

"The washer. I left the washer running when we left. It must have overflowed. Aw, *man*! First the arm, now this."

When Kerry had tucked in all three kids and had her own bath, she called Alex back.

"How goes it at Noah's Ark?"

"The landlord brought over a Shop-Vac. I'll leave the doors and windows open for a couple of days and hope for mild weather and that no mold grows."

"I wonder if you should have just bought your own Shop-Vac. Never hurts to have your own, especially in a big old house like mine. I mean, *ours*."

They had chosen the end of August to move in

together, to coincide with the ending of Alex's lease. Alone in her bedroom, she smiled, waiting for him to remark on their upcoming merger. When he didn't, her smile faded a little. She shrugged it off to exhaustion. He wasn't used to broken bones and broken washers all in the same day, while he was trying to work on a pet personal project.

"Boys all tucked in?"

"Tyler's asleep. They said Travis might wake up in the night needing more Tylenol."

"You sound beat."

"Aw, man. I'm dead on my feet."

"Alex?"

There was no reply.

"Everything okay?"

The pause lasted a few seconds too long for comfort.

"I don't know about this."

She froze. "What do you mean?"

"All I have is two kids and this dinky little house and it's already way more intense than I could ever have imagined."

Kerry lowered herself slowly to the edge of her bed. Moving day was only three weeks away. She had already started cleaning out the extra bedroom she'd been using for storage.

"What are you saying?"

"I'm not saying anything. I'm just a little concerned, that's all. Maybe I'm too old for all this change."

She huffed a laugh. "Don't be ridiculous. You're still young. Plenty of men way older than you father babies every day. There are even studies showing that older parents have advantages. They're usually making more money and are more emotionally mature."

"It's not just my age. I've been rethinking things. The farmhouse . . ."

"I admit, it could do with a little updating."

"Updating? How about a new roof, for starters? And with five kids, a dishwasher is going to be a must."

"My mother raised four kids without a dishwasher. I don't mind a few dirty dishes lying around."

"I'm neater than you are. No offense. Just because I'm moving in with you doesn't mean I can change who I am overnight."

"So? We'll hire roofers. And there's the Home Depot in Sherwood. What else is bothering you?" She fisted the phone, her trained legal mind racing ahead to defend her point of view.

"Where do you stand on the subject of air-conditioning? 'Cause if next summer's anything like this one . . ."

"What's with all the reservations all of a sudden? It's almost like you're looking for reasons to back out."

"I'm not backing out. It's just that taking on the boys was a huge undertaking. With them, I had no choice. They needed a home. Now you're going to have to go through the foster parent approval process, too."

She snorted. "Do you really think CPS would reject me?"

"A local attorney whose father is a prominent local judge? Not a chance. You're like Willamette Valley aristocracy—"

"Stick with the subject."

There was an ominous pause.

"I'm a stranger in these parts. That's fine, for a man who has nothing to prove to anyone except to himself. But when it comes to other people . . . I don't know if I've got what it takes to be a father to not just two but *five* kids, plus be a lover to you, all under the watchful eye of your brothers and Rose and the judge."

"I got past the fact that you're a cop."

"I'm honored."

"Sorry. That didn't come out like I intended, and you know it."

"It just seems like we're starting out with a lot of strikes against us."

"Do you think blending families is *ever* easy?"

"That's just it. I've never given it any thought whatsoever."

A sinking feeling came over Kerry. "I guess I jumped the gun. I was hoping that because I was ready for this, you were, too."

"Don't blame yourself. This is my fault. I never should have agreed to it so readily."

The sinking feeling coalesced into a distinct funnel shape and began slowly turning inside her. "Are you still coming over tomorrow?" she asked, hoping he couldn't hear the uptick in her breathing over the phone. The kids had begged to get together and they'd said yes, never imagining there'd be a reason not to.

"I'll let you know."

It was worse than she'd feared. "It's supposed to be rainy again."

"It's not fair for us to use your house as a refuge from the rain. But in light of how small this place is, and that my carpet will probably still be wet . . . and I don't want to disappoint the kids—*any* of the kids . . ."

Alex adored her girls as much as they worshipped him. Of that, Kerry had no doubt.

"Then take my advice and don't share your qualms with them," she said in a rising pitch. "You might change your mind again, and you can't be giving them whiplash like that. They're too young, Alex. They don't understand what goes into such a big decision. You'd be putting a burden on them."

She hadn't planned to use the kids as leverage, but here she was, doing just that.

"You're right. I won't say anything to the boys. I won't talk about it at all."

"It goes without saying I won't tell the girls either."

Maybe this was just a temporary case of cold feet, she thought after they'd ended their call. She would be able to judge better tomorrow, when she saw Alex's face and could look in to his eyes

Chapter Thirty-six

"Listen," said Kerry, looking up from her tablet, where she'd been reading the same passage over and over again. On this gray Saturday afternoon, even her favorite author couldn't distract her from Alex's misgivings about moving in together.

"Hear that?"

She and Alex sat in overstuffed chairs, sharing an ottoman. Alex was on his computer while Ella napped and the kids played in the attic.

"All I hear is the rain on the roof."

"Exactly." Kerry's bare feet hit the floorboards and her hands came down on the armrests. "It's not normal for four kids to be this quiet."

"I'm finally making progress on my blog. Why not let sleeping dogs lie? The last I checked, Ty and Shay were drawing and Chloé and Travis were trying on clothes from that old trunk."

They heard footsteps on the stairs.

"Whelp. You were right. Looks like that's it for today." Alex closed his laptop with a snap and turned to see all four kids hurrying over, their faces alight. "There they are. We thought you got lost. Hold it. Where'd you get those?"

Travis's hands were cuffed in the front. He grinned. "On the table next to your keys."

"Tyler," he snapped. "Did you do this to him?"

"He wanted me to," said Tyler, eyeing Alex uncertainly. "He's the one who took them."

"Don't you two *ever* touch these again, do you understand?" he said sharply as he reached up and deposited the cuffs into an old ceramic mixing bowl of Kerry's mother's on the top shelf of the buffet.

Shyly, Ty thrust a piece of paper under Alex's nose. A ruler stuck out of his back pocket.

Alex took a cleansing breath and straightened the hem of his shirt. "Now. What's this we've got here?"

"A plan."

Calmer now, Alex turned the paper around, looking at it from different angles. "Plan?"

"For how me and Shay want to make the attic after we move in here. See? I drew a straight line down the middle with a ruler, the way you taught me." He came around to Alex's side and leaned against him familiarly.

Kerry observed the cozy scene from where she was curled up in her favorite blue chair. When it came to kids, he truly had a gift.

"Here's the girls' side and here's the boys' side. And then, this here's going to be where me and Travis's fort's gonna be—"

"And this is my private area." From behind the boys, Shay inserted herself, pointing to a small square.

With some difficulty, Chloé wedged herself in between Shay and Ty. "And here's where I'm going to put my desk."

"Nice," said Alex.

From upstairs came a whine.

"Someone's up from her nap," sighed Kerry, rising to get Ella.

Alex glanced at Kerry's retreating form on the steps.

"Looks like you guys have this all figured out."

"We do," said Shay importantly. "Ty and I are going to ride the middle school bus, and Chloé and Travis will both be on the elementary."

"Chloé thaid I get to thit with her," said Travis.

"Annnnd," said Shay, "guess what else? You know how I always wanted to be a cosmetologist?"

Alex nodded.

"I changed my mind. I decided to become a teacher."

"That's awesome."

"I'm going to be a psychologist," said Chloé importantly.

"Me too," said Travis. He frowned at Chloé. "Whath a thychologith?"

"What about you, Ty?" Alex asked. "What do you want to be when you grow up?"

"A cop," Ty said shyly, "like you." Suddenly embarrassed, he buried his pink face in Alex's arm.

Alex's heart swelled. "C'mere, you," he said, tucking Tyler beneath his arm, giving him a giant squeeze.

Tyler's arms reached around his neck.

Not to be left out, Travis fell into Alex's lap, and Chloé embraced him from the opposite side.

Even Shay sidled over, perched on the arm of his chair, and touched her temple against his.

At the sound of footsteps, he swallowed the baseball-size lump in his throat and glanced at the stairs to see a wavy Kerry with Ella's sleep-dazed head on her shoulder and her thumb in her mouth, observing him with a face that radiated love.

Not ready? What had he been thinking? This was everything he'd ever wanted.

"What would you think of having a sleepover?" Kerry was addressing the kids, but her eyes were glued to Alex's.

Cheers erupted as the kids fell all over one another in their enthusiasm.

"Yay! Yeah, let's! A sleepover!" shouted the girls.

"Can we? Huh?" the boys pleaded, tugging on Alex's shirtsleeve.

A smile grew on Alex's face. "How can I say no?"

From that moment on, whether they were rearranging the attic, hauling a bunch of old junk out to the trash, or making pizza, he and Kerry were more acutely aware of each other's presence than ever before. The afternoon seemed to stretch on for days, the blasted kids never letting them out of their sight. They had an uncanny way of popping up just when Alex was about to steal a kiss or cop a feel.

At long last, supper came and went. Waiting for Kerry to put Ella to bed and for the rest of the kids to devour their popcorn and ice cream was a delicious agony. Finally, when his boys and her girls had finally passed out in their sleeping bags on the living room floor, they tiptoed upstairs, wincing at each creak of the floorboards.

When they made it to the top, Kerry held out a halting hand and put a finger to her lips. Blood pounding in their ears, they held their breath, listening.

The second Kerry nodded the all clear, Alex's hands snatched at her, but she dodged his grasp and scampered down the hall on her tiptoes, Alex hot on her heels, both giggling like teenagers and shedding clothes as they went.

Carefully, Alex closed the bedroom door, watching Kerry slip her bra straps down off her shoulders. He stepped out of his shorts, abandoning them in a puddle on the floor, and reached around to her back and undid the hooks and flung it across the room. Then he slipped his knee between her legs, toppling her backward onto the faded, patchwork quilt, both of them cringing through their grins at the screech of protest from the ancient metal bed frame.

It was steamier upstairs, despite the box fan beneath the window screen. In the country night at the end of the lane, they were finally free to do what they'd been fantasizing about doing all day. Hands dragged along curves and dips. The pace slowed. Smiles faded as their breathing deepened and filled their ears.

The time for rushing was past. Now they had the luxury of years stretching out before them. Alex lavished Kerry with attention, taking his own pleasure in pleasuring her until she was thrashing in sheets worn thin and soft with age. To keep from being overheard, they made their desires known using body language, finally forgetting to be quiet when, together, they fell over the edge.

In the middle of the night, Kerry felt Alex stirring.

"Did I wake you?" she asked softly.

"No. I've been awake for a little while. I was trying not to wake *you*."

"I guess neither of us is used to sharing a bed."

For a while, they lay facing each other in the dark, sharing trivial intimacies and comfortable silences.

"Something I meant to ask you. Why'd you freak out when you saw Travis with your handcuffs on? You were really bent out of shape."

"I should never have set them where the kids could get them. Childproofing is something I'll have to get used to. You're right, though. Cuffs give me the heebie-jeebies."

"That's funny. You must use them almost every day. Handcuffs are a tool of the trade."

"Ever since I was seven and I got this big splinter in my foot and the docs wrapped me up in a sheet, mummy style, while they dug it out, I can't stand the thought of being bound."

"Poor baby."

"Go ahead. Poke fun. You don't know what it was like, being tied up for hours."

"Sounds like you better stay on the straight and narrow, Detective."

"Know any good defense attorneys, in case I don't?"

She tickled his ribs, and he grabbed her hands, rolled onto her, and kissed her.

Chapter Thirty-seven

"Hey, sleepyhead," said Kerry. "Time to get up."

Alex opened one eye and reached for her, sitting on the edge of the bed, but she curved her body out of reach in the nick of time.

He propped himself up on an elbow and sniffed the air. "Is that bacon?"

"And coffee." She stood looking down at him with her hands on her hips. "Good coffee, not like the stuff at the NPD. Come on, before the kids eat it all."

"Mmn." He lay back down. "It's so warm and comfy under the covers here. You really should crawl in and see."

She sat back down and caressed his head. "I'd rather we were both downstairs before Shay gets up. She and I need to have a private girl talk. She's at the age where she's bound to have questions about you and me sleeping in the same bed."

"A little late now, isn't it?" he asked through a yawn, tracing a line from her shoulder to her elbow.

"I should have gotten it out of the way before, but everything happened so fast . . ."

"The idea of sharing a home is going to take some getting used to for all of us." He pulled her onto the bed and under the covers and began kissing her neck.

She lifted her chin to give him better access. "When I woke up this morning, I couldn't believe how lucky I was to have this kind, caring, sexy man lying next to me."

"You say that now," he said, slipping his hand inside her oversize button-down and cupping her breast. "But what happens if I take too long a shower and we run out of hot water, or I get called out on a case at two in the morning and wake you up?

"Or if you leave the cap off the toothpaste?"

He scooted lower in the bed. "I would never do that. But we should probably have a conversation about our wine budget," he said, suckling her.

"Noted," she murmured, rolling away from him. "Now, I've got to get back downstairs."

Reluctantly, he let her slip away. "Remember where we were."

She kissed the tip of his nose. "Oh, I will." She shot him a saucy smile, and he would have sworn the exaggerated sway of her hips as she left the room was deliberate.

Around the dining room table sat the girls in their PJ's and he and the boys in their rumpled clothes from the previous day, while Hobo wagged from chair to chair, begging for handouts.

"It stopped raining. Let's go outside after breakfast," said Chloé around a mouthful of toaster waffle.

"Sorry. I'm gonna have to put the kibosh on that," said Alex. He looked at the boys. "You guys smell like onions and old socks. Time to go back to my place to shower. Then we're going shopping for new school clothes. Can't have you going back to school in ankle pants."

"Whaths ankle panths?" asked Travis.

"It's when your pants are too short and you can see your ankles," said Ty.

Travis folded his arms and frowned in protest. "I don't want to go thopping. I want to thtay here."

"Please?" begged Tyler. "Shay said she'd show us her secret place by the creek."

Shay frowned. "You weren't supposed to tell!"

"Sorry."

"You'll have plenty of time to play down at the creek once you've moved in," said Kerry, sitting down to eat with them. "Only two more weeks."

Tyler slipped a piece of bacon under the table, and Hobo inhaled it without chewing.

"Hey! I just thought of something else!" exclaimed Tyler. "We're going to have a *dog*!"

"Don't you want a new cell phone for school, Ty?" asked Alex.

"Yeah!"

"I still can't believe the school actually requires them," Alex muttered to Kerry.

"Get ready. There're a few more things that have changed since you were in school."

"Do the kids still carry milk money? I have a big jar I throw my change into every night."

Kerry shook her head. "I pay for the kids' lunches the same way I buy everything else—online."

"Looks like I've got as much to learn as these knuckleheads," he said, snatching Tyler and giving him a noogie. His hair had grown back in, and he had lost that gaunt look.

"Aaaah! Cut it out!" Tyler laughed, his voice cracking, beating Alex with impotent fists.

"Oof!" cried Alex, doubling over, pretending to be hurt.

"I'll be your teacher," Kerry said to Alex with a wink.

She looked so damn approachable in her yoga pants, with no makeup on.

"Tell you what," Alex said to the boys. "If it's okay with Kerry, you guys can go out and play for a half hour. But when I say it's time to go, no arguments."

In a flash, the boys and Chloé were out of their seats and headed for the back door.

"Please carry your dishes to the sink first," said Kerry.

"Wait for me," said Shay, drinking the leftover milk from her bowl of cereal.

While the others were running down the porch steps, Alex took Kerry into his arms.

Shay turned around after rinsing her bowl and gazed steadily at her mother in Alex's arms as she made her way to the back door.

"She's going to be the tricky one," said Kerry when she was gone.

"What are you going to tell her?"

"That's what I'm most worried about. In Shay's experience, the guy always lets us down. I'll tell her that just because two men have disappointed us, that doesn't mean you will."

Alex pulled her close.

A moment later, she pulled back, draped her arms over his shoulders, and looked up into his eyes. "I'll tell her that, unlike the others, we can depend on you. And that we love each other and we're ready to live as a family."

"What about your mom and dad? I keep thinking I need to ask for your hand or something."

Kerry laughed. "My father can be a little intimidating. It's not like we're getting married, though. And even if we were, I decide what's best for me and my girls."

"I'm not sure which would be harder, asking him to marry you or telling him I'm about to shack up with his only daughter—in *his* house. My manhood is shrinking just thinking about it."

"I pay rent here."

"It goes without saying that I'll step up to the plate. I'm not talking about the practical end of it, though. Judge O'Hearn has made it very clear how he feels about cops."

"Oh, no." She winced. "Sorry. Let me handle him."

"No. Tell them what's going on if you want, but before we make this official, I need to speak to him myself—both of your parents—in person."

Later that afternoon, the shopping bags containing new backpacks and underwear and sneakers slung carelessly on the boys' beds, Alex took his laptop out back while the boys played in the yard.

"How come no bluebirds have moved into the nice, safe boxes we built them yet?" asked Tyler.

"It's too soon," Alex replied, only half paying attention. Then it occurred to him. "Did you think they would move right in as soon as they saw it?"

"That's what I'd do if I was a bird."

"It takes wild animals a while to learn to trust. Maybe we'll take the boxes with us when we move, if they're still unclaimed."

That cheered him. "Okay."

He watched Tyler pitch a ball to Travis, who had his tongue out in concentration as he shouldered his bat.

Livvie had warned him not to get his hopes up. But he couldn't help it. From the first nourishing meal he'd bought them, he'd gotten hooked on the high of being a father . . . giving of himself to vulnerable, defenseless beings with no thought to the cost.

About a week earlier, Livvie had confided that Greg and Deborah Pelletier had made the mistake of skipping one of their court-mandated counseling sessions. Perhaps, in their supreme arrogance, they thought they were above taking orders. Or maybe, when the judge told them how vital it was to follow their plan to the letter of the law, they weren't paying attention. Whatever the reason, every misstep would count against them at the next custody hearing. And each count against them was a count in Alex's favor. He knew he shouldn't, but he could already taste the possibility of adoption.

Then there was complicated, exasperating,

provocative Kerry. He used to have to dredge up fading memories to see her navy-blue eyes in his daydreams. Now he gazed into them whenever he wanted. Even better, he got to *touch* her. He would never take that for granted. What lucky star had guided them together after all those years?

Kerry and her two impossibly precious—that is, when they weren't annoying the hell out of him—angels. When he wasn't looking, Chloé and Ella had charmed and cajoled their way into his heart.

And then there was Shay, a former solitary like Alex, who was blossoming before his eyes into a self-assured young lady. She was going to be every bit as fiery as her mama, and he adored her beyond all reason. He couldn't imagine his life without any of them.

The boys came running over, pink-faced and sweaty. "Will you play with us?"

Alex regarded the boys, then his screen, then the boys again. And then he closed his laptop with a click. "Okay." He rose from his seat with a muffled groan. "Who batted last?"

Chapter Thirty-eight

Kerry's parents were watching Ella and Chloé so she and Shay could have some mother-daughter time under the guise of back-to-school shopping, without the hassle of the younger ones.

What a difference a year made, thought Kerry, watching Shay try on clothes and listening to her chatter on about her new friends and text them photos of clothes from the fitting rooms, getting responses like, **That's. So cute.**

Last September, Shay was still a kid. This summer, she got her first period. And today, Kerry had caved and bought her some bras. Bras! Sports bras, but still. Shay said all her friends had them.

The last stop was to Ruddock's for dinner, just the two of them.

"So," said Kerry as they slid into their booth. "How do you feel about Alex and the boys moving in with us?"

"I'm so excited! Coach Walker—wait. What am I supposed to call him now?"

"That's a good question. Why don't you talk to him about that and decide together?"

"Good idea. Let's see." She rested her elbow on the table and put her finger to her lips. "I could call him Alex."

"That *is* his name."

She grimaced. "It sounds so . . . I don't know. Weird. Like calling one of my teachers by his first name. Don't forget, Chloé and Ella are going to have to decide, too. Ella's so little. It'd be *really* weird, hearing *her* call him Alex." She thought some more. "You know what I'd really like to call him?"

"Hm?" Kerry perused the menu, trying to decide between a burger and a salad.

"Dad."

Kerry slid off her glasses and looked at her daughter, who was changing almost before her eyes. "You never even called Dick, Dad."

"That's because I was still just a confused little kid back then. Turns out, it's a good thing I didn't, huh? Now that he's gone, it's like he never even existed.

"*Dad* makes the most sense. I mean, think about it. It's short. It's easy to remember. Ella probably doesn't even remember her real dad, so she can just act like Alex's the only dad she's ever known."

"Alex isn't going to be your stepdad. At least, we have no plans for that."

"Dick *was* my stepdad, but what difference did that make? Did it stop him from leaving?"

Technically, Kerry had insisted Dick leave when

she found out about his affair. But she didn't want to spoil a lovely evening by rehashing the past. Shay was thrilled with her purchases, she wasn't too hormonal, and she and Kerry were getting along swimmingly.

"You know why I really want to call him *Dad*?"

"Why, sweetheart?"

"So that when people hear me say it in public, they'll think he really is my dad, and that I'm his daughter."

Tears stung Kerry's throat. Whether at home or at school, all Shay had ever wanted was to belong. Thanks to Alex, now she did. Because of him, she had friends at school and a male mentor in her life.

She reached across the table for her daughter's hand. "That's a wonderful sentiment. I think Alex will like it, too. He thinks the world of you, you know."

"I know," Shay said, her newfound confidence filling Kerry with maternal pride. But to whom did she owe that but Alex?

After dinner, when they pulled into Kerry's parents' house, Kerry brought Shay into her confidence.

"We don't have much time before Alex and the boys move in. I should tell Grandma and Grandpa what's going on with Alex and the boys so they aren't surprised. After you show them the things we bought, would you mind keeping an eye on Chloé and Ella so I can talk to them in private for a few minutes?"

"Sure."

* * *

To Kerry's chagrin, she arrived at her parents' to find Ryan and Indra comfortably ensconced at the patio table.

"I was cooking anyway," said Mom. "The more, the merrier,"

Ryan raised his glass to Kerry. "Let's drink to summer's last hurrah," he said.

Shay got out the bubble wand Grandma kept under the kitchen sink and ushered all the younger kids away from the table to blow bubbles in the gathering dusk.

Kerry hadn't planned on discussing her plans with Ryan, but time was running out. Besides, he would find out soon.

"Shay sure has grown up over the summer. Look how she treats her sisters. She and Chloé always used to be sniping at each other," said Mom.

"I give Alex all the credit in the world," said Kerry.

"Alex Walker?" asked Ryan.

By now, everyone in her family knew how the boxing lessons had opened a whole new world for Shay.

"She says she wants to be a teacher," Kerry said.

"She'll make a fine teacher," said Indra, watching Shay show her littlest one how to dip the bubble wand in the soap solution and then wave it.

"Walker shocked everyone when he took in the Pelletier boys. Chief Garrett above all. How's that working out?" asked her father.

"Alex was cut out to be a father."

"Father? Isn't that putting the cart a little before the horse? Precedent shows that in most custody cases, the courts overwhelmingly favor reinstatement of family rights."

"There's a hearing next week. I asked Alex—and the boys, assuming he still has them, which we have every reason to believe he will—to move in to the farmhouse."

Around the table, brows lifted.

"You don't waste time," said Ryan.

Indra frowned and said, "Ryan. Help me round up the kids. It's getting late."

But Ryan didn't budge. "What happened to Miss Independent?"

"I've proven I can raise my family on my own. But there's nothing wrong with wanting to share the load with a partner I trust. This will be good for both of us."

"I can tell Alex makes you happy," said Mom. "But five children are a lot for any couple. Are you sure that's what you want, honey?"

"It was my idea. We talked about it, and it's the right thing for us. I always wanted a big family of my own, just like the one I came from. Besides, it's like Dad said. There's no guarantee Alex will get to keep the kids. There's a hearing next week. We'll just have to wait and see. If he does get to maintain custody, whether it's for six months, one year, or forever, I accept them as a complete package. The kids all get along like gangbusters. And like I said, when it comes to my girls, I couldn't ask for a better role model than Alex."

"Have you picked a move-in date?" asked Dad.

"The weekend before school starts. But Alex insists on coming to see you both beforehand. You'll have plenty of chances to grill him then."

"Grill him?"

"I understand you didn't exactly pull any punches the first time I brought him here."

I will not let myself get worked up, thought Kerry. *I'm a grown woman. I know what's best for me and my kids.*

"That old house has seen plenty of laughter and tears," said Mom. "It was a good house to raise my family in, and it'll be good for you, too. I look forward to seeing you all there. It'll remind me of when you and the boys were small. Do you remember? Tsk. All that commotion . . ."

"That's what I loved about growing up there. Thanks, Mom." She went over to her mother's chair and bestowed a hug on her. *One down.*

Time to face her father. She hadn't forgotten how he had reacted to her first two disastrous breakups. Rather, *not* reacted. In Dad's day, men hid their true feelings, and her dad had been no exception. But Mom confided that for weeks afterward, he walked around with a cloud hanging over his head, burrowing in his study right after supper until bedtime.

"You really think it'll work this time?" asked Dad.

"I love him, Daddy. And he loves me, and my girls. I can tell by the way he looks at us, the way he would do anything for us."

"Then if you're happy, I'm happy," Dad said with a hint of weary resignation.

It wasn't the response she'd been expecting. She waited for the inevitable contingencies, but all he did was light his cigar and blow smoke away from the table so it wouldn't bother her or her mother.

He's mellowing, Kerry thought with a blend of gratitude and nostalgia.

"When would you and Alex like to come over?" asked Mom.

"Soon. This week or next."

"How about supper a week from tomorrow?"

"Let me check Alex's work schedule," said Kerry, pulling out her phone. "Perfect. He's off. You can count on us, then, unless something comes up."

"Let's see. You and the girls are four, plus three. Seven for dinner. Oh, my."

"Don't fuss. We'll pick something up."

"That would be good. I'll do dessert."

"I think this is going to work out well for everyone," said Kerry.

"Sounds like you're trying to convince yourself," muttered her brother, just as Maeve, his youngest, ran up to him crying over a stubbed toe, and he swooped her into his arms and carried her away from the table.

Kerry watched him carry Maeve away, hiding her trace of apprehension. *What if Ryan was right?*

Chapter Thirty-nine

"**A**re you ready for tomorrow?" Kerry asked Alex, picking at the nubby fabric of her beach towel.

They had taken the kids to the pool one last time before it closed for the summer.

"I'm trying not to think about the hearing. What with moving and school starting at the same time, I've had plenty of other things to think about. Canceling my utilities, packing, and making sure I'm not forgetting anything for back to school."

"You got clothes, right?"

"Check."

"Cell phone for Ty?"

"Check."

"Pediatrician and school paperwork?"

He sighed. "Double-check. Since there're two of them, everything takes twice as long and is twice as expensive."

"I hate to say it, but I'd hate even more to see you get hurt. Don't forget what Livvie said about getting your hopes up."

"In the same breath, she said compliance with the court-ordered counseling plan was imperative, and that the Pelletiers had fallen short," he said irritably.

He was counting on that to get him past this first hearing. After that, he would somehow get through the next, and then the next, until the day he could take permanent custody.

"Don't bite my head off. I'm on your side."

He swiped off his aviators and pinched the bridge of his nose. "From the first time I took them home, we were a family. It's like I can't even remember life before them. Who would have guessed I'd be so into being a father?"

Kerry leaned against his arm. "I would have."

"I'm in my element with them, Ker. Not to brag, but all I've ever wanted to do was help people. It makes me feel needed, showing Ty and Trav new things, listening when they have something to say, giving them the attention they deserve—every kid deserves. I love giving them what I didn't have. Tucking them in at night, going to sleep knowing they're safe and protected . . . I'm not saying it's easy, being a parent. It's the hardest thing I've ever done. But if I had known before how rewarding it was . . ."

Kerry smiled up at him, and he gave her a one-armed hug. "We have a great future to look forward to."

Alex looked out with paternal pride at where Travis dove off the board. He'd only had them a

short time, but if he had to give them up, he didn't
know how he could do it.

School started. Kerry deflated the pool and
shook out the sleeping bags and hung them across
the porch railing to air out before storing them in
the attic for the winter.

On the morning of the hearing Alex put the boys
on the school bus, as usual. He casually mentioned
that there was a hearing today. But he didn't dwell
on the possible results. No sense in worrying them
needlessly. He couldn't put them through the
agony he was about to endure, waiting for the outcome.

The hearing was held behind closed doors in
the judge's chambers. Livvie had promised to call
him the minute she heard the outcome.

Alex went about his day, jumping every time his
phone rang.

At lunchtime, Kerry texted to ask if there was
news.

"Not yet," he wrote back.

"Stay positive ☺," she replied.

Just as his shift was ending and he was headed to
his car to go get the boys, Livvie called.

"I know you've been sitting on the edge of your
seat all day."

At the tone of her voice, his heart almost
stopped. "Just tell me," spat Alex. "Don't keep me
guessing."

"I'm sorry, Alex. This is the worst part of my job.
They brought in a high-powered family attorney

from Portland. You know how life goes. You win some, you lose some. This time, they won."

Standing there in the parking lot, Alex's blood was pounding in his head so loud, it was all he could hear.

"I assume the boys are at the Community Center?"

"Yeah, but . . ." Surely they couldn't take them away from him, just like that. Could they? It was cruel and inhumane for all three of them.

"Someone from my office will pick them up."

"And then what?"

"Deliver them to the Pelletiers."

He paced the macadam, frantically racking his brain for an alternative.

"Can't I get them myself? At least give me a chance to explain to them what happened."

"I'm afraid I can't do that. You lost custody the moment the judge gave his decree."

"Livvie. Isn't there something you can do? This is so wrong—" He was blind with disbelief. "So unfair. Tyler and Travis have already gotten attached to me. They're going to hate this."

"I tried to prepare you for this outcome."

"I know, but this is going to tear their lives apart yet again." Who was going to help Tyler with his book report? Make sure Travis wore his jacket to school in the cool mornings? Be there for him when he got his cast taken off?

"I wish it had turned out differently as much as you do," said Livvie.

* * *

When Kerry saw Alex standing in the doorway of her office, her heart sank. She closed the door behind them and led him to one of two visitors' chairs.

"I can't believe it," she said, lowering herself beside him without taking her eyes off him, her hand resting on his forearm. "I mean, I always knew there was a chance they'd get them back, but . . ."

Alex dropped his head into his hands. "Is there no recourse? Nothing I can do?"

She sighed and shook her head, her hands falling into her lap. "I don't think so. I can try to find a good family attorney for you, but in my professional opinion, you'd be throwing your money away."

"What am I going to do, Ker?"

She squeezed his hand. "I know how badly you're hurting. But you still have me and the girls. You're going to move in with us, as planned. And somehow, we're going to get through this, together, one day at a time. You can't see it now, but every day will get a little bit easier, until one day you'll wake up and losing them won't be the first thing that comes to your mind."

His head sagged. He was way stronger than she would be in his place, thought Kerry admiringly. If she lost her girls, she'd be out of her mind.

"I was planning on taking the girls to the taqueria for supper. Want to come?"

He rose slowly. "I think I just want to be alone tonight."

"You need to eat."

He edged toward the door. "No offense, but I'm not in the mood to . . ."

To be around her tight-knit family.

Before he left, she pulled him into her arms and hugged him tight. "I'll give you space tonight to be with your feelings, and I'll call you first thing tomorrow."

The car was too quiet on the way to the taqueria.

"I'm not hungry for tacos," Kerry blurted. "Who wants to go to Ruddock's instead?"

"Me," said Shay.

In her rearview mirror, she saw Chloé raise her hand. "I do. Do you, Ellabella? Say 'me.' "

"Meeee," said Ella, grinning as Chloé raised her hand for her.

Midway through their meal, Kerry looked up from wiping Ella's face to see a man standing next to the table.

"Danny!"

With his thickly layered head of hair, he was as handsome as ever. She recognized the shirt as coming from the same local men's shop where her dad bought his clothes.

"Kerry."

Danny reached for her hand, but instead of simply clasping it as she'd been expecting, he bent his head over it and kissed the tips of her fingers.

Shay and Chloé's eyes grew round.

At the surrounding tables, the buzz of conversation abruptly ceased, bringing the low volume of Burt Bacharach's recording of "This Guy's in Love with You" to the forefront.

"I just finished having dinner with my parents."

He gestured toward an approaching older couple. "Mom. Dad. Look who's here."

Kerry pasted on a smile and fluttered her fingers.

But Mrs. Wilson was having none of that. She came at Kerry with open arms. "Kerry O'Hearn. My heavens. How long has it been?"

Ooof. Kerry reciprocated and was enveloped in a cloud of Chanel N° 5.

Not to be outdone, Mr. Wilson had to have his hug, too.

"Is this the little one I've heard so much about?" asked Danny.

"This is Ella."

"Hi, Ella," Danny said, cupping her chin as if she were ten rather than three. "Your Auntie Paige told me all about you. And you must be Chloé, because you have the prettiest blue eyes . . ."

Red-faced, Chloé turned her chin and squirmed in her seat.

Next in line was Shay, with her brittle ego.

"Shay." There was a wistful look in Danny's eyes, and Kerry knew they were both recalling the day Danny had proposed to her when she was already pregnant.

"Nice to meet you," said Shay, for once using her manners.

Kerry released a held breath. She should have known. Danny might be awkward around kids, but he had always had a way with women—of all ages. Hard to believe that, after all this time, he had never found someone else.

"How do you like Newberry?"

Shay shrugged. "I like it."

After a little more small talk, Mr. Wilson looked at his watch and mumbled something about a TV show that was starting soon.

"Why don't we go and let you and Kerry catch up?" asked Mrs. Wilson. She turned to Kerry. "We still live in the same house over on Seventh. Danny can easily walk home when he's finished."

Danny had the grace to look conflicted. "Are you sure?" he asked his mother.

She waved away his faux concern. "Yes, yes. We don't mind, do we, Bill?" she said with a hand to her husband's back, already edging him toward the door.

Danny shrugged and made an apologetic face at Kerry. "Since I'm already here . . ." he said, scraping a fifth chair over from an unoccupied table.

Around them, people shared satisfied looks and resumed eating and talking.

And when the nosy waitress came over and asked if he'd changed his mind about dessert and maybe he'd like that piece of lingonberry pie after all, he looked inquiringly at Kerry, as if to ask her permission. At her feeble smile, he dazzled the waitress with his own broad grin and said, "I don't mind if I do."

They must have looked for all the world like the perfect little family when Kerry noticed the door to the bar open and saw Alex come walking in with Olivia Bartoli.

Alex didn't recall driving home from Kerry's office. All he remembered was walking straight to his wine cooler, pulling out the first bottle his hand landed on, and carrying it out back to the patio.

But all he could see out there were the ghosts of the boys playing catch. All he could hear was their yells of discovery from the woods upon finding a squirrel's nest or a cool rock. Several minutes later, he realized he hadn't yet touched his glass.

He wandered back inside, at a loss for what to do with himself. Maybe he should have taken Kerry up on her supper invitation, even though it wouldn't have been easy, watching the authentic bond she had with her girls. No one could ever take *them* away from *her*.

Now he was stuck here in self-imposed exile.

He sat down on the edge of the couch and thought about Curtis Wallace, from the night they had met at the Turning Point and he'd told him about Kerry and Danny Whatshisname to the day Curtis had almost run him off his property, then fed him, until the day Alex found him having died the way he lived, by himself.

He checked his watch. By now, Kerry and her gang had already eaten. But he could still go get something. It would do him good to get out of the house.

He had parked and was walking toward the taqueria when he saw none other than Livvie walking toward him.

"Alex." She touched his arm and peered up at him.

She had the kindest eyes, he realized. Deep brown with gold flecks, like tiger's eye.

"I won't ask how you're doing."

The salt of tears he'd been holding in all day

stung his nasal cavity. He swallowed and managed a polite nod.

"I'm just leaving work. I was going to grab some food to take home. Were you—" She gestured toward the door of the taqueria.

When he didn't answer, she squared her shoulders. "I have a better idea." With a toss of her head in the opposite direction, she set off.

Alex followed her, robotlike, to her car, and sat there, his hands helpless in his lap, feeling numb and useless.

"After a day like today, I think we could both use a drink," she said.

A minute later, she pulled into the parking lot at Ruddock's.

Two adults having a grown-up conversation with no interruptions, no talk of school forms or vaccinations or Pull-Ups. How long had it been?

Livvie ordered for both of them, and instead of rehashing what had happened that day, she talked about the vacation she was planning to Hawaii in the fall. "Have you ever been?" she asked.

He shook his head.

"Oh, you have to fix that. Everything they say is true. There're white sand beaches where you can snorkel and actually hand-feed tropical fish. Fantastic restaurants. And the waterfalls and rainforests . . ." She feigned a little swoon.

Alex looked, really looked, at Livvie, forcing himself to focus through his gray clouds of grief. How had he never appreciated her no-drama demeanor, her simple enthusiasm for living life to its fullest? At the very least, she deserved an effort at participation in the thread of conversation she'd been carrying on all by herself ever since they sat down.

"Who are you—" He cleared his throat. "Who are going with?"

"An organized group of singles." She held up a hand. "Not what you're thinking. Most of us have vacationed together multiple times over the years and become fast friends. Sure, there've been a few who've paired off, but that's not the intent. Just a bunch of fun people who happen to be between relationships but aren't into taking a trip by themselves. If you want, I can see if there's still room for one more."

"Another round before you order some food?" the bartender asked them.

"I shouldn't . . ." she said, but when their eyes met, she arched a brow in a question.

If there was ever a night to have a second drink, tonight was it.

Alex slugged what was left in his glass and slid his glass toward the bartender. "Hit me," he said, only freezing up when he happened to glimpse across the dining room during the pour.

"Alex?" Livvie's eyes followed his line of sight to where Kerry and her girls were enjoying dinner with none other than—Danny Wilson.

"Alex?" Livvie tipped her head to catch Alex's eye.

"Huh?" Somehow, he managed to tear his eyes away from the intimate get-together. He looked down at the bar. "Sorry."

Her eyes fastened on Kerry's table, Livvie sniffed a laugh and slowly shook her head from side to side. "After all this time, they still make a great-looking pair."

"Do they?" asked Alex, staring hard at the surface of the bar, determined not to look Kerry's way again. "I hadn't noticed." Any misgivings about turning Kerry down earlier had vanished on seeing that she had a backup waiting in the wings, all set to swoop in and recover his lost ground.

"It's not just me who thinks so. Look around you."

She was right. Everywhere he looked, people were sneaking glances and talking softly behind their hands.

"That's a small town for you," sighed Livvie. "I don't mean to pry, but I can't help but be a little confused. Aren't you and Kerry . . ." She made a rolling motion with her hand. "You know."

"She invited me out tonight. I said no. Thought I needed some alone time."

Livvie fingered the stem of her wineglass and considered. "So, how does it make you feel now, seeing her with Danny?"

Alex jerked up his head. "Why does it feel like I'm being psychoanalyzed all of a sudden?"

"Sorry. Force of habit."

"No. I'm sorry." Livvie really was nice. "I didn't mean to—"

"You're right. I might have been projecting my own desires on to the situation."

Despite his anguish, Alex grinned. "Spoken like a true counselor."

"A slightly *tipsy* counselor." She slid off her barstool and tugged the strap of her bag over her shoulder.

"You leaving?" Out of deference, he stood as well.

"I liked getting to know off-duty Detective Walker a little better," she said, taking one last sip from her half-full glass. "But I think you have some sorting out to do."

Alex bent over and kissed her cheek. "Sorry I wasn't better company. You go ahead. I'll walk back to my car. Night air'll do me some good. Thanks for making me smile. Didn't think I had it in me tonight."

Livvie smiled back at him, though her smile didn't reach her eyes. "Maybe someday I'll find someone who can do the same for me." Then she turned and walked out into the night.

Alex steeled himself not to look at Kerry's table, but a familiar peal of girlish laughter broke his will. It was Chloé, giggling at the pie on Ella's face. He raised his finger to the barman. "Check, please."

Chapter Forty

The next few days passed in a haze. Signs of the boys were everywhere Alex looked in the small house. The neatly made twin beds still sat forlornly in the office he'd sacrificed for them. Gone was the wreckage of dirty clothes and sports equipment that used to litter the room. He'd packed up most of the clothes he'd bought them and delivered them to CPS. But the next day, after work, he'd gone looking for bird food in the storage area out back and found their baseballs, gloves, and bats still there.

He shut the door, went back inside, and opened the fridge to spot a half gallon of whole milk and the apples he'd bought for their school lunches. He gathered the apples into his arms, carried them out back, and hurled them one by one into the woods for the deer.

His phone rang.

"You ready for this?" Kerry asked. She had already broken the ice by telling her parents he was moving in. Tonight was the night they were going to make it official. "Dinner. Right." He felt numb. "Our order at Happy Family should be ready at six. I got you walnut shrimp, like you asked."

He rubbed his temples.

"Is everything okay? You don't have to do this. My parents will understand. It hasn't been an easy week. For any of us," she added with a tinge of sadness in her voice.

"No." In all fairness, Kerry had suffered a loss, too.

"Can you stop by my place first and we'll drive over to their house together? Ella's too big for me to carry her, and if I let her walk, we'll never get there. After dinner, maybe you can help me put the kids to bed and we can have a moment to ourselves."

"Sure."

"Great! See you soon. You're not nervous, are you?"

"Why should I be?"

She laughed, but it sounded forced. "You shouldn't. Don't worry; everything will work out fine."

The sky smelled like rain.

"What does your fortune cookie say?" Chloé asked Alex.

"I didn't open it yet."

"Open it!"

"Open it," Shay repeated.

Alex cracked the cookie in half and pulled out

the slip of paper and read, " 'Wherever you go, go with all your heart.' "

Kerry leaned into him and laid her head on his shoulder.

"Shay, race you to the end of the lawn," said Chloé. The girls tore off running.

"Can I get you anything, Alex?" asked Rose. "More ice cream?"

"No, thanks."

Rose paused before taking his plate away. "You didn't care for the shrimp?"

"Just not hungry tonight, I guess."

"Should I—?"

"No, you can take it."

"So. Are you ready for this?" asked the judge, with a nod to where Chloé and Shay chased each other up, down, and around the flagstones and landscaping, hollering at the tops of their lungs.

"Alex?" said Kerry.

"It was a rhetorical question, Son," the judge said with a definite edge to his voice. "But I think it still deserves a response."

Rose gave Seamus a warning look.

"He's right," said Alex.

He looked at Kerry full-on. "Something happened today you need to know about."

Kerry looked at him with bewilderment. "What do you mean?"

Alex struggled for words. "I came to a decision."

"What are you talking about?"

Rose stood and began amassing a pile of empty foil tins and used napkins. "Seamus," she said, "would you carry Ella into the kitchen for me? There's a new coloring book in a drawer in the buffet."

"Now? There's finally a decent breeze coming off the Coast Range."

"*Seamus.*"

"Coming, dear." Seamus stood heavily and gathered Ella into his arms.

When they were alone, Kerry said, "You're making me nervous," with a shaky laugh. "Whatever it is you have to say, just say it."

"I don't know how to tell you this."

"Just tell me. Whatever it is, we'll deal with it, together."

He looked her square in the eye. "I can't move in with you."

Kerry just stared at him. "What do you mean? I thought it was all settled. We already told the girls . . ."

"I know, and I'm sorry. But it would hurt them more if I moved in and then left. They've already endured that twice."

Kerry blinked and raised her hands to the sides of her head. "What's changed?"

"You know what's changed."

"The boys? What's that have to do with us? I told you before the hearing, I wanted you with or without them."

"I was never meant to be a father. I don't deserve to have a family."

Alex might as well have punched Kerry in the gut with one of those big, fat leather gloves, because all the wind was knocked out of her.

"Why do you say that?"

"I don't know how to be a dad. I wasn't fathered

right from the beginning. Losing the boys is just another sign."

"You're having a crisis of self-confidence. That's all. You'll be fine. You've seen how the girls are around you. They revere you."

"I don't want to let them down."

"How are you going to let them down?"

He ground his jaw. "If I hadn't sent the boys outside that day, Travis might not have a broken arm right now."

"The fun and adventure he had in the short time he was with you more than made up for something so minor as a cast on his arm. You were the best thing that ever happened to those boys."

He gestured toward their grand surroundings. "I don't belong here."

"Of course you do."

"Don't you see how your father looks at me? Your brothers? They don't think I'm good enough. They'll always be watching me, waiting for me to stumble."

Kerry got up and began to pace like she was querying a witness. "I don't care what they think. And you shouldn't either. The only thing that matters is what we think of each other."

"No, it's not. That's wishful thinking. The reality is that we're constantly going to be on defense. Every time your father looks at me, he's going to be wishing I were Danny."

"I can handle it."

"It's not just that. Every time you have to recuse yourself, I'll be the one to blame. Our being together will result in lost income for you."

"A case here and there."

"A case here and there will add up over the span of your career. Maybe an entire college fund's worth. You say you don't care now, but you might feel differently down the road."

"We'll have your income to make up for it."

He shook his head. "If you were with someone else, you'd have his income without having to give up any of your own."

"This is unbelievable."

Her parents had ventured a few tentative steps back outside. On hearing Kerry's shrill tone, Rose turned right around and ushered Seamus back in.

He shook his head. "I'm sorry, Ker. I'm not doing this to hurt you."

Chloé came running up to the table, dewy and out of breath. She frowned. "Are you guys fighting?"

"No," said Alex.

"Alex," pleaded Kerry.

"You *are* fighting," said Chloé.

Betrayal, hurt, and anger mushroomed in Kerry like the charcoal-colored clouds in the western sky, but she couldn't release it here, at her parents' house, in front of her kids. She was forced to swallow it back, leaving her insides feeling constricted.

Shay jogged over, looking for her sister. "Come on, Chloé. I thought we were going to see who could be the first to find a four-leaf clover." It didn't take seeing everyone's facial expressions for her to realize that something was amiss. The tension was embedded in the dense atmosphere.

The kitchen door opened. "Chloé! Shay! Come inside. It's starting to rain."

"But—" stuttered Chloé.

"Right *now*."

Heeding their grandmother's call, the girls scampered off grudgingly toward the house.

"Again, I'm sorry to put the girls through this."

"It's nothing they haven't been through before," Kerry replied, emotion thick in her throat. She began gathering up their things. "By the way," she said, a sweater folded over her arms. "What were you doing having drinks with Olivia Bartoli the other night after you told me you wanted to be alone?"

"Oh. Okay. Here we go."

"What's that supposed to mean?"

"I could ask you the very same thing."

"Danny was having dinner with his parents. He saw me and the girls and stopped to say hi."

"From where I sat, it looked like a little more than just saying hi."

"I'm sorry if it bothered you that I was talking to Danny after you turned down my dinner invitation."

"Whoa, whoa, whoa. We're getting way off track here."

"Okay. So let's get back on message. You remember when I said I was going to talk to Shay about us? About you moving in? You want to know what she said?"

His shoulders tensed, while dark splotches began to appear on the stone pavers surrounding the sparse shelter of the portico.

He was doing well to brace himself, because this was going to hurt him. But she was glad. She wanted him to hurt as badly as she did.

"That she wanted to call you *Dad*. You know why?

So that people would assume she was your, quote, 'real daughter.' "

Alex hung his head. In the near dark, Kerry saw his jaw working.

"I think you should go," she said.

The only sound was the soft patter of the rain.

"Let me drive you home."

"My parents can drive us."

"What are you going to tell them?"

"Does it matter?"

"I'm sorry," he repeated.

He rose heavily, and Kerry watched him set off on the path to the front, where his car was parked, raindrops staining on his shoulders, his footfalls on the pavers tapping out a slow drumbeat of regret.

A few seconds later, she heard the solid *ka-chunk* of his car door, followed by the swish of tires on wet pavement. She kept watching as his car drove down the lane, until the red glow of his taillights disappeared.

The wind whipped her hair, skeins of it sticking to her damp neck, pulling when she dragged her fingers through it.

The back door opened again. "Kerry. Honey. You're going to be miserable."

From behind her mother emerged a tall, blocky shape that came walking toward her.

This was going to be the worst part. Telling her dad that his foreboding was right, and she'd been played for a fool yet again by a man. A cop.

"I suppose you put two and two together from what Chloé picked up," she said as her father reached her. "Go ahead and say it: 'I told you so.' "

"You're defending him."

Dad's voice wasn't as judgmental as she'd been expecting.

She huffed a laugh. "Force of habit."

"I don't have to tell you about extenuating circumstances," he said. "I wish there was the ideal partner out there for my little girl. But I'm old enough to know he doesn't exist. We all have to do the best we can and hope the good outweighs the bad."

"What am I going to do?"

"The same thing you've always done. You're going to go on taking care of your children. You've still got your mother and me." He put his arm around her and tugged her into his comforting bulk.

"Let's go in," he said finally.

The next day, Shay was furious. "Now everything's ruined," she wailed. "First Tyler and Travis, and now Alex."

"I know how much you wanted Alex to be part of our family, but it just didn't work out."

"Nothing ever works out!"

"Alex made me promise not to tell, but remember that day Aunt Indra got hurt? He said the word, *crap*," said Chloé importantly.

"Big mouth!" Shay hurled back at her in Alex's defense.

Kerry swallowed the lump in her throat. Now her poor judgment was causing a rift between her children. "Don't talk to your sister that way."

"I miss Ty," said Shay.

"I miss Trav," echoed Chloé.

"You can still be friends."

"How?" Shay said. "We don't all go to the same school. And Tyler had to give back the phone Alex bought him."

"I understand there are enough new kids signed up for boxing that they've been given the green light to keep the program."

"But no way are Ty and Trav going to be allowed to take it."

Kerry pressed her lips together. She had thought about pulling Shay out of boxing, too, but that would only be punishing her for Alex's actions. And technically, Alex wasn't the head coach; Gene was.

"What about all the plans we made for the attic?"

"Speaking of the attic, I need you to roll up the sleeping bags hanging on the porch and carry them up there for the winter."

"I will. Later."

"Don't forget."

"I'm going up to my room," mumbled Chloé listlessly.

"Why does this always happen?" asked Shay.

Kerry turned from watching Chloé shuffle upstairs.

"It was too soon. I never should have let Alex get so close to us in such a short amount of time."

"It's your fault he's not coming back."

"Relationships are complicated, Shay. You'll learn that as you get older. When something goes wrong, it's hardly ever just one person's fault."

"But no one ever stays with you. They all leave.

Just like my bio dad, and Dick. They left. And now Alex. What is it with you?"

Guilt filled Kerry to overflowing. She could have changed course at any step of the way. Made different decisions. Yet, after she had vowed to put her children first, she still let Alex in.

Shay's phone rang. "Mayree!" she exclaimed, her mood instantly brightening. "You finally got your own phone!" She headed outside to talk in private.

Kerry didn't mind being shut out. She was just glad Shay had someone to distract her, even if it was her former best friend back in Portland. She didn't have to worry about Mayree making Shay homesick. Shay had gotten past that, thanks to Alex.

Or so Kerry had thought, until fifteen minutes later, when Shay came back inside.

"I wish I could go back to Portland." She swung her new backpack filled with supplies over one shoulder, the way she'd seen the high school kids do it at the pool.

"You're going to injure your spine if you keep lifting your book bag like that."

"Stop telling me what to do! I don't want to be in this house anymore! I hate it here!" She stomped upstairs.

Beneath the kitchen table, Hobo panted nervously and whisked his tail across the floor, scattering toast crumbs.

There was no use arguing with a dejected, hormonal thirteen-year-old girl, even if you were a crack defense attorney. *Especially* if you were her mother. And especially when she was right.

Chapter Forty-one

Before long, Shay became caught up in the swirl of texts and phone chats with the friends she'd made over the summer. Kerry was relieved. It helped her forget about losing Alex, if only a little.

The dinner hours were filled with Shay and Chloé talking about their teachers and who had the most homework and filling out activity forms.

And then, one morning, Kerry got an automated phone call from Shay's school, letting her know that Shay was absent.

Shay, absent? There had to be some mistake. Kerry called the school office to talk to a real person. "What do you mean she's not there? She got on the bus this morning. You'd better check again."

But Shay had been a no-show in homeroom when attendance was taken, and was not in her first-period class.

Kerry hung up and called her mother.

"Is Shay there?"

"Why would she be here?"

"She's not at school. Please tell me she's with you."

"She's not here, honey."

"Who's not here?" asked Kerry's dad in the background.

"Shay's missing," replied her mother. "Kerry got a call from the school."

"Dad's putting on his shoes. He's on his way over to the farmhouse right now," she continued. "He'll call you as soon as he gets there."

Kerry paced her office. *Maybe I should run home.*

No. There was nothing to worry about. Shay probably cut school as a way of acting out. Typical teenage stuff. She supposed she'd better get used to it.

Minutes later, her phone rang. "Did you find her?"

"I've looked everywhere," said Dad. "She's not here."

"Are you sure? She has to be there!"

"I went through the entire house, calling her name. Where else could she be?"

Ryan strolled into Kerry's office, looking puzzled. "Everything okay?" When he saw Kerry's stricken face, he went over to her and cupped her elbow. "What's wrong?"

"Shay's missing. She's gone."

"She can't be *gone*. When was the last time you saw her?"

"This morning, when she left for the bus." Kerry pulled away from her brother and pressed her fingers to her forehead.

"Dad. Ryan's here with me. I'll call you back."

"She can't have gone far," said Ryan.

"She's not at school or at Mom and Dad's," Kerry said, her voice rising ever higher, "and Dad said she's not in the farmhouse."

"Panicking won't get us anywhere. Was Shay angry when she left this morning? Do you think this has anything to do with the trouble you've been having with Alex Walker?"

"No. I don't know." Her stomach sank with fear. "These days, everything sets her off. Her former best friend back in Portland got her first cell phone and has been calling her, making her homesick all over again. I can't seem to do anything right . . . you're right. I should call Alex.

"Dammit!" she said, pressing the phone to her chest when her call went to voice mail. "He's not picking up. He's probably working a case.

"Alex. Call me as soon as you get this voice mail."

She texted him too, for good measure.

Then she called the school back to make sure they hadn't made a mistake after all, and Shay was sitting in the cafeteria eating the substantial lunch she'd packed for herself.

But no.

Kerry paced, one hand on her hip, clutching her phone, the other pressed to her forehead.

"Have you heard back from Walker?" asked Ryan.

She shook her head.

"I don't want to be an alarmist, but it might not hurt to get in touch with the chief of police, if only to find out his whereabouts."

She'd been thinking the same thing but been

reluctant to take that step. Calling the police took things to a whole new level. "You're right." She looked at her phone, then had another idea. "I'll just go over." She had an overwhelming urge to see Alex in person. To share her escalating fear.

The police station was an easy walk from her office. With every step, she thought of him. She yearned to pour out her anxiety to him, to be taken into his arms, to lean on his strong chest. He loved Shay. He'd be as worried as she was. He would know what to do.

When she was informed Alex wasn't there, disappointment flooded her veins. She asked to see the chief instead.

Chief Garrett took one look at her face and escorted her back to his office and closed the door behind them.

"Do you know where Alex is?"

The chief narrowed his eyes.

Kerry had no illusions about how the local police viewed her. The chief had seen her out of professional courtesy and the high regard with which he held her father.

"I need to know. It's urgent."

"Took some time off. Why?"

"My daughter, Shay, never showed up at school this morning."

"She mention anything about going someplace lately?"

"She recently got a call from her best friend from when we lived in Portland. But she has no way of getting there. I've been trying to get in touch with Alex to see if he might have seen her. Alex and his foster children were supposed to move in with us and then, as you know, he lost the boys, and . . ." She threw her hands in the air. If she wanted help, the chief needed to know all the facts. "To make a long story short, we broke up. Shay's at a difficult age. She was very affected by what's happened. She's very attached to Alex, and vice versa."

Chief Garrett massaged his lower lip and thought for a minute. Then he picked up his phone and made a call. "Ms. Bartoli. What's the latest you have on the Pelletier boys?" Following a brief pause, he filled her in on Shay's situation. "Appreciate it. I'll be standing by.

"Sit tight," Garrett told Kerry. "That was CPS. She's going to check with the school to see if the boys are present and accounted for."

"What about Alex? Why isn't he answering my calls?"

The chief measured his words. "Maybe he just needed to unplug for a little while. People don't do that nearly enough anymore."

His phone rang. "Yeah. Well, I'll be." He eyed Kerry as he listened to the caller.

"What?" Kerry rose and flattened her hands on the chief's desk. "What did she say?"

Chief held up a finger as he finished his phone conversation, frustrating Kerry to no end. "Bet you dollars to doughnuts we're going to locate them in a park somewhere between the school and the Pelletiers' place with stomachaches from too many Slim Jims and grape sodas from the Thrifty Market. Right."

He hung up. "Travis and Tyler Pelletier were no-shows at school both yesterday and today." He smiled blandly. "Could be at home, nursing summer colds."

Kerry sniffed in derision. Neither she nor the chief believed that for a minute. They were both thinking the same thing: *Or maybe they're trying to make their way back to Alex.*

Chief stood up and walked around his desk. He opened his door and stood in the doorway, signaling it was time for her to leave. "We're checking into it. I'm going to give a shout out to Patrol to keep an eye out for all three of them," he said, walking her through the hallway to reception and on to the exit. "We'll also ask at the bus station. Try not to panic. It's a beautiful day and it's only been a few hours. There's a good chance Shay'll go home after school as usual, believing she got away with cutting."

"I appreciate your help. You'll let me know immediately if you hear *anything*?"

"Will do. Likewise for you."

Gerald Garrett stood in the doorway and watched Kerry O'Hearn stride away. Passionate woman. Solid upbringing. No wonder Walker was so smitten with her. Too bad she had gone over to the dark side. The county could always use another top-notch prosecutor.

Back in the summer, Gerald had seen with his own eyes how close Alex and Kerry's daughter were, the day of the boxing exhibit at the Community Pool. And after Alex lost the Pelletier kids, he'd been visibly shaken. He said he needed a little time to clear his head. Claimed he was checking out some resort town in BC and would be turning off his phone for a while.

Gerald returned to his office, sat down, and tried to call Alex without success.

Within seconds, the ancient desk phone jangled. He picked it up on the first ring, believing it was Alex calling him back.

"Have you heard the news?"

Gerald leaned back in his springy chair. "Now, Seamus, don't start thinking the worst."

"Easy for you to say. It's not your granddaughter."

"Your daughter was just in here. I'll tell you the same thing I told her, which is the kids probably just cut school and they'll show up any minute now."

"Kids? Who else is missing?"

"Pelletier kids."

"Jesus."

Gerald could almost see his friend rubbing a hand down over his face.

"When Kerry got involved with another cop, I knew it'd be nothing but trouble."

"What's Walker got to do with this?"

"Are you kidding? I smell him all over this. Everything was fine until he came into the picture. Kerry was back home with her girls. The farmhouse was filled with a family again. And then she gets tangled up with this guy, and he gets it into his head that he can take on two little troublemakers with no experience being a parent, and next thing you know, he's reneging on moving in with her and loses the kids to boot. And now they're gone, along with Shay. Don't tell me he's got nothing to do with it."

Gerald teepee'd his fingertips and considered.

"Where is he? Where's Walker? I want a word with him. Now."

"I don't know."

"What do you mean, you don't know? The man works for you, does he not?"

"He took some time off."

"Well, if that isn't a strange coincidence. Where'd that son of a bitch go? So help me, Gerry, if you're going to put Alex Walker ahead of thirty years of friendship—"

"Hold on," Gerald said. "Let me think." What was the name of that town Alex was headed to again—assuming that was really where he had gone? It started with a K.

"You better think long and hard. That is, unless you don't mind the mayor, the town council and *The Trib* getting an earful about you and old Curtis Wallace's still. I hear you just bought a couple of bushels each of Winesap, McIntosh, and Jonathans from Stillman's Orchard."

These days you could walk down the streets of Newberry openly smoking a joint, but get caught making a batch of giggle juice and you'd be facing felony charges. All because Uncle Sam wanted his share of the taxes. Gerald could see the headline already: POLICE CHIEF FIRED FOR ILLEGAL MOON-SHINE STILL. "You wouldn't."

"Wouldn't I? Try me."

"Pretty hypocritical, given how many gallons of that 'shine you've bought from me and Curtis over the years." But then, what if Seamus was right? He thought of all the people—rich and poor, young and old—people of all stripes he'd seen herded through his processing center in cuffs throughout his career. What if Alex had something to do with the kids' disappearance?

"I want answers, and I want them now. Put out feelers. Call in old favors. Whatever it takes to get my granddaughter back."

"Lemme see what I can find out," said Gerald.

Crazy, how Google unearthed more information in seconds than you could get from slogging through the traditional channels in days. But then, what could you expect, given the nature of bureaucracy? Gerald's departments' radios weren't even hooked up to the staties,' let alone the feds.' Officers across all agencies had learned to swap personal cell phone numbers if they were ever going to get anything done.

"Sorry, Alex," he muttered as he punched in the number of the Royal Canadian Mounted Police. "They say one is the loneliest number. I just hope you're smarter than you are lonesome."

Chapter Forty-two

Alex was sitting at his gate, waiting to board his flight back to Portland, when three officials wearing black service caps with gold bands and vests over button-down shirts approached him.

"Are you Alex Walker?"

He stood up. "I am."

"Turn around and put your hands on top of your head."

The clink of metal made his heart start to race.

"What's this about?"

His arms were being twisted backward and he heard the familiar snap of the cuffs closing.

"What's going on?"

"Right now, you're being detained for questioning in a missing child case."

"What the hell? What missing child?"

He was led away, a cop clutching each of his arms and the third following close behind. All around him, bored passengers lifted their heads from their phones and paperback novels and stared.

"We'll talk about it when we get to the substation."

They led him to a windowless room barely large enough for a table and three chairs. The acoustic tile walls were pockmarked with dents from angry fists. The only decoration was a clock and a video camera in a corner near the ceiling. Then he saw the large eye screw embedded in the center of the table.

"Guys," he said, trying to hide the panic swelling up in him like a balloon, "is all this necessary? I'm one of you. I'm a detective with the Newberry, Oregon, PD. I'm not resisting."

"Hang tight," said the lead officer in clipped tones as he attached Alex's cuffs to the eye screw. "Be right back."

What else could he do? Alex knew from long experience what *hang tight* meant. They might be back in a minute. Or it might be hours he would have to sit there, unable to scratch an itch or reach anything beyond six inches from the table's center while they got their ducks in a row in preparation to interrogate him for whatever crime it was they suspected him of committing. How many times had he done the very same thing? Now it was his turn in the hot seat. Sweat poured off his forehead and his heart pounded like a drum. He sucked in deep breaths. Tried squeezing his eyes shut so he couldn't see the cuffs encircling his wrists. But no matter what he did, he couldn't escape the iron bands cutting into his skin with his slightest movement. He was hopelessly trapped.

He watched the hands crawl around the clock as he racked his brain, trying to figure out what he'd done wrong. Was he being mistaken for someone else?

The airport intercom announced that his flight was boarding.

"Aaaagh!" He yanked his wrists against the eye ring with all his might, but it didn't budge. Every second was an agony, every minute felt like an hour.

He yanked at his shackles again. He couldn't breathe. He imagined all the oxygen was slowly being depleted from the cramped room.

"Passengers on Alaska Air flight 346 to Seattle. This is your final boarding call."

Anguish added to his panic. Until this morning he'd lost almost everything. His parents, his old partner, the boys. Ruined what he'd had with Kerry and her kids. But he'd still had his crime-fighting comrades. If there was anyone he could count on, it was them. Now, even they had deserted him.

Alone again, naturally. Just like the song. Just like Curtis.

He lay his head down in despair.

After what seemed like an eternity, the door finally opened and fresh air rushed in. Slowly, Alex lifted his head. The cool air evaporated the sweat beaded on his forehead, and a detective entered.

Alex rubbed his raw wrists.

"Where are Tyler and Travis Pelletier?"

That's what this was about? Ty and Travis? Alex

shook his head. "Last I knew, they were back with their parents, in Newberry, Oregon."

"They've been reported missing."

"Ask my superior, Chief Garrett of the Newberry PD. I have no idea where Tyler and Travis are. They have a long history of running away. Tell the chief to scour a two-mile radius around their house. They're probably hiding in someone's shed."

"Funny. That's what *he* said."

"*Huh.* Then why . . . ?"

"You lose custody of the boys, then you leave the country around the same time they're reported missing?" The detective sighed. "How about a thirteen-year-old girl by the name of Shay O'Hearn?"

Fingers of fear uncurled inside Alex. *Not Shay.* Despite their youth, Ty and Trav had a little street savvy about them. Painful as it was, he had survived losing the boys. Kerry couldn't lose Shay. She'd shatter into a million pieces. He licked dry lips as his pulse started pounding anew.

"The American authorities think the two may be connected."

Kerry must be beside herself. His juices began to flow again. He rattled his chains. "Let me out of here so I can help look for them. Do you really think I smuggled them across the border? Were there three random kids on the flight manifest?"

"That's being looked at now, as we speak."

There was the sound of a bolt sliding back, followed by the door opening. "He's free to go," said another detective. "There were no kids matching their description on the passenger list of his arriving flight."

"See? Now, get me out of these things." He held out his arms and was soon freed.

"You might have checked that before you hauled me in here," he muttered, rubbing his sore, reddened wrists.

"And let you slip through our fingers and fly off to Australia? The Far East? We had probable cause, and we had you contained here, in the airport."

Wasting no time, Alex squeezed past the Mountie, exited the substation, and jogged to the ticket counter, where he was told that if he ran all the way to the gate, there was another departing flight he might be able to catch in time to meet his connection back to Portland.

Before his plane even touched down in Seattle, he pulled out his phone to call Kerry, only now discovering her frantic texts and voice mails. Without taking time to read them, he punched in her number.

"Alex! Where have you been? I need you."

He wanted to reach through the phone and clutch her to him and tell her everything would be all right.

"Have you found Shay?"

"School just let out. I came home to see if maybe someone dropped her off, but so far, nothing. Please, come soon. Come home."

"My flight's boarding now. I'll be there as soon as I can."

Fewer than two hours later, Kerry rushed out onto the porch and into Alex's arms. She clung to him fiercely. "Where were you?"

Alex closed his eyes and sucked in a breath redolent of pine and lavender and stroked her hair. "I'm here now."

Out onto the porch came her father, holding Ella. With him were Rose, a balled-up hankie in her fist, and Chloé.

Alex held Kerry at arm's length. "Have you searched the grounds?"

"My dad and the neighbors did a cursory sweep, but Chief Garrett is convinced she's with the boys, downtown, so he's focusing on that area. It's only been eleven hours, but it's going to be dark pretty soon. I can't bear to think of her out there somewhere all night."

Keeping one arm around Kerry, he reached out to Chloé with his other, pulling her into a group hug.

"I'm glad you're back," she said, peering up at him with trusting blue eyes.

He swallowed the plum-size lump in his throat.

"Who's that?" asked Kerry, at the sound of an approaching car.

"Livvie," Alex replied. "Maybe she's got news."

He and Kerry met Livvie as she climbed out of her car.

"Alex. I had a hunch I'd find you here. You didn't see my calls?"

He shook his head impatiently. "What is it?"

"The Pelletier boys have been missing for two days."

"They were absent from school, too," Kerry told Alex.

"Not just truant. Gone. As in overnight, and the parents never reported them missing. We only found out when we followed up with Greg and Deborah, after the school informed us of their absence. You know what this means, don't you?"

Alex and Kerry exchanged cautiously hopeful looks.

Everyone from the house had followed Kerry and Alex into the driveway.

"Not a judge in the country is going to give them back to the Pelletiers now," said Kerry's father.

"Do you hear that?" Kerry gave Alex a quick squeeze.

"Any news on Shay?" Livvie asked Kerry.

Kerry shook her head.

Alex knelt in front of Chloé. "You remember when Shay was going to take Tyler and Travis to her secret place?"

Chloé nodded solemnly.

"Where is it?"

Chloé shook her head slowly from side to side. "Shay'll get really, really mad at me."

"Chloé. Listen carefully. This isn't a game. Shay could get hurt. Look at your mom. She's already hurting. You have to tell me. I'll tell Shay I made you."

"Well, I can't really explain where it is in words."

"Then take me there."

She looked around at the circle of worried people. "Just you."

Alex stood and met the eyes of Kerry's father.

He nodded his ascent. "What are you waiting for?"

"Let's go," Alex told Chloé.

Inside the screen door, Hobo barked.

"Let Hobo loose," said Alex.

"He'll run away," warned Chloé. "Then we'll have someone else to hunt for."

"Or he might help us," said Alex.

Kerry dashed inside and jogged out with Hobo on a leash, extending the hand loop toward Alex.

Alex and the dog followed Chloé out of the backyard, along the edge of the meadow, slightly downhill to a swath of white oak some sixty feet tall or more until they came to a log lying across the narrowest section of a brook. Alex crossed, turned, and reached for Chloé's hand to help her over, while Hobo splashed through the water.

They came out into an oval-shaped patch of ground cleared of trees but choked with fern, wild iris, and brambles. There was a rustling sound in the weeds and the leash went taut as Hobo strained after a rabbit.

Chloé looked around with a frown. "It looks different. I can't see the path."

"The foliage is at its peak this time of year. Look. I see it," said Alex, pointing to spots where the long grass lay faintly flattened. "Someone passed this way not long ago."

It was the perfect place for a hideout. To the right was the brook in the stand of trees, and to the left rose a steep hill.

When he heard voices, he broke into a run, pulling up short at the sight of sleeping bags arranged around a campfire.

Tyler leaped to his feet, his eyes as big as saucers. "Alex!"

"Alekth!" In his panic, Travis didn't watch where he stepped and stumbled on a rock.

"How did you . . ." said Shay, stunned.

"You okay, kiddo?" asked Alex.

Chloé stomped clumsily up behind Alex, red-faced and out of breath.

"Chloé!" snapped Shay in an accusing tone.

"You should be thanking your sister. Everyone's been worried sick. Chloé saved the day."

"I did?" Chloé asked, blinking up at him, brushing her hair out of her eyes. There was a small twig tangled in it.

Tyler looked around wildly for an escape, his body gathered up like a spring, poised to flee.

"There's no need to keep running," said Alex, approaching him gingerly, the way he'd approach a wild animal. "All the running is over. We're going to be together, now. For good."

Tyler relaxed a little. He and Travis exchanged suspicious yet hopeful glances.

Alex called Kerry on his cell to let her know Shay was safe.

The day before, when the boys had appeared from out of nowhere just as school ended, Shay had hustled them onto her bus, forging a note to the driver saying it was okay to drop them off at her house. Back at the farmhouse, she'd collected some food and the sleeping bags draped on the porch railing and taken the boys to the secret place to spend the night, returning before Kerry got home from work. This morning, she had pretended to walk up the lane to the bus stop but detoured around the meadow and joined the boys here.

They left the sleeping bags to be retrieved later.

Alex was amazed at how quickly the boys could

shift gears, especially the younger one. Walking out of the meadow, they were already romping with Hobo, no longer stiff and anxious.

"Did you see that?" asked Travis. "A bluebird. I wonder if ith looking for a home."

Alex tossed an arm around Travis's shoulders. "We can fix that."

Travis gazed up at him and grinned.

But Shay lagged behind the others, looking sullen and defeated.

Until she saw two girls running full speed across the meadow toward them, excitement all over their faces.

Chloé turned around. "Look, Shay. It's Mia and Addison. Their moms have been calling to see if you were all right. I guess they were worried about you, too."

A grin spread slowly over Shay's face.

Later that night, he and Kerry were sitting out on the lawn, watching the lightning bugs, drinking a glass of wine, while five kids were safely tucked into beds upstairs.

"It's nice here," said Alex, looking up at the moon.

"I'm glad," said Kerry.

"Your house is so . . ."

"So what?"

He took a deep breath and then let it go. "Homey."

"After being unsettled for so long, I was craving homey again. Something safe and solid. What about you? Tell me about the house you grew up in."

"Contemporary Craftsman with big stone pillars out front and long curtains in the living room." He gave her a sideways glance. "My mother had excellent taste."

"Sounds nice."

He huffed. "Decorating was all my mom cared about. She had a successful interior design business in Vancouver. Started it before I was born. Bad timing to have a baby. I always felt like I cramped her style. The memory that sticks in my mind is of her walking out the door, dressed to the nines, leaving me to figure things out on my own."

Kerry reached over and took his hand. "I'm sorry."

"Hard to miss something you never had."

"Where was your dad?"

"He was a lot like Greg Pelletier—never around. He had a store that sold home hardware and lighting fixtures. That took up all his time. He didn't see the shift away from brick and mortar to Internet commerce coming until it was too late. Retail has always been tough, but especially in those days. When I was nine, he died of a heart attack. After that, my mom moved from her rented space into the building where the store had been."

"I hate to think of you growing up lonely."

"Don't feel sorry for me," he said, sitting up straighter. "I survived. Taught myself how to ride the bike they bought me. That gave me the freedom to go out and find things to do outside the house. Hang with other kids."

"Just look at you now. You have this rich, rewarding life. You serve the community every day in so many ways, through your job and your volunteering. And now, you have your children."

They gazed out at the silhouette of the mountains, inhaling the scent of juniper released by the late summer heat that seemed to emanate from the earth in waves, even though the sun had already set.

"I grew up feeling useless. Never knowing what I was here for. Who cared for me enough to want me around. What kind of legacy I'd leave behind." He looked over at her. "Now, I know."

Epilogue

Two months later, a Sunday afternoon in November

Travis opened the back door of the farmhouse and in bounded Hobo, his feet covered with mud. Ever since Travis had moved in, the leash hung, unused, on the coat rack. Hobo was never far from Travis's side. "Come thee, everyone!" shouted Travis from the doormat.

Kerry dropped her newspaper to the kitchen table and got to her feet.

"Hobo!" She ushered the dog back to the door by his collar. "Out!"

"Thome bluebirds are building a netht!" continued Travis. "Down in the houth we hung in a tree by the thtream!"

Shay and Ty were on the floor, frowning over a thousand-piece jigsaw puzzle scattered across the large, square coffee table. "Cool," said Ty as he worked a puzzle piece in.

Alex came in, briskly rubbing his hands together to warm them. "I thought the western bluebirds should be getting ready to fly south for the winter, but it turns out, the mountain bluebirds stay here in the Willamette year-round."

Chloé put a bookmark in her book and set it carefully atop the towering pile that threatened to topple over. "I'll go see it with you," she said to Travis.

"You will? Come on! Let'th go!"

Kerry grabbed a pink hoodie from the hooks by the door and dangled it, swinging, in Chloé's path. "Sweatshirt."

"All riiiiight." Chloé snatched it and tore outside after Travis.

Then Kerry disappeared mysteriously up the stairs.

Alex looked after her as he slipped off his jacket and hung it on a hook. He heard the latch close on the bathroom door. She seemed a little out of sorts these past couple of weeks. He wondered if it was cause for concern.

Then again, she had just started working on a new case, and with five kids, a dog, and him to deal with, who wouldn't be tired on the weekends?

He sat down with his laptop, praying for five minutes of quiet to jot down some notes from a bottle he had opened last evening. If he were honest, he'd begun to regard blogging with more dread than anticipation. There were other things he liked better, like kicking a soccer ball around with his boys, reading to Ella—even the challenge of trying to figure out adolescent girls' mood swings.

No sooner had he logged on when his phone rang. With a sigh, he rose and strolled into the dining room as he slipped his phone from his pocket.

Minutes later, Kerry came back downstairs as Travis and Chloé appeared on the porch waving drooping pussy willows.

"Wipe Hobo's feet," Kerry said, handing the kids an old towel through a crack in the door.

Then she sprawled back in her favorite chair, resting her head on the upholstery, and blew out a breath.

"I got news," Alex said from the middle of the living room as Hobo bounded in, ecstatic, followed by the kids.

"Down." He shooed Hobo off the couch to his rug in front of the fireplace as everyone looked up from what they were doing.

"That was the chief. He said yes to my invitation to Christmas dinner." He'd forgiven the chief for suspecting him of kidnapping as soon as he'd heard how that had come about.

As for Seamus, he'd changed his tune from the moment Alex brought his granddaughter out of the woods and into his waiting arms. He'd even invited Alex to join Rotary, where Alex got satisfaction from speaking to high school students about a career in law enforcement.

Though her brothers would never tire of giving him a hard time, he was learning to give it right back to them, gaining their grudging respect for doing so.

Kerry paled.

"I know you're beat from getting the paperwork ready for the house closing and the mortgage and everything, but the roofers are under strict orders to have the roof done early this week, and the pounding will be over with."

"At least we have a dishwasher," said Chloé, ever the optimist.

"I should have cleared it with you, but what with Chief's wife's staying with her sister in Boise while she recovers from her operation, he was going to be all alone for the holidays. Don't worry. We can order the whole Christmas dinner pre-cooked."

Kerry lolled her head to the side.

Now he was getting a little concerned. He took a step closer. "What's that in your hand?"

She rolled her head back to meet his eyes and held up a plastic stick.

He frowned. "What?"

Shay leaped up from the floor, dashed over to Kerry, grabbed the stick, and held it in Alex's face.

"Hold on," said Alex, patting the pocket of his flannel shirt, then looking around the room. "Where are those reading glasses I got at the drugstore last week?"

"I saw them on the table in the foyer." Tyler dashed out of the room and was back with them in a flash.

"Thanks, Ty." Clumsily, he unfolded them and slid them onto his face and frowned at the stick until a pale blue symbol swam into focus.

"A plus sign. What's that mean?"

"Don't you know *anything*?" asked Shay with a roll of her eyes and a teenage, supercilious grin. "We're having a baby!"

A thrill ran through Alex's body. He sank to one knee before Kerry's chair, opening his arms, gathering Shay, with Ella hoisted on her hip, Chloé, and the boys into a circle.

Gazing at Kerry with wet eyes, he opened his mouth, struggling as he always did to find the right words. But how could he possibly describe the fullness of his heart, aching with pride and gratitude and, at long last—belonging?

"Shh," Kerry said. Nestled in her favorite chair, surrounded by those she loved best, she smoothed her thumb across the frown lines between Alex's eyes.

"You don't have to say a thing."

His devotion was as plain and simple as the ray of autumn sunshine streaming through the window onto his shoulders. Because deep down, that was what Alex was. What he had always been. Solid. Steady. And true down to the core.